Just Another Day

Cochran Affair

Taz Will

ISBN: 1939764068
ISBN-13: 978-1-939764-06-5

1 TREASURE

"Well it was great doing business with you all and I look forward to us working together in the future." We shook hands with everyone and headed for the door.

"Dang Treasure you just closed a deal for me that I didn't think would ever happen."

"That's what family is for Corey!" We decided to get a bite to eat before we headed home. We stopped at a café and ate on the patio. I love sitting out with Corey, he's Deangelo's best friend, and I've known him since forever.

"Treasure I'll be back I need to make a couple calls, it'll take a minute so don't leave until I get back." I just stared at him; sometimes he's worse than Deangelo. Always being so damn over protective like I'm a baby and need them to watch after me. I raised my lemonade up and he walked off.

"Xavier, right?"

"Stop playing Mr. Player, how have you been?" I stood up to give him a hug. I met Harlem Player a couple years ago down south. He's working on a couple projects for us because he's a contractor. He's so fucking sexy; all I do is blush

1

whenever he comes around.

He's a cold drink of water on a record breaking hot day. I used to tease him all the time about resembling Will Demps, I think that's why he's decided to rock dreads now. He's a honey complexion, body built like a Gladiator and solid as a rock. Harlem's a Pork and Beans thug turned mogul, he started off small but has contracts all over the place.

He works with all the celebrities and it was just by luck I met back up with him. I'm sure glad I did because he helped us make a lot more money. He barely charges us anything for it; I guess I still have it. "It's been too long Treasure, you still with your guy?" I tried to get out of his arms and sit the hell back down but he's holding my waist just right. Yeah I said it, he holding my ass just right. "Why you going there? You trying to get me in trouble?"

"You know I wouldn't do that but I have to say you still sexy. I'm hurt you won't give me a shot though!" I looked at him and was lost in his hazel eyes; they make my body want to see them from a different angle. I have to snap the fuck out of this; before I can look away he kissed me. For a second I want to kiss him back then I decided it's not worth it so I pushed him away.

WHOLLY SHIT! "NO! COREY!" He pulled Harlem around and punched him right in the face. Corey looked at me with some seriousness; I put my hands over my mouth. That look told me to shut the fuck up! He whaled on Harlem until Max pulled him off.

Corey walked over and grabbed my bags and damn near ripped my arm off pulling me to the car. I didn't know what to say or where to start. I know Corey's mad; he sat in the passenger seat up front with Max. I know he don't want to say anything to me but I have to try. "Corey!" I called him, then again. He raised the divider up so I know I'm in for it when we make it home. We stopped and I sat there waiting on Deangelo to pull the door open screaming at me. Max helped me out and Corey walked off into the house.

I was surprised that he took me to the villa; I just knew he was taking me straight home. I need to explain this shit to him; I'm not goin' let this chance slip past. I walk inside; Corey sat out on the porch so I grabbed a bottle of water and sat across from him. It's hard looking at Corey; he looked so disappointed in me. My heart pounding like it's about to break free from my chest.

"Treasure what's going on with you? Do you know what Pandillero would do if he found out that nigga hugged up with you, kissing all over you and shit?" That's the one thought that should've come to my damn mind when I was fucking his ass looking into his eyes.

"I know Corey, it was a misunderstanding. I shouldn't have let it go that far I know that. Please, Corey! Please, don't tell Deangelo, it was nothing." He looked up at me; I'm waiting for him to tell me I'm out my damn mind to think he wouldn't tell.

"Treasure, Pandillero love you, he would kill that nigga himself for what happened!" Corey did *not* have to tell me.

"I know but I don't want this to turn into something it's not." He stood up.

"Let's go so you can go home. You can tell him or not, that's up to you. But if I think you doing him wrong, I'll shut it down and kill yo' ass myself and deal with Pandillero later." I hugged him and hurried my ass back into the car before he changed his mind.

2 DEANGELO

Max called and said they were heading in so I went up to the room, turned on the game and waited for T to come up. "What's up T, how that deal go?" I was waiting on her to come over to me but she took off her shoes and headed to the bathroom. "Fine baby it's done, how was your day?" I got up off the couch to see what she was doing in the bathroom.

I couldn't help but laugh; she was brushing the shit out of her teeth. She looked up at me. "Damn T, yo' breath must be off the chain you running in here brushing like that." She shook her head and finished up. "Whatever Mr. Man, I just had a weird taste in my mouth. I had to get that shit out." I laughed and watched as she started taking off her clothes.

"What's up Deangelo? You standing there like you scared don't be scared!"

She closed the shower door and laughed. "Come on now T, I ain't eva scared!" I hurried up and jumped out my clothes and got in with her. I walked up behind her and turn her into the wall, her ass pressed right up against my man and I'm solid.

"Now what was all that shit you were just talking?" "I said..." I gut bust in before she can finish. She wasn't ready so she screamed out and tried to push me back. I wouldn't let her budge though, I had her body pressed flat against the wall and it was no way she was getting out. "What you say T, I didn't hear you?" I smack her on the ass, she moans and tries to push back again but I'm working that ass. She shorter than me so she taking more of me than I thought she could.

She started to get louder then she was quite. "Deangelo...I, no, hurt!" I can't do shit but laugh, she can't even get out a full sentence. I kissed her neck and stopped jabbing her ass and let her breathe. I step back and let her bend over. Even with the little bit that I had in I can feel that back wall that I always try and break the fuck down. She put that ass up and I'm ready. "You still think I'm scared T?" She didn't say anything I was banging her back out, all she can do is push off the wall to stop from smashing her head against it. "You can't hear me T?" She tries to say something but I hit real good and hard and she moans again, put that ass up more and held her head back.

I kiss her on the neck, pull out and get out the shower. I grab a towel and sit on the couch while she walked over pouting. "I know you don't think that's it?" "Yeah T, I'm scared remember!" She moved the towel and start stroking my stick, she spit down on it and my mouth dropped. I'm waiting on her to put her lips on him, she keep stroking making sure I'm wet. She has both hands going

5

and I can feel her breath as she holds me close to her mouth. I'm waiting on her to take me in, she didn't, and she kept going. Her hands were twisting and stroking, my man loving it. All I need is for her to put her mouth on me and I can let this shit go.

She get up and tries to walk away, I grab her wrist as she look down at me. "Naw remember, that's it." She smile and start to laugh, I don't see shit funny. "I see you still want to fuck with me T huh?" I put her ass up against the bed post, put my arm under her thigh and locked the post in my hands. All she was doing at first was screaming out then nothing again. I watch as she tries to take it all in. I can see she's taking in air but she damn sho' ain't letting any out. I slow down to give her time to breathe; she grabs my hips and pulls me back in hard.

That's it; I kiss her, put my foot on the rail of the bed and start nailing her ass. She's off the ground and I have her body resting all on my man and forearm, I'm doing some damage to T. The moment she bit my chest, it was like she hit the eject button. I'm shooting my load off in her like a fire hose putting out a flame. I pulled her legs around my waist and laid her on the bed, we fell asleep still joined as one.

3 TREASURE

"See you later Husband!" I kiss him and don't want to let his ass go.

"You sure T, you know I'll tell them to go without me and stay here with you." I should take him up on his offer but I know the girls will be just as mad as his friends if we call off the parties. "You just don't party too hard and make sure you show up, don't try and pull no hangover shit on me." There's no chance in hell that will happen unless somebody put some shit in his water.

"Stop playing T, I love you don't hurt nobody." He damn near had to pry his self out of my arms; I wave to them as they all speed off. I watched the long train of motorcycles speed off down the long winding road. "You need to hurry up girl and change so we can get this party started!" Sammy said as I walked back in the house. We all began to sing, "Let's show 'em how it's done, let's take a trip to victory 'cause were number one!" Everybody was on the floor laughing; the thought of that song being trapped in our minds had us over the top.

I changed and Sammy met me in the hall, I'm so happy to have her in my life. We've been friends since my family moved into the county back in junior high. We were tight and held each other down for years; she's one of my best friends. "Okay Treasure, when we stop you have to put on this blindfold before we get out the car." Everyone in the limo was turned up to the fullest; all we did so far was shop and eat dinner. I can tell this is going to be an interesting time; they've already started the party. I put on the blindfold; I can hear music blasting as we make our way inside.

I feel them cuff my hands to a chair and I'm going to kill Sammy when I'm freed. They take off the blindfold and in front of me stood some of the finest mother fucking men I've ever laid eyes on. I'm not into strippers but seeing these men, from now on they'll be the Greek Gods that I imagine. Poseidon with his trident, hell he making me wet just looking at his ass. Hermes and his wand, Hephaestus and that thick ass hammer, Hades and his shits scarier than a three headed dog.

I mean the list just went on, Dionysus and that long ass thyrsus. Ares body is made just like he had on golden armor, Apollo, that statue has nothing on this man here. I'm lost and they're standing there booty buck ass naked! I'm not about to look the fuck away.

"Sorry Treasure but you can only look, they can only come as close as they are now so you just have to endure!"

"Really Sammy, this it?" She laughed, danced around then came behind me. "Yep, that crazy ass Bateador said he would kill me if they touch you. You may not be scared of him but fuck that shit, I believe his ass." I shook my head and laughed at the thought of Corey threaten Sammy.

I know what she talking about though; I took it for what it was worth. After she told me the rules of this here adventure, I was released from the chair. I sat back and enjoyed laughing at everyone else. These men were hot; I mean shlongs damn near on the floor. We had a blast. I was exhausted from laughing my ass off by the time we made it to the hotel.

I felt like hell trying to get up to meet with our mothers the next morning for breakfast and shopping. I wasn't even drinking and by the looks of my girls, they all looked like shit. We managed to make it through the day with all the older women and were in for a delight that none of us expected later that night. The doorbell rang and Pam came over to me, she smiled and walked me over to the chair in the middle of the floor. "Sorry Treasure baby, you know the rules!"

All I could do was laugh, I was weak when the music started and out came the hottest, sexiest, most well endowed men I've ever seen. I thought last night was something, these brothers here are straight out of this world. Right in front of me stood Egyptian deities, there was Geb, Horus, Lah, Maahes, and the list continues.

I can't believe these old Betties have it in them. All I hear are those damn whistles and clackers that Pam and my mother have. They're having a good time smacking men on the ass. I thought I would die watching them get lap dances and stick money in the shoe strings they had on as draws. We had a ball, I was so fucking horny all I was thinking about was Deangelo and how much I wanted to satisfy this craving.

I still couldn't think straight the next morning; Shay had come over and was getting on my last nerve crying about seeing Deangelo. I wanted to see him as much as she did but I had other reasons on my mind. I waited 'til our mothers left to check on the venue and we went to see Deangelo. I wasn't letting Shay stick around too long so I took Ms. Jackson with us. "Treasure you think you slick!" Prime said as they all laughed, I didn't care if they knew where we were going. I pushed them off the elevator and made them wait on the next one and headed to see my baby. I was on a mission to get down that long ass hall. Ms. Jackson old ass was taking too long, I wasn't about to let her stop me.

We knocked on the door, he didn't answer. Damn why didn't I get a key to his room before I came all the way over here? I started banging on the door then I heard him come over. "We missed you Daddy," he smiled at what we said and hugged us; I waited as he talked to Shay. I have his dessert but he has something I need before he can get any of that. Shay was out the door and back down the hall, I couldn't have been happier. We talked and I couldn't focus on any fucking thing he was saying.

My baby was more than happy to see me I could feel it; the thought alone was creaming my ass. How in the hell does he do it? He's like a high interest earning CD, only gets better over time; damn I love being on top of him. I said something back to him about luck and my coochie was raring to go. The way I been getting teased the past couple days, I need to taste his ass real quick to cool me off.

I moved back off of him and unlatched his belt. He enjoyed my anticipation so he let me do all the work on getting his ass free. The site of his third arm made me smack my lips like I was trying to get moisture back in my mouth from chewing that hard ass bubble gum from back in the day. I tossed around the cough drop to make sure I had just enough succulence in my mouth to get it good and covered. I looked up at him as I slid my man into my mouth. He was thick so I had to get my snake on and adjust my jaw if I wanted to get him in.

I figured I would just work with the head first, I let everything in my mouth ooze out down his man. I ran the cough drop over the tip a couple times then pulled him out and blew on it. I watched as his eyes closed and for the first time he broke eye contact and his head went back onto the couch. I adjusted again and sucked him in more, I made sure to keep it nasty. I licked and sucked his balls and gave them just enough of a blow to make his toes curl.

He put his hand behind my head and I tried to hit the back of my throat with his man. I stroked him faster and smacked his man all over my tongue. I was enjoying every second of getting him off. He tried to stop me from getting what I was after but I dug my nails in him forcing him to let me have what I came for. I kept at it all the way until he released in my mouth. I drank his ass back and licked up all of the mess I made off of him.

My baby was sweating like hell, he looked like he could barely breathe his chest was moving too fast. I teased him and climbed back on him. He wasn't going to let me have all the fun, I know he's ready for dessert he turned me over. "Wait Deangelo my hair, I can't mess up my hair." I know it'll be too fucking long for me to get my hair fixed again, that will set the whole day back.

He helped me then tried to check me about getting his initials put on his dessert. How the hell he thinks it got there? I sure couldn't put those little bitty ass letters there by myself. Hell it was awkward enough having the lady at the spa do it. I was surprised when she told me that it was a specialty and many people came in and had it done.

I was tired of hearing his mouth I pushed his ass down so he could cool me off, his tongue always turns me on. He wasted no time getting me to cum. His fingers hit right on target and the more he moved them up and down the faster my breathing was. He worked his tongue so fast across my clit it felt like a vibrator set on high speed, the first time I came I had to hold on.

I lifted my hips and tried to pull away but he held on. I could feel my body drench his fingers but he kept going. He stopped long enough to suck every last drop of my cream out then he sucked my lips and started right back with his handy work. I didn't have enough strength in me to go any longer after he kept me going the way he did. My legs were numb and I couldn't control them anymore, they were shaking too bad.

The last one had me begging for him to let me rest, I had to pull his ass off and close my legs as tight as I could. He laughed at my attempt to get up. My legs wouldn't stop shaking so he carried me to the bathroom and sat me on the counter. I watched as he laughed and talked shit, he started us some water so we could take a bath.

I climbed down off the counter and leaned over into the mirror looking back at him. "Come here Daddy, I need you to dick me down." He smiled and walked over. I stared at him as he kissed my neck; the feel of him pushing his self inside of me made me put my head back. He grabbed my neck and I looked back in the mirror examining him as he moved in and out. He backed out as I continued to wait, I smiled and he slammed forward damn near lifting me off the ground.

"Ahhhh, Deangelo! Do it again baby!" I pushed back off the counter back down to my feet and opened my legs more. He put his hands under my shoulders holding me in place. I braced my hands on the edge of the counter so I can feel it all. "You ready?" I looked up at him; he pulled out and started to hit my ass with everything he had.

The only thing I can do is arch my back to try and make more room for what's coming in. I can feel his ass in my throat his man buried so deep inside of me. I'm trying my best to breathe but I can't, he knocking the hell out my ass. He slowed down giving me the same amount of distance with his strokes.

He stopped and I put my hand over my mouth. "I know ya'll hear me cause I can hear ya'll! Terentia I know you in there!" We looked at each other and laughed, Deangelo moved us closer to the bathroom door. "Kathy she's not in here!" He yelled back at my mom banging at the door. "You a got damn lie Deangelo, I can hear ya'll down the fucking hall!" We both laughed. "Come on Kathy can I watch this movie in peace?" he said and closed the door to the bathroom.

4 DEANGELO

"What's up Pandillero man, you look nervous as shit standing over there. Yo' ass scared now!" Marco said.

"Man that nigga terrified, look like he sitting his ass in the box waiting on the mufucking verdict," Cargo said.

"Man Pandillero wasn't this scared before a fight, now look at him," Rook said as they all began to laugh.

"Leave my son alone he ready for this, he just getting his mind right. He know what he want and what he has so let's give him a minute," my father said as they all continued to laugh and walk out the door leaving me in the room alone.

I sat there looking at a picture of the two most beautiful women in the world; I would do anything to keep them happy. I paced back and forth. Not from fear of what was about to take place this evening but from not seeing them and not knowing if they're okay. I wanted to be with them, I know it's not traditional but hell, are we traditional? Why do I have to wait?

Shit, who is it now, bad enough I haven't seen T and my Princess in two days, who the hell is it knocking—now banging on my damn door? I walk over and don't even ask who it is, I snatch the door open, and all I can do is smile. "We missed you Daddy," T and my Princess say as I pull them both into my arms.

"I missed ya'll too. What ya'll doing here anyway, shouldn't you be getting ready?" My princess climbed into my arms, I pulled T in close to me as she put her head into my chest.

"Daddy I have a pretty dress, I can't wait for you to see it."

"Princess I can't wait to see your dress."

"Daddy can I go get some cake now, Granny said I can get some dessert when she comes back. Can I daddy? Can I?"

"Go ahead Princess so mommy can give me some dessert. I want some too." I put her down and T laughed Shay runs out the room to Ms. Jackson who's waiting on her in the hall.

"Why you tell her that Deangelo? You know you wrong for that." I hold T and kiss her before she can say anything else.

"Look at you T. What you doing here?" We make our way to the sofa; T sits on my lap and faces me. "I missed you. I can't stay away that long, what you think?" She licks down the side of my neck. "T you just don't know how bad I wanted to come see you two, hell I didn't want to leave. You know they say its bad luck to see each other before the wedding." She sits up and starts to pout.

"Now I see where Shay gets that from, what's that all about?"

"You sound like luck is the reason we're here." I kiss her on the cheek.

"Baby we're here because I love you and you love me." She smiles and looks me in the eyes.

"Good because I've been missing you too much to be worried about luck. The way you stabbing me I know luck has nothing to do with anything."

"So I guess all them punk ass strippers yo' ass thought was gone be all over you has nothing to do with the way my dessert leaking on me huh?" She laugh and shake her head looking like she caught.

T scoots back off of me and I watch as she gets down on her knees and starts to unbuckle my belt. "T you know we only have three hours 'til the ceremony, why you doing this to me?" She smile and look up at me, wrapped her mouth around my head and worked it with her tongue. I can feel something extra while she doing it and the smell is familiar. She let go and sent an icy blow across the head, I let my head fall back.

T pushing it, I should've known something was up. She doesn't have a cold but that cough drop she using is just what I need. T put my man on her chin and used the bottom of her tongue on the tip of my man swiping it from side to side like a windshield wiper. She goes back to sucking on my head then licked all around my shit causing a frenzy inside of me. By the time she sucked on my nuts they had already been ready from the moisture that she sent down to 'em.

I put my hand behind her head, she made her way back up; she put both hands around him and let me do her in the mouth. I looked down and she pulled away showing me the mess she making. It's so nasty the shit turned me on more. She cleaned it up and started doing it all again, some kind of way she went deeper.

The deeper she went the more I stood up. I can hear her gag and feel the back of her throat as she swallowed with me still inside. I want to see her make the sound and hear it again so I lift her jaw so she can look back up at me. She did it again and I loved the sound, my man getting harder just seeing the glimpse of the tears forming in her eyes.

The moment she started turning her head and moving faster with her hands I was losing control. T annihilating my ass. I want to stop her, I can feel myself about to burst, she pulls her nails down my chest, the pain and pleasure is too much. "I'm coming T!" I manage to get out, she look up at me, spits down on my joint, lick it up and go back at it.

She pull my man out and hit it against her tongue, I can't hold it any longer. I feel the intensity; I have to let it go. I tried to move her back so she wouldn't get it in her hair but she digs her nails into my legs and take it all in her mouth. I watch as T swallows then cleans the rest of it up while looking me in the eyes. I'm sweating and breathing so hard I can barely catch my breath.

"What was that you were saying about luck?" She sits back on my lap and kiss up and down me. I kiss her and she sucked my tongue in. "You right T, luck has nothing to do with this, we're destined to be together!" I pick her up and turn her onto the couch. "Wait Deangelo my hai..." "Don't worry T, I got you." I lift T up so that her shoulders are against the arm of the couch then pull off the dress she wearing. "What you don't like panties anymore?" "I know what I want so why complicate things with panties?"

I smile and kiss her again then whisper in her ear. "I hope you did that little design by yourself. I know you didn't have some stranger playing around with my dessert." I look her in the eyes and we both laugh. "I had some help but you don't have to worry it's yours that's why the design is there." "T who you hav—" T laugh and push my head down, I bit the inside of her thigh making her laugh even more.

I'm more than excited when I trace my initial with my finger then with my tongue. I can feel T breathing harder as I make my way further down. Once I reach my target her body is convulsing more than she anticipated, I let her have it.

5 TREASURE

We finish up and Deangelo walks me back to my room. My mother came out before I make it in. She looks like she wants to fuck Deangelo up for lying to her. We laugh it off. "I love you too T. See you in a minute." He close the door and I change while Deangelo's Aunt Laura and our mothers bicker at me about what I just did.

I thought I'd never hear the end of it; they act like we've never had sex before. I change into my custom made dress. I'm surprised they were able to pull it off in such a short period of time but they did. It's a beautiful ivory color, fitted, with a low back; I'm on top of the world after I look in the mirror. Laura helped me with my shoes and went to answer the door. I turn to walk down the hall and Corey stood there with the brightest smile on his face.

"Sis you killing it in that dress baby!"

"I know right? You think Deangelo will like it?" He made a bizarre face and grabbed my arm.

"If he don't I'll kick his ass and show you to him again." We laugh and walk out the door.

"Corey thank you for everything, I know we've all been on a crazy journey together. I'm so happy that you're here."

"Treasure I wouldn't miss this for the world. Pandillero den had me all over the place watching your ass. You know how many people I had to keep track of you? What make you think I would miss this?"

"So I guess I should be blaming you for everybody thinking I was crazy when I thought people were following me?"

"Nope, that was all Pandillero; I was just doing what I was told." We laugh more.

"See you later Treasure." Corey kiss me then walk off as my father walks over to walk me down the aisle. "Now baby you sure you want to do this? I have a car outside if you're having second thoughts." I look at my father; I can't believe he just said that.

"Daddy why would you put that in my head?"

"Baby I want you to be happy either way so stop acting surprised and let me know what you want to do." I kiss him.

"I want you to not let me fall; this dress is more than half my weight." He smile and kiss me then pulled my veil down and we started our walk.

I'm shaking like a runaway slave in the dark waiting on a carriage to go past once those doors opened. My mind flicking back through so much shit it's making my head spin. By the time I reach Deangelo I'm in tears. I can't believe that after all the shit we've been through we're finally going to be together. I wanted to kiss my baby when I saw his eyes all watery, he's just too cute.

I can't wait to say I do, and when I heard him say it, I was out done with emotions, I didn't want to stop kissing him. We could've made love right there while everyone ran out the room I don't care. Shay hating ass had to come running over and Deangelo can't resist picking her up. I'm so happy I can't wait to get back in the room so my husband can put my ass to sleep.

6 DEANGELO

After we had another go in the tub I walk T back to her room and gave her a final kiss. "I'll see you in half an hour T, don't go disappearing on me." I hold her in my arms. "I'll see you there Mr. Joseph," she said and kissed me again.

"Girl get in here! I know ya'll heard me banging on the door earlier. Deangelo you think you funny, don't play with me!" T's mother Kathy said as she walked away from the door.

"I love you Deangelo."

"Who don't love me T?" I said as we both laughed again.

"I love you too T. See you in a minute." I watch her walk inside and I pull the door closed.

After I make it back to my room I sit around with my boys for a minute. We all had our hair cut up and we were ready to make our way to the ceremony. All my worries ceased as soon as I walked into the venue and took a look around. All my family and close friends and T's family and friends all stood by while we waited. The moment I see T coming down the aisle I'm in love all over again, I'm choked up and I don't care who sees. It's like each step she takes I see a glimpse of everything that brought us to this point.

Coaching her softball team, keeping her out of trouble, teaching her how to fight, how to drive, watching her exceed on the court, even the look on her face at her graduations. I also see the bad things like, when they held her in the alley, her beating the shit out that dumb ass broad, me having to put up a front. Trying to convince her to leave with me in Washington, losing her and not knowing where she was at.

Forcing her to go see Doc. That one actually made me smile at the thought of afterwards when she smacked the shit out of me. Her flipping the plate over into my lap and having to leave after she sent me away. The pain in her eyes at the funeral. And about the same pain I saw when she learned that difficult lesson from that pussy ass nigga.

By the time T made it to me all I can think about is her and Shay. All I ever need in my life is standing right in front of me. Her father lifted her veil and I saw those walnut shaped cognac colored brown eyes. I watched her as the tears began to get trapped in her long curly eyelashes. That was enough for me, after we said our vows we embraced as husband and wife. My baby girl came running over; I pick her up and kissed her as everyone congratulated us. We made it back down the aisle, my princess ran off to play and I took my wife back to the room to celebrate. Once we took care of each other I held T in my arms while we rested in the bed.

"Come on baby we need to get ready to go, we're already late thanks to you." She walks to the bathroom.

"So you sure you want to go to the reception? You know we can chill out here."

I watch her walk back out the door towards me; I can't take my eyes off the way her hips moved. She turned and did her infamous stand. "You sure you don't want to join me in here? Because you know we have to go." I shook my head and let my dick pull me right behind her.

"Alright Mrs. Joseph hurry up, we only going to be here for a minute." She hit my arm. "Don't say that, I remember the last time you said that then you left me." She put her head on my shoulder, I pulled her head back up and kissed her forehead then all over her face as she laughed. "You don't have anything to worry about, I'm not going anywhere. Bateador will be waiting on you when you come out so hurry up."

The second I stepped off the elevator I see Kathy coming past me fast. I can hear what has her on the move so I stop her. "Hey Kathy, I got it." She stared at me. "That's her problem; ya'll always spoiling her, she need her ass beat that's what she need!" She turned and walked away. I walked towards the crying and see Shay kicking and screaming while my mother tries to calm her down. Shay took one look at me, jumped up and ran into my arms. "Princess what's all this about?" I wipe away her tears then kiss her on the cheek; she buried her head in my neck and wrapped her arms around me. "Daddy, Gran Gran said I have to change into another dress. I don't want to change, this dress pretty Daddy."

I laugh as my mother looks over at me. "You sure you don't want to change, I saw the other dress, and it's pretty too." Shay look up at me with her puppy dog caramel colored eyes and a pout on her face. "I don't want to change Daddy, I like this dress." Her lips begin to quiver.

"Alright Princess you can wear that other dress some other time." Shay hugs me and kisses me on the cheek. My mother walks over and pops me in the back of the head, shakes her head and walks away. I don't care what they say, she don't have to change if she don't want to. They should've known that before they even picked that shit up for her.

We waited as T came down the elevator with Bateador then we all headed into the reception. It wasn't long before we were kissing Shay goodnight as they carried her out of the party. We had a good time with all our people. "So husband did you have fun tonight?" T asks as we make our way to the car. "As long as I'm with you, I'll always have a good time wife." Instead of going home we went out to the water, we watched as the sun came up then we went in.

7 TREASURE

After the wedding we headed to our honeymoon in Turks and Caicos, it's beautiful. We're staying at a place that everyone calls Mothers or something. Deangelo closed my eyes as the boat made its way closer to the house. When I saw it I fell in love with it. It has a pool right in the entry of the damn place and it's huge. The stairs wrap around the pool and it has furniture sitting all around, it's something else. The inside is fresh and open; the colors are relaxing; it has rooms on top of rooms. I feel like we're still standing outside.

I started dragging Deangelo around from room to room he stopped me once we reached the kitchen. "Look T, this cool and all but think about this for a second. This place has fourteen beds, hella chairs, couches, desk; you name it, not to mention all the bathrooms, showers and beach." He just gone ruin my fun like that? "What you telling me that for? We can still go look around." He sat me on the counter and started biting on my thigh.

"T I don't want to look around I want to have my dessert all around this bitch. We can look around when I'm dicking that ass down." I push him away, jump down and ran away from his ass. "You gone have to catch me first!" He drops his shirt, shorts and came after me.

After the honeymoon I was beat, I felt like I needed a vacation just to heal from all the shit we did there. Deangelo coochie whipped ass always ready to go. Seem like every chance he gets he's pulling me away. I guess he's catching up on lost time. He doesn't care where we're at, the store he'll pull me in the bathroom, the beach, the closets at home, the car it don't matter.

I know Ms. Jackson tired of walking in on us. I'll never forget the look on her face when she walked in on the last time. Deangelo was standing and had me upside down eating the hell out of me while I went at him. She opened the door to the shed and damn near died. He put me down and we laughed for weeks about that shit every time Ms. Jackson came around. She didn't think it was funny she gave me a packet of little yellow dots and told me to put 'em on the door if we were in there.

8 DEANGELO

It wasn't long after the wedding that we moved into our new house. "I had a call today, I have to head back and straighten some stuff out." T looks over at me, I know what she's going to say so I walk out the room and wait for her to finish with Shay hair. Hell I know this about to be ugly; she closed the door behind her. I turn around and watch as she comes over. "Deangelo, when are you talking about and how long?" I pull her into my arms and kiss her chest; hopefully this will take her mind off the question.

"I see whatchu doing and it's not gone work Mr. Man!" She tries to get herself together and put her nose on mine. I didn't say a word, I slipped my finger right past her and played around with her clit and listened as her lungs picked up. She moaned so I put another one in. I roll her onto her back, dropped my pants and went in before she can speak a word. I pull her right leg up onto my chest holding her left leg down under my right leg. I work her in and out, slow and steady bringing myself out just before my head was all the way free.

The slower I go the more I can hear her kitty talk to me about what's happening. She arches her back and tightens her walls around me so I let go of her leg and free her other one. I lean down and pull her closer by her shoulders. She can't move, the more she tightens the faster and harder I dig in. I lick her ear and whisper, "A couple weeks, I'll only be there for two days and I'm back out. You think I'm goin' leave all this? Don't worry T I got you, two days that's it."

"Oh, oh, ummmmm!" was all she said, I felt her legs shake and the wetness cover me.

A month later I'm cruising down Hall Street watching all the cars, bikes and trucks put on a show. "What's up Pandillero, good to see you Big Dog. Hate that I couldn't make it to the wedding; I heard it was off the chain though. How Treasure and the baby doing?" Lil C said as I walked up.

"It's all good, I know you had that thing to take care of but T good, they both good." We stood around for a minute watching the parade of cars and shit come by.

"Aye Pandillero, you ready? We shutting it down up the way so we need to hurry up before five o comeback around," Flight said, we all headed into the drain pipe. I can see Bruce tied down in the chair in the center of the pipe. "Aigh't let's make this quick." I put two shots in the front of his dome.

"Now that that's out the way, I don't care what the fuck they offering, and where you think you can run, you will be found! If anybody want out its good just say the word and you out. We not on that bullshit! It's too much money out here for the take so if you want out just say it. If you in this room there's no fucking way your hands should touch shit! If yo' crew not tight you need to fix it. I'm out; Bateador will be taking over for me." They all looked surprised and started looking at each other.

"You out-out? Or you just stepping back?" Cargo asked as he looked around.

"Let's just say he'll be running the cleaners," Bateador said as we walked back out onto the street then we went our separate ways. The next day we finished up everything we needed and headed to the airport. "Alright man make sure you meet up with all dem niggas out in Jersey. Everybody already out there right?"

"Yeah Pandillero they left out the other day. Check this though, I don't have all the details but you remember that hitter from out in Washington?"

"Yeah the one that's sleep." How could I forget that piece of shit? He lucky I didn't see his ass or I would still be going at him right now.

"I been on that shit still and the one connection I found so far was that bitch Loretta notarized some of that nigga shit." "You mean Loretta, Loretta?" He looked at me and shook his head. "Really? We need to call up the Judge now don't we."

9 TREASURE

I sat down to tackle Shay hair, it's too thick and long, she's tender headed so that doesn't help much. I see Deangelo walk in and look at me like he ready to go. I tried my best to hurry up then he told me that he had to go back to St. Louis. I really don't have a problem with it but he didn't ask me to go and the look on his face said that he going to put somebody to rest. I sat there thinking about it while I finished up her head. I need to come to terms with what he does and accept all the bullshit not just some of it. I grab some water and head up to talk with the Grim Reaper.

"Deangelo, when are you talking about and how long?" He sat there, I know he don't want to tell me but he don't have a choice. I'm getting my answer one way or another. He start kissing all over me, I'm losing track of why the hell I came up here. I have to focus he has me under his trance though. His fingers started dancing around my coochie and I forgot about the shit. My mind gone, I want to feel him deep inside me, his fingers are great but I want that eleven inches.

I'm in heaven, all I can do is scream with joy when he hit. He just staring at me, my legs shaking I'm cumming and it's about to break free. I try to tighten up so I can hold out a little longer. He not having it though, he locked my ass up and told me what I wanted to hear. Two days ain't shit but this juice is so I popped and let it out.

After Deangelo left Ethan said he'll be stopping by before he headed home and I can't wait to see him. Shay with Ms. Jackson at a birthday party. I'm walking back and forth waiting on him to pull up. Max thinks I'm crazy but I don't care what he talking about, it's been too long since I've seen Ethan.

He couldn't come to the wedding so I still need to cuss his ass out about that. I see him pull up and I'm running out the door. "Ethan! I missed yo' funny acting ass!" I run over and hug him before he can close the door. "What's up Mrs. Treasure?" He pick me up and spin me around, we walked back in the house.

"Come on Treasure I know you about to hit me with it so go ahead." I threw a pillow at him he caught it and laughed. "You damn straight. I know you busy but you could've at least come to see me before the wedding." We sat around after that talking about all the changes that have happened with us over the years. Ethan's still a playboy not willing to settle down, no kids, great career and southern fed.

He used to be just a young tender but now he's all grown up. Everything about Ethan makes women want to be down; he has body, brains and is too handsome to not want to stare. They keep saying he favors George Wilson, but I beg to differ; Ethan's way finer with true grey eyes and all. He's my best friend and I'm down for him and that's all that matter to me. The time is flying past and I'm dreading him leaving but the way he ignoring his phone I know he has to go. I walk him out and we said our goodbyes.

After Ethan left I'm teed off because I tried to call Deangelo but of course it went straight to voicemail. I put that shit on the back burner and sat around with Shay. The time was passing; I know Deangelo will be home soon, I was getting extra excited waiting on him. I went shopping at this little store that you couldn't see inside and picked up all kinds of shit.

Ms. Jackson took a look in my bags after I came home and said she was taking Shay to her house for a couple days. I just laughed and kicked both dey asses out the door, I sent everybody away after that. That is except for Max, he said he wasn't going anywhere until Deangelo came back. I told him to sit his ass out front then, he laughed and walked away.

I hook the room up putting all the shit around, getting ready for my baby to come home. I handed Max a note. "Can you give this to Deangelo before he comes in?" He looks at me and shake his head no, I asked him why not, "I'm not supposed to be here, you remember you sent me away." We laughed and he took the note from me. I hear Deangelo come in and just like the note said he went in the shower downstairs and was back out headed my way. I waited in the bathroom until he got in the bed and I walked out.

His eyes are big and beaming right at me as I took my time walking across the bed, I was about to take off my heels. "Naw T, leave them on, you can lose everything else but leave them on." I stand right over his ass letting him take in the view. I move up over his head so he can take a look at what he about to get. He pulled me down to his mouth and I let him get a sample.

I stand back up and sat on his lap then moved his arms up and whispered in his ear. "So you get over there and you send me to voicemail huh?" He smiled but before he can say anything I handcuffed his ass to the bed. He looks up to see what he chained to and laughed. "T I was busy, I couldn't answer when you called." I nodded my head, stood back up and grabbed my new rabbit fur flogger.

The look on his face is priceless, he know he in trouble and it's nothing he can do now to stop what's about to go down. "That's your final answer?" "T I kno..." I hit his ass, his man stands straight up, I guess he shocked that it really didn't hurt. It do sting though, every time he tries to talk, I'd hit him again.

I tortured his ass for hours and he was right back up after he bust. By the time I unhooked his ass all he could do was roll over and put his arms around me, we were knocked out cold. We had a couple days to get right and he made sure to get me back every chance he could. Shay came running in the door to him and he's cheesing like he hadn't seen her in years or something.

10 ESSENCE

"Excuse me Ms. Donahue, your two o'clock is heading to the conference room."

"Okay Tammy, come in my office and help me after you show them in." Alright bitch pull it together, you need to go in here and go to work. I start walking back and forth talking to myself trying to get enough courage to face these men and get the money I need out their ass. I've been trying to meet them for damn near a year and the closest I came was a fucking teleconference. We couldn't even get them to let me have a damn video conference. The more and more I stand around, the more I feel like my damn life on the line. I know I need their account and I'm willing to do whatever I need to do to make this shit happen.

It ain't stopped me in the past and it damn sure won't stop me now. I've been hanging on by a thread since the market went down. I'll lose everything within a year if I don't close this once and for all. I'm not going back to the club!

I refuse to do that and if I was lucky enough to fuck my way out of there I won't hold back now. Shit, just thinking about the club back in the Bronx makes me cringe. All the bullshit I had to deal with and them drunk ass niggas in there every night. I was so broke I was going in on my off days fucking and sucking just to make some extra cash to get my tuition paid. I'm not mad either because it was one of those off day hump days that those tricks from the league came in the door.

"Come here you!" I looked around to see who was calling me. "Over here baby girl." I look back and see a shadow in the corner. The closer I came, the more I wanted to hurry the fuck up. It was still dark as hell but this nigga was fine as fuck from what I could see. I think he's white but by the sound of his voice I know better. "What's up Daddy, you want a lap dance?" Look at his lips this shit can't be real; I turned around to get him to answer my question.

He smacked the shit out my ass, not a look at that ass smack but a daddy, 'What did I tell you?' smack. It sent a chill over my body; I turn back around and ask him again. "Damn Daddy, you want a lap dance or you just want to smack me on my ass like you own it?" He thought the shit was funny. "Girl sit yo' thick ass down! I don't wanna fucking lap dance and you way too fucking fine to be in this hell hole given 'em."

I wanted to walk the fuck away from his smart mouth ass, don't knock me when yo' silly ass the one paying bitches to do the shit. Hell, if these niggas didn't come in this bitch it wouldn't be open so he has some nerve to talk shit to me. It don't matter, he sound like he ain't about to put out any dough any fucking way. I know he has to be on the team, I figure he's a water boy with dry pockets. I turned around and bounced my ass away from him.

I took a few steps and he was in front of me, I damn near smack the shit out my own ass once I realized it was Superstar. This nigga is the team and my dumb ass about to walk away like a damn fool. He came right up on me; I looked him in his eyes. They said he has some sexy ass hazel eyes but I never knew just how fucking demanding and intense they could be.

Something about Superstar telling me to run, like he's Jack the Ripper or some shit. His eyes were telling me everything I need to know about him. He maybe famous but I can see the anger and death in his shit. My body wanted to run and fast but something was overriding my thoughts.

"Don't get all scared now baby girl. Where you think you going?" I looked at him and took a step back, I'm feeling real uneasy. He moved closer, every step I took back he came forward. I was backed up against the wall. He had his hands pressed right above my head staring down at me, what the hell?

"I was about to go do my job, you don't seem like you want company so I need to do what I have to do." I'm trembling and I think he's getting off on it by the way he's smiling and what a smile it was. I wanted to look away but he pulled me in, his eyes and his smile eased my fears. He leaned down to my ear and I turned my head like he was yelling at me but he whispered.

"What is it that's so important to you that it has you working in here? Drugs, money, the thrill, what?" I know he don't think I do that shit, hell if I wasn't trying to make it through school, I wouldn't mind flipping burgers. I have plans and I'm ready to do whatever I need to to make that shit happen. My mom's died when I was nine from drugs, I'll never get involved with them and I try not to even associate myself with anyone that does.

"Come on sweetheart speak! I know you not that scared, look at all dese people around, I won't do shit to you in herrre." Hearing his words didn't make it any easier. I was more afraid after that than I was when he backed me up against the wall.

"No, I don't do drugs and its' not a thrill. I need the money to finish up my degree; once I have that I'm out of here." He looked at me then leaned back towards my ear. His cologne's sending waves through my body; his hand is wrapped around my waist so I won't move away from him.

"Yeah I bet every bitch in here say dat shit." I had enough of his insults, I stepped forward. I tried to walk around him but he blocked me without touching me with his hands in the air. The smile was gone and he looked at me like I had just ticked him off. I was back against the wall looking—hell begging for security to come and rescue my black ass from him.

"I don't like when people walk away from me when I'm talking to 'em. It's rude. I know you know better than that shit, act like you have a little bit of class baby girl. I know it might be hard but hell, you can pretend right?" I couldn't figure out what the fuck Superstar wanted from me but like I said, I was feeling like he was getting a thrill out of fucking with me.

"Can you please just tell me what you want? I told you already I need to do my job if you not down. It's rude to be smacking on my ass and not paying me to do it. As hard as you hit my shit you should be paying me double for doing that alone." He leaned back in and said something to me in another language. I didn't know what the fuck he said but the way it rolled down the side of my neck; I wanted his ass to say the shit again. He started laughing because I didn't respond.

"I said do you want to ride with me?" I started to say, 'Hell no! I don't want yo' crazy ass all in my fucking face!' He didn't give me a chance though. He took off his coat, wrapped it around my shoulders, grabbed my hand and led me out the back of the club.

He opened the door to his blacked out Maserti for me and I saw his security jump in two trucks. We pulled off and they were behind us. He didn't say anything; he didn't even turn on the radio. I sat there not knowing what the fuck he was trying to do to me or where he was taking me. Then he pulled along the side of the road, I looked up and it was a dead end, only left or right.

I heard the cars behind us do the same. I'm straight terrified, I just know this crazy ass nigga is about to send my ass to meet my maker. He turned and I jumped for the door, I'm ready to get the fuck out the car. "Calm down baby, I just want to talk to you for a second." He laughing and shaking his head at me.

"What's your name sweetheart?"

"Storm." He shook his head and looked down.

"Come on baby girl, you fine, you thick and built like you from my hometown. Boo look, you need to find a better career, you scary, can't keep a nigga attention and you can barely shake yo' ass. I thought you said you were in school? You acting real slow like you can't keep up with the conversation. Let me ask you so you can understand. What name were you born with?" I had way more than enough, I'm not about to let him keep treating me like I'm the scum of the earth. He had his fun and laughs for the night now I'm out.

I opened the door, threw his coat down and started walking back. He came and stopped me before I even made it to the back of the car. "I'm sorry baby girl." I turned and looked at him; I had tears in my fucking eyes. I wiped the shit away then he walked me back to the side of the car. I watched him reach in; get some tissue and his coat. He put it back over my shoulders and wiped my eyes for me. "Look, I just want to talk with you for a second." I shook my head up and down. "You see the fork? I'm about to ask you some questions, if you tell me the truth we get back in the car and go left together. If you lie to me then you can get a ride back in the truck and they'll pay you five g's for your time."

Hell, he said I was slow; this dumb ass nigga about to pay me five g's just to answer some questions. I've only been with his ass for less than an hour. I wanted to laugh at how dumb his ass was but I was more intrigued about what he wanted to ask me.

"You sure you don't do drugs? Not even pills?" I shook my head and he told me to use my words like I'm a damn child.

"No I don't use drugs. To be honest I have a strong gag reflex and I have trouble swallowing pills." He thought that shit was too funny. He has tears coming out of his eyes he laughing so hard, I had to laugh with his ass.

"Don't worry; I think I can help you with that." We laughed even more at what his crazy ass said.

He started drilling me, what am I taking up in school, do I have kids, money, where do I live, and do I have a car. You name it he was asking; I was surprised he didn't ask when my last menstrual cycle was. I told him everything he wanted to know. "So what's your name?" I told him and he smiled. "Essence is a beautiful name, it suites you. Here Essence, write your name and social on this."

I looked at him like he's the crazy one, he started laughing again and I had to laugh with his ass again. "Look Ma, I wanna know who I'm dealing with that's all. If it's too much to ask then you can get that ride with them back and get ten g's." I didn't even bother to look back at them, I put it on the paper, and he waved a guy over and gave it to him.

"You want something to drink Essence?"

"Yeah but you probably don't have what I'm looking for." He turned his head like he didn't hear me.

"What, alcohol?"

"No, I don't drink alcohol, I really only drink milk. I know it's crazy so go ahead and laugh at me again Superstar." He didn't laugh at all; he smiled and asked if I was running game on him. I told him no and he waved over to the truck like he had a cup and next thing I know they were bringing over two small bottles of milk. We stood there talking and drinking then he looked at his phone and read something.

"So Essence can you have some faith in me and ride or you want to head back?" I don't need time to think about shit.

"I'm down!" He opened the door and that was history.

He took me to his three bedroom loft off of Mercer Street in the city, we didn't have sex. He wined and dined my ass before he sent me to a doctor to get my ass checked out. I was good though, hell I didn't have anything to hide so I made it happen. When we did have sex, I would've never guessed in a million years that he ate pussy like he did. I mean his tongue game was on a million and his stick was a strong nine. He made that bitch jump when he was in the cookie.

41

He taught me how to suck him just the way he liked it. I was too eager to learn, it was no time after that I was hitting my trachea with his shit.

After a couple months he moved me in my own condo. He bought me a car and paid for the remainder of my tuition all I had to do was go to school. Whenever I would slack off he would tell me to remember the fork and I got back on my game and did what I had to do. I never went back to the club after that, I never went back to the Bronx. That fucked up motel I was staying in, I never saw that place again. I didn't go back for shit and I was happy that I didn't have to, Superstar took care of me.

I was kind of upset that he didn't want to really be with me in public. I mean, he flew me out on trips and shows and shit like that but whenever the cameras were around I was sent away. I was still alright though because I had plans and if I wanted anyone to take me serious I couldn't be that bitch. When I graduated he was front row and center. By the time I made it off the stage he was parked in the back. He made me feel like I was on top of a mountain; I thanked him for everything he did. I graduated top of my class so I had a job and I told Superstar that I would no longer need the condo or the allowance he was giving me. He laughed.

"Aw now you too good for me?" I hugged him and told him I wasn't saying that. He looked out for me and I couldn't be more appreciative that he did. He tried to get me to keep the car but I told him I couldn't.

I started working and that was really the last time that I saw Superstar. He was in and out having a real hard time with the fighting and shit. When I found out he was facing jail time, I reached out to him but he never responded. I figured he was at his fork making moves that he needed to make and didn't want to talk. Hell, if I would've known better I would've tried to really be with Superstar but I had to do better than live off a man. I had to choose my own destiny and I was ready.

11 TREASURE

"Deangelo look at this." He came over and read the email. "T why you want me to help this chick anyway, she seems like she nothing but trouble." I couldn't believe Deangelo, acting like he doesn't want to help. I felt bad for her when they said she was on the verge of going bankrupt. She built her shit from the ground up and I know a good thing when I see it. "Because Deangelo, it's a great opportunity to branch out. And I know you want me to stop hounding you about it so do this please." He smiled at me and shook his head no.

"No what?"

"No T, you need to do something for me first." He just don't know, he ain't said shit I can't handle.

"So you ready now?"

44

"T get yo' head out the gutter, is that all you think about?"

"Yeah, most of the time why? Don't you?"

"Hell yeah, bring yo' lil nasty ass on. I'm hungry, can you handle that? If so, I can handle your little rescue mission for you."

"Hell I'm trying to feed you. I just asked if you were ready."

"T I got you when you finish cookin' and you know it." I was too happy to feed my baby. I was about to cook anyway so hell, I'm winning and I know I'm getting mine later on too so I got his ass twice.

"What's up Sammy? You heard anything back from the Essence Dreams yet?" She put her glass on the table like it was heavy; I'm surprised it didn't break. "Yeah I did, her trick ass secretary called over and said they needed a face to face. If it doesn't happen then they have to meet with some serious investors." We both were laughing at the thought.

"Yeah okay tell us anything. Has Corey called her or Deangelo?" She shook her head no. I don't know how the hell they plan on making this happen if they not even gone call her ass. I had Sammy call her secretary while I called Deangelo telling him they could take a five minute conference call with her. She agreed so about a week later we were all at the house and Sammy called me.

"She said what Sammy? Tell her this is it, we not doing video anything, she can take the call or we walk away." Sammy told her what I said then an hour later Sammy called back and patched her in. I couldn't believe this bitch; she's really trying to get her sexy on, she damn near whispering. Corey getting annoyed though, he kept telling her the connection was breaking up and she cleared that shit right up.

After the call she tried to get a direct number but I banged on her ass. It wasn't like they were going to give her a number anyway. They got up and went about their business. I just can't believe this trick trying to play them like that though. I'm starting to lose the little bit of respect that I have for her ass.

Seem like every day after that Sammy was calling me with some shit about how she need a face to face with them to reassure her ass. Bitch is not slick, my panties then dropped on more than a few occasions hearing Deangelo voice over the phone. She begging like this after one phone call, she would lose her mind if she was to see them in person. I'm not worried but I wouldn't put that bitch alone in a room with either one of them if I had my way after all she doing.

I told Sammy to call her ass up and say I was their secretary, she did. I told her that I can meet her and whatever we discuss will be approved by them. This bitch hit me with I'm not qualified to have the conversation I was having with her now. Then she told Sammy she was meeting with some investors in a month and if they didn't have a face to face, she would go with someone else. She hung up the phone; we thought we would die laughing at that bitch, she begging to see dey asses. "Girl she is on a mission to meet her some Mr. Joseph!" Sammy thought that was so funny.

"Don't play with me girl, I got something for her ass. I'll get them out there I just don't know when yet."

"You crazy as hell sending yo' husband to meet with her ass. You know why she wanna have a face to face right?"

"Who the hell I look like? I'm not a duck and I know when a bitch trying to fuck."

"Yeah whatever. I hope you going along with them. I keep telling you that Tammy bitch ain't shit. That trick play for both teams, she come at me sideways again and I'm bound to take a flight there myself."

"Sammy please, you know you like those carpet munchin' ho's! That's why yo' ass ain't got a man." I was laughing hard as hell.

"I'm not falling for that shit! Stay out my business trick, you know damn well I don't get down like that. I'm still not tellin' you shit about if or who I'm seeing or sexing skank."

"That nigga a ho! Stop savin' yoself for him. We not in high school anymore so stop trying to front."

"I don't know who or what you're talking about. You need to be worried about sharing yo' man with them ho's and not who in between my damn legs."

"Whatever Sammy, let me get to work because you think you slick pushin' my buttons about this trick. I wanna show this bitch how stupid she really is." We hung up and I made the calls I needed and put the shit together. All I have to do is get Deangelo and Corey to go along with it and meet the damn girl.

I see Corey coming in from playing basketball; Deangelo still outside so I have my chance to talk with him. "Corey, I need you to do me a favor." He looked at me with a straight face.

"Nope! Talk to Pandillero." He turned and walked out the house. I'm weak with the way he played me out, my ass laughing hard. I'm sitting in the damn door jamb laughing like I'm losing my mind. He looks back at me and walked back over.

"Man whatchu want now Treasure, stop being so damn silly. What?" I had to take a minute and clear my eyes.

"Corey can I get a wedding gift from you?" He about to walk away. He wants me to tell it and stop playing around with his mean ass.

"Corey I really need you and Deangelo to go meet with the owner of Essence Dreams in two weeks. It should be short and simple, I can give you what I have and I know you'll work out the rest. Can you please give me this?" He looked at me, pulls out the chair and sat down.

"What's in this for you Treasure something up, why you want this so bad, it's not that big a business."

"I don't really but I want to help her." He got up.

"If you gone lie to me then I'm out."

"Okay, I did just want to help at first then she started hounding trying to get at ya'll. Now I want to show her that she can do it without a man."

He chuckled, "So what you plan on doing to show her Treasure?"

"Nothing really." He turned and walked away. I'm behind him trying to keep up without getting Deangelo attention on us.

"Okay Corey, I'm goin' jinx the contract." He turned around and shook his head. His eyes said all I needed to hear and I'm about to go the hell off if he blow up my spot without me getting a chance.

"It's just going to say if she fucks up I'll own her ass." He look at me and then back at Deangelo.

"You know you wrong right? What you think Pandillero gone say when he finds out what you plan on doing to her? Please believe if you don't tell him I will." I smiled and walked over to where Deangelo was and whispered in his ear.

"Baby I have some pineapple slices in the freezer. I'm gon' hide 'em and they'll be all gone if you don't come upstairs with me." Corey came walking over and I laughed and walked back in the house. By the time I make it to the door I hear, "Really, game over like that?" I see Deangelo come running towards the house so I ran upstairs on his ass. I told Deangelo the best way I know how; I let him cover the pineapples in his favorite dessert. He was game but he made me promise not to do it no matter what. I'm sure she'll get the point so I did.

I called Sammy back and told her to setup the meeting, she thought I was crazy sending my man in to talk with her but I'm not worried. I still want to help her get what she need even if I do have to force her to open her eyes and not her legs. When the meeting was set she was calling Sammy to thank Deangelo personally. We both laughed hard at the thought of her actually seeing them. I would love to be the clock on the wall when she sees what she can never have. I already know Corey wouldn't like her, he so fuckin' picky it really don't make any sense. Deangelo on the other hand, he know better so I'm not worried about him, I'm more interested in what she'll do.

12 DEANGELO

"You know who this Essence chick is that T trying to help out right?" Bateador looked over at me.

"Who don't know Storm? That's punk ass Superstar gal from back in the day."

"T doesn't know that she know Superstar. I don't know why T wants to waste time on this chick." He laughed like he knows something that I don't know.

"Man you know she trying to see if you'll buckle under pressure!"

"Bateador get that shit out of here! T would never bet against me."

"Yeah okay! Why else would she be pushing for us to go out and meet this chick, she could've closed this by herself." I never thought about it until he asked me. This a small thing that I know T could've worked out. She didn't have to go through all the trouble she has trying to get us to go out here.

"What's up Pandillero you quite over there, Treasure on your mind?" He laughed and I couldn't help but laugh.

"I don't know, now that you said something I know T could've worked it out and took the damn business over. Looking over the shit she gave me Storm is about to be back on stage coming soon." We both laughed and jumped in the car.

"I'm just hoping she not on that fuck to get in my pocket's type shit. Ho's be killin' me with that shit, act like a nigga have to pay to get some pussy or something. Maybe dem ugly, busted, broke niggas, but I damn sho ain't one of 'em and I hate when a chick try and play me like one."

"Nigga please. I can tell by the way she was rappin' on the phone she'd do just about whatever to get what she want. I'd bet money on that shit nigga."

"On errthing Pandillero, I wouldn't even waist my money like that. I'm tellin' you now; I don't have the time or patience for no shit today."

"Damn nigga, thought you liked being at the top? Shit you said it was easy to lead from the front and make all the calls." We laughed as he bent the corners towards Essence Dreams.

"It actually ain't that bad. It's feeling responsible for the fam like I do. I never realized just how close the family is to shit that can get them in two fucked up boxes. On the same note, you can't trust these niggas out here for real, only ones you can trust is yo' family. Anyway, it ain't shit you need to worry about Pandillero."

"I know it's not but I have yo' back no matter what. If you need me to help then so be it. I told you already, it's time to let that shit go. I wanna talk wit' a

51

couple of 'em anyway to see if they ready to let that shit be."

"You know damn well ain't nobody tryin' to hear that shit. I'm not even tryin' to hear it so how you wanna kill this time? We damn near two hours early." I laughed and shrugged my shoulders at him.

"We can stop by Tone place first; I need to make sure he has what he needs anyway. I been tellin' his ass I'll get out here for 'bout a year now, I bet he be hella surprised to see us walk in." Bateador drove to the new recreation center and we talked to Tone. By the time we left out of there we were almost running late for the meeting.

13 ESSENCE

Now all I have to do is go in here and kill it, not saying that I won't fuck these niggas to get what I want because I know I will. I see Tammy my secretary come in the door.

"I hope you have your stuff together Essence!"

"Shit, is it that bad? Girl tell me before I pass out." She looked at me with her eyes wide open and shook her head from side to side.

"Just tell me. How they look? Do they look as smart as they sound? What?"

"Those are some fine ass brothers! I'd be surprised if you can concentrate; you better try and look away because that Joseph, I wanted to..."

"Okay Tammy! I'm already scared now you have me wanting to change outfits. Matter fact, move so I can."

I put on a tighter black skirt suit and my five inch heels. "Mr. Taylor looks like he'll bend you over and put you to sleep in no time. They didn't bring too much with them except a packet for you." This bitch been gone way too long, I thought they setup all kinds of shit for her to take this long.

"Damn Tammy what took you so long to come in here?" She looked at me and started laughing.

"Girl I was trying to get a threesome with their asses, that's what took me so long! I love my job but I'm willing to start over if they were willing to get at me. I don't care who can see." We laughed all the way into the meeting at what she was saying; I had tears in my eyes. I open the door and it seems like I was smacked in the face with the definition of handsome and drop dead gorgeous. I bet this what the Bermuda triangle feel like 'cause I feel like I'm all lost without direction seeing these men.

"Hello nice to finally meet you I'm Ms. Essence Donahue, you must be, Mr. Joseph?" He smiled and shook my hand, "No I'm actually Mr. Taylor, and this is Mr. Joseph." He stepped aside and the way Mr. Joseph stepped up and looked at me, I know he's top dog and the one I need to make sure I pay the most attention to.

"It's nice to meet you Ms. Donahue; you sure do drive a hard bargain. I thought you were going to come track us down if we didn't agree to meet with you." I didn't hear shit he said, I was agreeing with what Tammy said and thinking about kicking her ass if they fucked her instead of me.

I smiled and don't want to let go, I don't give a fuck about that ring on his finger. Shit it's shining so fucking bright my ass want to count the big ass diamonds on that bitch. "You ready to start?" Mr. Taylor said and there my ass goes again. I feel like I'm drooling just hearing that come out his mouth. There's something about looking at Mr. Taylor, he reminds me of someone. He's fuck-me-good sexy but his eyes scream dangerous situation. I can feel he don't play games and he's probably a beat a bitch down and have no remorse type a nigga.

But shit he's fine; I'd take an ass whooping from his fine ass if he fucks me right. Tammy came in with the rest of the stuff I need so I put on my show for them. Tammy thinks she getting over. Any other meeting she'd run out and get an extra lunch break on my ass. Today she sitting right across from them and every time I look at her, which isn't often, she's smiling all in their faces. I'm not mad because I made sure to show them what I was working with. And I'm down for a foursome if they want to make this happen.

Once I finished, they looked at each other, it seems like they want to get a moment alone but neither of us were leaving. I'd kick Tammy the fuck out if they asked but I'm not going to risk the chance of letting them get away. Mr. Joseph said something that sounded like, "Me lizuke cha;" I guess it's Greek but I don't understand what the hell he saying then he looked over at Tammy. I know she doesn't understand.

"I'm sorry Mr. Joseph, we don't understand, can you speak English it would really help?" They laughed and Mr. Joseph said something else, Mr. Taylor stopped laughing, looked at Tammy and said something. I don't know what the hell going on. Then they had a full conversation going back and forth, we can't take our eyes off of them. Even with the language barrier I feel like they're speaking to my heart. My coochie taking the most punishment because of it.

I don't want to sit my ass down, I know I'm soaked and I'll leave a print if I do. I stood there trying to keep it together while they talked. "Ms. Donahue we have some concerns..." Mr. Taylor said, he made me feel like maybe I should've studied up a little more. These men are smart and it doesn't take a rocket scientist to figure that much out. "Now if you can work with that we have a deal," Mr. Joseph said. I'm willing to work with more than that. I want to jump up and down, hell, I really want to fuck.

14 DEANGELO

"Excuse me Ms. Donahue, your two o'clock is heading to the conference room." We follow Tammy, her secretary, back to the conference room. This girl throwing her ass hard, we were trying not to laugh at her crazy ass. "Do you all need anything? Can I bring you two anything to drink?" We told her we were alright. We figured she'd go get Ms. Donahue so we could get the hell out of here.

She didn't, she started pushing shit around the table like she doing something, putting her ass up in the air and shit. Then she walked up front and just so happen to knock over some paper clips. The way she bent down to pick 'em up had us about to break out of there. The tiny ass skirt she wore was barely covering her ass to start with. Now she's bent over at the waist and we can clearly see the bottom of her ass. If I was twenty and single and not damn near thirty one and happily married; I'd let my man spit all over her. She doing way too much and the last thing I need is for T to be on my ass about some wack ass girl.

We waited for about ten minutes, she still picking up paperclips. I ignored her trying to pass the time for this meeting to get started, I decided to text T. I know she'd want to hear how they were trying to play us. She thought it was hilarious. "Excuse me, Tammy right?" Bateador said, she said yes then came over and leaned on the table to where you could see all her shit. Bateador didn't find it amusing at all, he stood up and walked to the door and opened it. "We have about five more minutes to wait then we leave." She walked over and left out the room.

"Damn Bateador, why you didn't just pick her ass up and drag her out like you did Prissy dusty ass back in the day?"

"Don't remind me, I still wake up in cold sweats thinking about her musty ass climbing all over me trying to fight and shit." We both laughed.

T called me and told me absolutely nothing, I teased her about trying to find out how the meeting's going and she played it off like she didn't care. "Look T, if you want this so much why didn't you do it yourself?" She said because she wanted her man to do it for her. I laughed, told her I love her and hung up.

"Told you Treasure fucking with you," Bateador said as he sat on the end of the table.

"Man T is not fucking with me. If anything she fucking with Storm here. You know damn well I don't want shit Superstar has and he damn sure won't get what I have." We both started to laugh again.

58

The doors opened and Bateador stood up from off the table and by the time I did he was in front of me. This girl thick, I see why they call her Storm, she real cute. She not my speed at all though, too much of everything, clothes too tight, hair too fake. Hell, seem like everything's fake once I looked at her up close. Pounds of makeup, I'm cool with her from a distance, she one of those pretty chicks that do too much and fuck up.

"Hello nice to finally meet you I'm Essence Donahue, you must be, Mr. Joseph?" Once Bateador told her his name I shook hands with her and introduced myself.

I don't think she heard a word of what I said. She just standing here still holding my damn hand and smiling like she day dreaming. I pull my hand away and she still has her hand there. I hear Bateador grunt like he annoyed by the way she's acting; I need to find out what's up with him. Once again his patients are running thin; he asked if she was ready.

We sat down as she put on her presentation. It's cool; we already know exactly what we're thinking. Most of the time I stared off into the room thinking about all the shit I need to do. I can feel Tammy watching me and whenever I look over she'll give me the "free pussy" face so I turn back around. Something about that chick telling me if she had the chance she'd chain me to a bed against my will. Psycho spewing all out of this girl, I can't wait to fuck with T about it. I know she'll get a kick out of the thought of me being chained to a bed.

I didn't even realize she was finished until Bateador tapped my chair. I looked back at him and she wasn't talking anymore so I play it off. I asked her if she spoke Greek then looked over to see if Tammy understood. I don't even know why I asked I know the answer but I had to say something. She said she didn't understand, Bateador knows what I'm doing. We laughed about me being caught not paying attention. I ask Bateador if it's something up with this Tammy chick because she looks nuts. He stopped laughing and looked at her.

"Naw man she just wants to get fucked that's all."

"She crazy as hell if she thinks that's happening. I know T would beat the sleeves off her if she saw this shit here."

"You don't have to tell me. Treasure would fuck the two of them up if she was here with us right about now. I know you zoned out but the paper flew off the desk. Storm bent down to get it an——" I don't want to hear what he about to say.

"You damn right, I don't want to know shit she did."

"So what you think, you want to stop back at the gym after this? Feel like going a couple rounds or what?"

"Bateador you want to talk about this now, they looking at us like we crazy."

"Man they don't understand shit we're saying!"

"Shit on the real I did want to try out some of that new equipment they had in there."

"I know I was thinking about hitting the ring with Senior, get a quick lesson, tighten my shit up a little bit."

"You can have that shit nigga; I'll fuck around and be here until next week fucking with his ass in the ring."

"So we going or what Pandillero? We can be in and out in about three hours."

"Yeah man it's cool I can burn some energy before I take my ass home. I'm not coming back for a minute."

"Yeah whatever man let me wrap this up real quick then we out." I let Bateador do his thing while I went back to thinking about spanking T ass for having me deal with these crazy ass girls. I guess she getting me back for all the times she had to deal with the bullshit. Now that we're married, I don't know how I couldn't see all the shit I did to T back in the day.

15 TREASURE

Everything was good; I was taking care of business so Deangelo wouldn't have to be in the streets. After he told me he was out, I couldn't have been happier. He let me work my magic and that I did. I was shocked when he said he was okay with me going to Miami to meet with some investors. I don't know why I was acting crazy when I found out Corey and six other people would be shadowing my every move. Corey didn't shadow at all, he was right there like I couldn't cross the damn street by myself. It was all good though, after the meetings Corey didn't have a problem with me hitting a couple clubs so I was happy.

The last day I was there I met up with Sammy and I couldn't wait for her crazy ass to finish up. We worked out a deal together for her a makeup line so once we finished up the paperwork we were partners and we headed out to celebrate. The clubs in Miami always jumping and I was having a blast with my girl.

"Why Corey always look like he about to kill somebody?" Sammy said as we looked over at him from the bar.

"Because he is always ready to kill somebody. Why the hell you think?" She looked at me like I just told her she had shit on her lip; I put my hands up and shrugged my shoulders. Hell, what else she want me to say? He is ready to kill some damn body, that's probably why he really brought his ass down here anyway. I didn't tell her that though, we headed back over to our little area.

"Excuse me." I feel somebody grab my wrist, at the same time I feel an electrical current rush past my fingers up my arm. Seem like it shot all the way across both my breast instantly awaking my nipples. Then it trickled down to my stomach and was hovering in between my thighs. I turned around and damn near dropped my panties. Then I remembered I didn't have any on so my eyes were all on him. How the hell can someone have this type of effect on you before you even see them? A touch? I need to get it together. Sammy started hitting my damn arm like she having a panic attack. Hell I am too and it's the best panic attack I've ever had.

"I had to stop you Miss you are beautiful, they about to play my song. I wanna know if I can bring you on stage and sing it to you?"

"I'm good, maybe you should get one of these chicks in here that are thirsty because I'm not." That was a bald face lie; I'm straight dehydrated lookin' at his ass. He laughed and bit down on that juicy, thick, soft, I-bet-it can-make-me-cum-faster-than-I-can-blink lip of his.

"My bad, what's your name?"

"Treasure."

"You sho' right, you are a treasure. But um, I'm not looking to pour my thoughts out to a thirsty chick. I'm asking a grown, sexy, woman to join me." I feel my coochie explode, he held out his hand and I took it. My heart thumping all the way up on the damn stage.

Usually I hate when people look at me, especially large crowds but I have to admit, looking at him there's no one else in the room. They dropped the beat and he turned coming toward me, "Soon as ..." I couldn't stop from smiling and fucking his ass with my eyes. He moved around me and he wasn't up on me but the little touches he did make had my ass trembling.

I said fuck it and let the song move my body to the beat. I didn't do too much but I jammed out like there's no one else in here with me. That is besides him! At the end of the song I feel someone wrap their arms around my waist, I looked over at Corey and didn't see him. Something about this feeling was different though and his scent gave him away. I feel a kiss on my neck and I know who it is.

"Give it up for Mrs. Joseph and my man Pandillero." I turn around and kissed my baby, he walked me off the stage. "Good looking man but next time don't get that close to my wife." They laughed and we were sitting back in our little area, I just sat there looking into his eyes.

"You know you wrong for that right?" He starts to laugh then Sammy ran back over.

"Why I couldn't get a treat, that's jacked up Pandillero! If it wasn't for me she wouldn't even know who Trey Songz is." She sat down pouting, Deangelo looked at Corey, he got up and put his hand out.

"Come on man damn, this punk ass nigga will sing to yo' ass too." Sammy jumping up and down, she grabbed Corey hand and they were walking over to the stage.

"I know you like his ass so I hooked it up for you. You deserve it wifey." I put my lips up at him.

"Does that mean I can get that one celebrity fuck?" He grabs my thighs and I'm damn near on the floor laughing.

"Hell naw you can't! What the fuck this look like? I wish that nigga would have some of my dessert. We cool and all but that nigga ain't stupid." We laughed and kissed then I heard the crowd go crazy, Sammy was all over his ass. She didn't hold shit back she damn near fucked his ass right there on the stage, we watched and danced.

I had to go into the doctor and find out for sure if I was pregnant or not. I was having all kinds of cravings and my mind was all over the place. Once I found out I was lost on how to tell Deangelo we were having twins. I planned to tell him at our one year anniversary. We had a blast, Deangelo out did his self with the whole day; I was showered with gifts and all kinds of shit.

We were at dinner afterwards and I was nervous as shit trying to find a good time to give him the gift I had for him. He too worried about getting dessert and he ready to go. But from what the doctor said our full blown sexcapades will have to be toned down a notch if I don't want any complications. Who am I kidding, we will have to bring our shit way down. No more back tricks, tight spots, or beatings, it's going to be hard not going at it.

He took the news well and I'm happy that he has my back, his excitement made me want to put it on his ass but he wouldn't let me. At least he wouldn't let me get it how I liked it the most. He's giving me just enough to keep me begging his ass for more. The doctor put me on bed rest so I spent months sitting around the house; I was so big I just stayed in bed.

It was cool because it gave me a chance to really get some shit done that was long overdue. Deangelo and Shay were bonding more and more; they were in and out the house. He was spending so much time gone I was starting to get jealous. If it wasn't Shay it was Corey and I was kind of pissed that Corey hadn't bothered to come see me since I been in the damn bed.

16 DEANGELO

After I returned from my trip I was straight, I had a couple months to plan for our one year anniversary.

"So T, are you having a nice one year anniversary?"

"Yes! How about you?"

"It's cool I guess?"

"What, cool you guess?" I had to mess with T I know she'll get worked up about what I said.

"Yeah, I mean I would like to get the hell out of here and get back so I can get my dessert."

"Really? Why you wait this long, I could've gave you yo' dessert a long time ago."

"Would you like the dessert menu? I can bring the cart over and show you our selection," our waiter said.

"Naw man, no one has the dessert I'm looking for on their menu." I said as we laughed even harder.

"But before we go I have something for you." She pulled out a box; I thought it was a watch or something. "What's this?" Before I can get the rest out I see the stick that's under the fabric. I look over at T and she has no real look on her face. I guess she don't know how I'll respond. "You serious? We're having a baby?" I'm too happy to hold it in. I want to jump up out my seat and run around the restaurant showing people the damn thing. "Babies Mr. Man, babies." Babies, I got up and hugged T, then I realized I may be hurting her so I let go and got down putting my head onto her stomach.

"You really happy or you just saying that?" T asked as she sat down on the bed next to me. "Why you say that T? Why wouldn't I be happy? They mine right?" T got up and tried to storm away. "Where you going?" I grabbed her and put her back on the bed. "Don't do me Deangelo that's not funny!" She turned her head away from me while I laughed. "Stop playing T, I know you not about to cry over a joke. I was just playing I'm sorry, I see yo' ass about to be crazier then you already are."

She smiled as I wiped her tears away then started to squeeze her thighs to make her laugh. "You still didn't answer my question." I stopped tickling her and pulled her up.

"T why wouldn't I be happy?" I wanted to understand where this was coming from.

"I mean, you went this long without having kids. I would think you didn't want any."

I pull her body closer to me. I moved back, rested on the headboard, lifted her and slid her right onto my man. "I told you already, I had a baby five years ago. What part of that you don't understand?" She tried to adjust her hips but I put my arms around her so she couldn't move. I can feel her walls blocking me and I can see she's in a good sense of pain. "I know bu..." I force her down a little more; she stopped talking and let out a moan from the blow.

"T you the only person I have ever done this right here with. That's because I wasn't going to risk having a child with anyone that wasn't you. You're the only woman I've ever loved enough to do this with, I stayed strapped. Like I said T, I love you, Shay is my baby and these two are mine as well." T locked down on my man so tight I felt my jaw dropped down, I can barely inhale.

"Why you still playing with me? Who else would I be pregnant by?" I still can't move hell I can't breathe from whatever it is that just bit down on my man.

I feel her go tighter, I put my mouth around her nipple and sucked on her, I don't want her to see what she doing to me. "I'm sorry, I didn't hear anything?" With those words she slammed her body forward taking all of me with what seemed like even more pressure around my shit. I'm beat after she wouldn't let up, she kept at it swirling her hips, bouncing up and down. I nutted so hard all I could yell was, "Uhhhhhhhh!" She put her hand over my mouth, I can't be quite. I know my mother is across the way and she probably can hear me but I had to let it out.

T laughs and put her head onto my shoulder, I'm sweating like a railroad worker. I can still feel myself shooting in her as she slowly rocks her hips and sucks on my ear. She still has a lock on me, I pull myself together and kiss her palm as she let go. I catch my breath and look up at T as she laugh and kiss my face.

"T I know those are my babies I was just messing with you."

"That's what you get for messing with me!" She climbed off the bed and I fell the hell over. I feel like I had my ass kicked and need to rest.

"Deangelo get up! Deangelo!" I feel T grab my man as I opened my eyes. "I'm up baby."

"Come look at this, hurry up yo' ass been sleep all day." What she mean I been sleep all day? I look over out the window and its dark as hell outside. I look at my watch and its nine thirty. I know it was about eleven this morning when I came in the room. I can't believe she wore me out like that, I showered and got dressed.

"Good to see you today son, you must've had a rough time this morning? I didn't know you were a screamer," my mother said as I proceeded down the steps, I laughed and ignored what she said. I'm too hungry so I went in the kitchen, after looking around I didn't want what was there. I look over the plans T had for the hotel then we set off to the restaurant and had dinner.

"See I told you the stock market is the dirtiest place to clean money," T said.

"Yeah you did T and it is paying off. But enough of that, what the hell you do to me earlier?" She laughed and looked away. I paid for our meal and we headed back towards the house.

"So you gone tell me or what?" T stopped walking and turned into my arms.

"Nothing, I didn't do anything to you but broke yo' ass off!" We both laughed.

"Yeah tell me anything T, I got yo' ass though."

T was put on bed rest shortly after due to complications, I was feeling like shit about the whole thing. I know it's my fault what happened to her in Washington. If it wasn't for that, she wouldn't have suffered as much as she has. There was nothing she could've asked for or wanted that I wasn't willing to give her. I spent most of my time with her and the other time with Shay, we're thick as thieves. T couldn't go with us so she thought we were leaving her out. I would tease her about being jealous of my princess and she would let it go.

T was busy anyway, I would've never thought that she would be so into my life style; I still remember when I told her. I thought she would want me to stop. Which she did and she wanted me to stop murking cats but I explained to her I was only doing what I had to do. Now since we're out of the states, I haven't had to do any of that no how so she's good.

Seemed like in no time she had the money going in so many different directions there was no way in hell it could be connected back to anything. All my peoples had to do was spend their money at one of the shit load of operations and that was it. Within a month they would see it in whatever stock they wanted. Like I said, shit was running like clockwork.

17 ESSENCE

With the help of Mr. Joseph and Mr. Taylor I found that I could make way more capital if I implemented the plans that they sent over. I learned real fast that even though Mr. Joseph was the boss, Mr. Taylor was the one that was more of the enforcer. He was on my ass on a regular making sure I wasn't deviating from the plan. I didn't speak with them often but when I did get a call I was working hard and I needed a break. Mr. Taylor sent me out to LA to meet up with his partners out there and said if I pulled them in I would be ready to partner up with them.

I was nervous as hell when we had our meeting, Tammy ass didn't bother to stick around for that, she was in and out in no time. It was cool because I worked my ass and all I could think of was those tricks at the club. All they saw was a big booty and a smile so that's what I gave their asses. I was in and out, we headed for dinner to celebrate and of course Tammy found her ass back in our company for that. They were going hard. All I kept thinking about was how bad I wanted to celebrate with Mr. Joseph ass. Something about him was stuck in my throat and I wanted to get a chance to swallow his ass back to see how he tasted.

I excused myself and went to the bar. "Excuse me; you don't happen to have milk do you?" The bartender looked at me like I lost my fucking mind. Then he said he would have to get it from the back. I wanted to ask him why the hell he was telling me that and why was he still standing there. I said okay and waited.

When he finally came back it was good and cold, I wanted to finish it all back with one gulp but as long as it took him I had to savor the moment. "Excuse me, can I get one of what she having." My face was hurting I was smiling so fucking hard. I turned around and couldn't help but put my arms around Superstar.

"Damn Essence you not hogging all the milk still are you?" I was too happy to see Superstar.

"You know I am. I wanted to drink it all when he gave it to me but he act like they have a shortage back there."

"Aw yeah? What about that whole gag problem you have?" I thought I would fallout laughing, I hit his ass.

"Nope, I don't have that problem anymore you helped me with that remember. I know you haven't forgotten?" He waved down the bartender again and told him to keep 'em coming. I sat there with Superstar just staring at him. I wanted to ask him why he didn't call me when he was in trouble but he seem like he didn't want to talk too much about his self. I told him briefly why I was in town and that I was doing well thanks to him. He was happy for me and that made me feel good that he really cared enough to help me when I felt like no one else was there for me.

"So Essence, you wanna take a ride with yo' boy?" I stood up. "You know I'm down." I left there with Superstar that night and just like old times he was working wonders on my ass. I was feeling like I was over the moon again and all my worries were out the fucking door. I had sometime before I needed to head back so I spent an extra two days rolling around in the sheets with Superstar.

I was having a ball, something about Superstar was different he wasn't as straight forward or over the top like he used to be. I was too hurt when he called me and told me that he couldn't make it over to see me before I left. Then I found out he was taking some chick to the awards so I flew back and kept it moving.

I went right back to work, Mr. Taylor was sounding like my daddy when I made it back. He seemed like he was aggravated that I took the extra two days. He said I could've done a million things in those two days that I wasted. I just stepped it up and remembered the fork. I worked my ass off to make the shit happen and it seemed like Mr. Taylor didn't give a fuck. He pushed my ass to work even harder. Technically I'm working for them now so what can I say?

I did and it paid off, they were ready to back me and I took a loss with the sixty forty spilt their way but it was still worth it to see my dream. It was only temporary though. Mr. Joseph said he wanted to see me succeed and they weren't looking to takeover they just wanted to make sure I was ready. Once I hit my goal the power would shift and I would be back in the driver seat, I was cool either way.

18 TREASURE

After the babies I didn't have a choice but to get right. Max had my ass in the gym working the shit out of me. I was dropping weight like crazy and the muscle tone was better than ever. I couldn't believe how he worked me over the way he did. I know Deangelo loved it; every chance he got his ass was all over me, not like he wasn't before. He knows I have that, 'Yeah, I'm available body,' not that, 'I have three kids body,' and yes it is a big fucking difference.

So many of these chicks out here let these fools brainwash they ass telling them they thick. Next thing they know they thick ass just sloppy. I'm looking good; I love to look at my abs in the mirror. I could've been a professional in the ring working with Max ass. Whenever I'm boxing with him I have to show off my body and my moves. It's the only place I can do both, Deangelo would have a fit if I stepped out half dressed. I can only imagine how he would act if he saw me fighting somebody. I remember back in the day when he would come to my karate practices. Whenever I looked over at him he would be looking like he was holding his breath or about to explode in anger.

"Come on Treasure push!" I'm so tired of hearing Max tell me that shit; I'm trying to knock his fucking block off. Every time we go around the ring he always act like I'm missing something or leaving myself open. He damn sure doesn't mind popping my ass every now and then when I don't listen. It's cool though because I learned to stop getting popped real quick. Hell, he had me doing it all, kickboxing, karate, he was even trying to get me to do some shit called Capoeira. I'm not into all that though. I just want to get the weight off and be able to beat a bitch down if they stepped up.

After I got out the shower of course I was right back in once Deangelo saw me. I got a call from Sammy about Essence Dreams. She said they were doing big things and that Corey said he was sending her out to LA to meet with Scoot Ink I know the owners from back in the day. I called him and told him it was a good investment and he invited me out. Once I told Deangelo, I was surprised he was okay with me going out there. Of course I had to take Max with me but it's all good. I need to hit the gym while I'm out there anyway.

I met up with them for a brief minute then sat in the back and watched, she walked right pass me when she came in the room. This bitch was damn near butt naked, the shit she had on was so tight it could've been body paint. I had enough, I text Mr. Calvert and told him that I still stood behind the business. While we were at the gym he said they were in and they were going to celebrate. He asked if I wanted to go but I turned him down and asked if he didn't tell her

I was there. He said yes and I was out. I called Corey and let him know she still pulling that dumb shit and to lay it on her ass. I already know he's down; he didn't like how she was trying to trick they asses when she met with them.

The business was doing great; she was really making her way in no time. She did all the shit she needed to do and I was truly happy for her ass. The deal was done and all Deangelo had to do was sign a couple forms and the shit was finished. He was out of town so I sent it to her and then the bitch slipped up.

Sammy called me and told me she was pushing to thank him in person and I wasn't about to have it. I thought she got over the shit but I see that wasn't the case at all. She couldn't reach him so she kept trying asking Sammy if she could take him to dinner. It sounded like this bitch really needing to get at his ass.

19 DEANGELO

We still hadn't tracked down Loretta; I talked to Schultz who's now on the Supreme Court. He said she was on the move but she would turn up. I'm pissed that she got away but as long as I have him in my pocket; I know she's going to be found sooner than later. Bateador running shit back in the states, he's holding it down so I have no worries on that side. Whenever he could get away we would meet up and catch up on old times.

"What's up Treasure? I see yo' lazy tail still in the bed," he said coming in the room.

"Corey come here, I missed you. Why you always have to drag my husband away and not come to see me when you here?" T said as she hugged him while he sat on the bed beside her.

"You know I always want to come and see you, knuckle head over there always try and make it like I stress you out or something." He leaned over and kissed her head. I just sat on the couch and looked away because I can feel T looking over at me.

"Really? Deangelo why you always trying to keep me in this house anyway? I told you I was alright." She tried to sit up. Before I could move Bateador helped her. The sound she made must have worried him because he looked shook after she made it. "I see why he doesn't want you up all that noise you making. Damn Treasure you big as hell! I don't even know how you moving around with all that going on." T laughed and wiped a tear from her eye.

I can tell she's in pain but she playing it off like she's alright. "Corey I'm fine, I was just thinking about you the other day. You remember when you kicked Chucky ass for trying to hit me?" I watched as they both laughed. "Really Treasure? You know that was nothing compared to what Pandillero did to his ass." "Oh really? He must've left that out. All I remember is him standing there smiling like the shit was funny." She tossed a pillow over at me, I caught it and laughed.

"Alright enough of this, let's get out of here man I see T losing her mind." I stood up and walked over to kiss T. "Good, you can help me up because I'm going downstairs." Bateador looked like a deer in headlights and started shaking his head from side to side. T looked over at him and hit him on the shoulder.

"Stop Corey, you not funny." Then she looked back at me.

"Baby please help me out this bed, I want to go downstairs. Stop acting like I'm handicap and can't do shit. All I need is for you to help me out this big ass bed and I can make it the rest of the way." I shook my head telling her no but she pulled the sheets back and started to try and get up anyway.

"T, why do you need to go downstairs? You know Shay not here, I'm about to leave so how you gone get back up here? I know you don't think Ms. Jackson gone help you back up here."

She looked up at me and started to pout then she turned to Bateador. "Corey can you help me? I know you don't want to go play no basketball." Bateador jump up off the side of the bed and start making his way around to help her up. "Man look at yo' weak ass, I got it! Damn, you can't ever say no." We all start to laugh.

I helped T to her feet but she was moving so slow I decided to carry her down. We sat around all day just talking about old times. Bateador telling her about how I had him or other people chasing her around the country. Her telling him different shit, we let go and had fun. We ordered dinner and after Bateador was out the door, I was lugging T back up the steps.

A couple weeks later T gave birth to our beautiful sons Deangelo and August, I was proud when they were born. T was surprised that I wanted to name our youngest August after her first husband, she cried too hard. I know he's still in her heart. After I found out everything that happened to him and how he took care of T, I respected the man. I sort of wished I could have gotten to know him instead of the way I did go at him. I say sort of because he still wife'd up and had a baby with my T. After T left Washington I remember tailing the nigga for a couple days hoping she would contact him.

I never understood why T was into his ass, he seemed like the type that stayed in the mirror more than a female. I was done after he hit up the nail shop and had a pedicure and manicure. I thought the nigga was suspect, then we overheard him and his potnas at the club they had on post. Come to find out these niggas were pickin' up chicks by doin' that funny shit. The chicks at the nail shop were all over him and his boy from the time they went in that mufucka. I thought they knew them or were regulars, he didn't seem like he was trippin' off the ho's. His boy was all over 'em though. I even saw him and the girl from the hospital walking the one white chick up to his room.

Before our wedding I went to check in on T and she was at the shop, next thing I know my ass was in the chair. I can't stunt, that shit felt hella good. T put me up on game and told me that her ex-husband used to go but only if she went with him. When I asked her why she told me I'd see. The entire time I was sitting there I could feel all eyes on me, not like I wasn't used to it. T got up and went in the back for something and a couple chicks came over to where the lady was scrubbing my feet. I turned them away but it was like even women who were walking past the shop were stopping in.

When T came out the back the place was jumping. I was sitting up front kicked back reading a magazine not paying attention to shit. I look up and T standing there with her hands on her hips, "Why you playin' wit' me Deangelo?" I didn't know what the problem was, "What I do T?" She pointed to the two ladies, one was massaging my foot and the other was doing my shoulders. I asked her again what the problem was.

"They don't offer this shit here! Why the hell you letting them touch all over you? These birds don't even work here Deangelo."

"How the hell was I supposed to know that? I thought ya'll work here." I moved and they stopped staring at me like I'm in the wrong.

"Deangelo I told you women see a man that takes care of himself and they think he'll take care of them. You know everything else why don't you know that?" T laughed as I stood ready to leave.

"You know how many ugly niggas could come up if they knew getting their nails cleaned and feet scrubbed would get them chicks? Hell, I need to write a book to help those niggas out, I'd be rich!" We both laughed.

All in all, I'm grateful that he took care of them the way he did. Any other nigga once they found out T was loaded would've tried to take her for all she had. Not him, he didn't touch a dime and still held his own and took care of them. I respect that and like I said I sort of wish I had a chance to really meet him.

Shay was the perfect big sister, she helped out every chance she could. I wanted to be around for everything, diapers, crying, feeding. Hell, I even had a couple drinks from those jugs T carrying around. I never knew breast milk was so good, hell I love breast, especially T's. I was getting mine just as much as the twins.

20 ESSENCE

It was game on, I'm too happy that the deal is done; all I need to do is get Mr. Joseph to sign. He couldn't make it out for the party so I was a little upset. I still want to fuck and once he signs on the dotted line, I'm going to take my chances. He called Tammy and said he would send the paperwork over, I damn near begged her to tell him to let me take him out to dinner.

He turned me down of course but that's not stopping me, once I saw him in New Orleans about a month later it was game on. We spoke briefly then he headed out. I sweet talked the bail hop to let me in his room and I'm too happy when he did. I changed clothes and put on this sexy ass teddy with my heels. I'm walking back and forth waiting on his ass to come in the room.

I thought maybe he wasn't coming back so I was about to leave, then I heard someone at the door. "Mr. Joseph can I thank you the right way?" I said as I walked around the corner towards the door. "Yeah bitch, have a seat," was all she said when she walked past me and took her coat off. I grabbed my bag up off the floor and picked up my shit.

"I'm sorry; I must have the wrong room." I was headed back down the hall. "MAX!" she yelled and some gargantuan Russian looking dude opened the door and stopped me from going out. "Come on back in here ho cause you not leaving until we talk." I'm not one to fight but this bitch not gone keep coming at me like she crazy.

"I said I had the wrong room, can I please just leave?" She stood there and shook her head no. Then she turned and walked to the love seat and sat down. I walked over and sat on the couch. "So you were trying to fuck my husband?" I looked at her like she farted, "I don't know who your husband is." She giggled and shook her head.

"Why you want to play with me? You know damn well who my husband is so answer the question." Shit fuck her, bitch not dealing with a punk.

"If you're talking about Mr. Joseph, yes, I am trying to fuck." Now what bitch? She clapped her hands and laughed.

"I see you a tough bitch."

"What do you want and who are you?" She blew out hard like I'm getting on her last nerve she picked up a bottle and took a sip. "I'm the bitch th..." she said a bunch of shit that I wasn't trying to hear. Then she act like she never seen good pussy before. I forgot what I had on anyway; I rolled my eyes and went in the bathroom to put my clothes back on. Damn think Essence, how in the fuck are you going to get out of this shit? I sat in the bathroom trying to figure out just how I can back the hell out of here without this bitch calling the police.

The last thing I need is for her to have me arrested for breaking in here. Shit that would definitely sink my business. I know once Mr. Joseph finds out him and Mr. Taylor will back out and that's the last thing I need right now. When I came out she was sitting at the table waiting on my ass. Max big ass was still standing in front of the door.

I walked over and sat down. "So Ms. Essence Donahue, you want to fuck my husband or you want to never contact him again?" I didn't say anything she still didn't answer my question so why answer hers. "I'm sorry who are you?" She put her hand up and that bitch had rocks the size of bowling balls. I'm surprised she can hold her hand up without help. I need to put on shades the way the light is hitting off that damn thing.

"That's not telling me anything." Still, fuck her!

"Okay, I see you slow. I'm Terentia Joseph; Mr. Joseph is my husband. If it wasn't for me they wouldn't have known anything about Essence's Dreams. If it wasn't for me calling out to LA and backing you, there was no way in hell that damn near strip show you put on would've worked. Yeah I was there; you probably didn't notice me sitting behind you though. Hell I don't have a dick so why would you. I called Mr. Taylor and told him how you put on that show. So guess what, that contract you signed boo boo is not everything you think. You really need to hire a lawyer instead of smiling in any good looking man's face and signing shit. Especially not my fucking husb—" I cut her off.

I stood up because I know what the deal is and it ain't shit this bitch can do about it. "What the fuc—" Who is she any fucking way? Her dumb ass probably just sits around leeching off his ass. She cut me off and walked around the table and stood right up on me. Then the guy came back in the room like he waiting to help her jump on me or something.

"Look bitch, I told you once you don't fucking want this here, so sit the fuck down and shut up! How the fuck you gone try and be mad, you sneaking in my mother fucking husband room trying to fuck him?" She did have a valid point there; I wanted to laugh in that bitch face. Then I thought about it, I sat back down so I can hear what she has to say. I'm too mad, just the thought of what she said about the contract and me needing a lawyer set my ass off. I don't know what I was thinking.

"Now where was I? Oh yeah, so the contract says basically this, you piss me off and you lose everything. That's even if you hit your goal, see." She slid me the documents. "Read this here, matter fact; just hire a lawyer I'll tell you. It says that for the life of this business or any branch fo...Terentia T Joseph will gain full control of sai..."

I'm in tears when she read me that shit. I looked in the contract and most of it was mumbo jumbo but her name is on it. Damn is all I can think, I want to fuck myself up for being lost in dick and not being about my business. Now this bitch at any time can take my shit away from me and it doesn't sound like there's shit I can do about it.

She slid me a box of tissue. "Bitch please, save that shit for someone who gives a damn. Like I said, piss me off and you're done!" I'm about to beg this bitch to see what the fuck she want.

"I'm sorry Mrs. Joseph, what do I need to do to make this right?" Shit, I'd screw her ass too if that will make her happy. Wouldn't be the first time, those dike bitches loved me in the club back in the day.

"Max adesso so chi sono. Ho pensato che ero io?" She started laughing saying something in I guess Italian to the Max guy, he started laughing. She said something else looking at me but I didn't understand so they started laughing again. I guess that shit run in their family because that was the same shit they did to me and Tammy. So maybe they were talking shit about us then too.

She stopped laughing and looked over at me. "You don't have to do shit but your job! Don't piss me off and we're good, besides, I don't have time for another business anyway. Make sure you stay the fuck away from my husband. Try not to even be in the same state with him and you should be fine. Don't call, email, you thought you were slick too with the video shit. I was on the floor when Sammy told me that.

Then you try to make it like you had other investors because you couldn't get a sit down with them. You are really funny. It doesn't matter though, just don't look at my husband, hell, and don't even dream about his ass. I know he been on your mind. You only met him once and you ready to fuck? I know they had rules about that type of behavior in the Bronx right?"

I felt my face swell up and get soaked, I'm crying like a baby hearing those words. Then I hear Max say something and I turn to look at him. It's Mr. Joseph; I look down quick and wipe my tears away. I'm still heaving and huffing though wondering why I didn't think about the fork before I came up in this damn room. "What's this T? What you doing here? What's going on Ms. Donahue, you alright?" I didn't even look up; I just kept my head down. I waited as they did that language shit and I'm too embarrassed, all I want to do is die. I hear him chuckle then he started to walk towards me but she said something and he laughed like he was highly pleased.

"Look Ms. Donahue, I see you met my wife and by the way you crying now you see she don't play games. I gave you my word about not wanting to takeover your business. I truly do want to see you succeed and so does my wife believe it or not. If not, she wouldn't have told us to help you. Even now she said she wanted to help you but I know you didn't understand what we were saying and I apologize for that as well."

"Okay Mister, wrap this shit up!" I understood her ass that time and she didn't seem like she wanted to help my ass. He came closer and sat on the table. I still wasn't gone run the chance of slipping up and pissing this bitch off. I closed my eyes and looked down.

"Like I was saying, I gave you my word and my word is final. I'm the least bit interested in you; don't get me wrong it's nothing wrong with you." I can hear this bitch laugh and sit down. "I love my wife and even if she wouldn't have come here today I would've sent you away. So just take care of what you need to and if you want anything you need to talk with Mr. Taylor or my wife." He damn straight, I'll talk to Mr. Taylor but I'll never talk to that crazy bitch another day in my life.

"I know you thinking you'll never want to speak with her again but she can really help you. Don't let the chance pass you by to learn because if you know better you'll do better."

When he said those words to me I thought about the night at the fork, Superstar told me the same thing. Now that I put the pieces together, they have to know Superstar. Maybe that's how she knows about the Bronx, I can't believe Superstar. It's okay though, I'll never speak with his ass again either. He did a lot for me but I would never think that he would let me risk my dreams dealing with them and not tell me. I cried even harder once I let that shit sink in.

"Alright bitch get out, I'm tired of hearing yo' ass cry!"

"Come on T, why you have to go so hard on her?"

"Don't do me; this bitch trying to fuck you now she sitting there crying like a damn baby. Bitch need to keep up with where this is going." She came over to me and I hear her popping her fingers in my face. I'm so fucking annoyed it took me forever to look up at her ass.

"That's right bitch, look at me. That's my husband and you can cry all you want. His word maybe final but my ass is queen and like I said, stay away! Do what the fuck you have to and that will be that!"

I want to beat this bitch ass; I stood up and pushed the chair out from under me hard. I'm tired of her shit; she already won so she doesn't have to keep at me like she is. She smiled and didn't even flinch. I can see Mr. Joseph out the side of my eye holding his head down shaking it from side to side.

"I told you bitch this ain't what you want. You want to try me and see what's behind the door with the letter T?"

I couldn't help but laugh at what that bitch said, I was shaking my head now, she smirked like she daring me to move. Then everybody in the room was laughing, even her, like it just sank in what the hell she said.

"I understand, I apologize and it won't happen again. Can I go now?"

"Bye bitch!" she said and threw her hand towards the door. I hurried up and got out of there.

I didn't bother going back to the room to get the overnight bag I came with, I went straight to the airport. I need to get back to Memphis as soon as possible.

When I spoke with my lawyer about what that bitch said I was too hurt. Come to find out, it don't matter what business I start she can still take control.

I asked if I can back out and he said no, it's like I signed my life over to the devil. I can't even sue them because I had more than enough time to seek counsel and was too dick blind to see what the hell I was doing. I was crushed; all I can do is stay away and handle my business.

21 TREASURE

I had no time to deal with Essence, that trick must've lost her mind if she thinks she taking Deangelo to dinner. It don't matter at all to me; we talking about a nigga who gets upset if I shower before coming from the gym and he's home. I was headed down to New Orleans to surprise my baby. By the time Max and I got to the hotel I saw him speaking with whom else? Essence.

I know why her ass is down here, she's opening up an office in the area. Deangelo's on the list to sit in on some bullshit ass conference. I watched my baby play her ass right to the left. Then again I don't know if he knows I'm here or not. Either way it doesn't matter, I know she didn't know who I was so when he pulled off we walked right up to the front desk.

I went to the counter and got a key for his room. I over hear her off on the side telling this barely legal bail hop that she was Mrs. Joseph and was trying to get into her husband room. I looked over at Max and asked him if he heard her crazy ass.

She didn't understand what I was saying because I was speaking Italian and she wasn't even looking in our direction. "So what do you want to do? You want me to get her ass out of here?" I looked at Max like he had lost his damn mind. "Hell naw I don't want you to get her out of here! I want to see just how far this crazy ass bitch will go to get at Deangelo. So before I forget try not to call his ass, I can see you dialing his damn number now." He looked away like his ass didn't understand what I was talking about.

The bail hop came past and I gave him my key to give to her ass, I gave him some money and he was too happy to do it. I gave her sometime to get good and settled in. I want to see just how far this bitch willing to go. I walked in and had Max stand outside, as soon as she heard the door she was asking if she could thank him. I damn near died when I saw the shit she had on and the look on her face. "Yeah bitch, have a seat!" I walked right past her and took a seat. She tried to grab up her shit and leave. I called Max and he stopped her ass so she didn't have a choice but come sit down.

She tried to lie again but I'm not having it, she sat right on down. You can tell a stripper, they never close their legs. This bitch was sitting like a straight nigga, legs wide open. I asked if she was trying to screw him and she played like she didn't know who I was talking about; I had to laugh at her ass. I mean she knows this his room. If I walk in with a key after she begged for a key wouldn't she know who my husband is?

They say common sense not common so whatever. I have to give it to her, she has balls, and she said she was trying to screw him. The look on her face said if he walked in right now she'd do it and not give a damn about me sitting here.

"What do you want and who are you?" She trying to get smart, I have to take a drink before I tell her ass off.

"I'm the bitch that's about to fuck you up and make your existence end if you say the wrong thing!" She jumps up like I'm still not qualified to be having a conversation with her ass.

"Who are you and how do you plan on doing that?" She played like she wanted to figure the shit out.

"Like I said I'm that bitch!" I stood up and she jumped up like she don't care if it's about to go down. I looked at her ass, "Bitch please, you don't want it. Go put on some clothes, I'm tired of seeing yo' pussy looking at me."

I sat waiting on the ho to come out the bathroom, didn't take her that long to jump out the shit she had on now she wanna take all day. She came back in and I let her have it. "So Ms. Essence Donahue yo..." Then she tried to play again I'm starting to get real annoyed. I thought this girl had more sense than she's showing; I'm starting to think I was wrong about her from the beginning. I showed that trick my ring. Once I tell her about what has her sitting over there all brash she gone want to kiss my shit.

"That's not telling me anything," she said with a stank ass attitude. She even had the nerve to squint her eyes like my shit was small and yawn on my ass. She got me hella good with that shit. I was about to laugh, she straight act like my ring don't mean shit to her ass.

"Okay, I see you slow. I'm Terentia Joseph; Mr. Joseph is my husband. If it wasn't for me they would not have known anything about Es..."

First this bitch wants to know who I am now I struck a chord when I brought up the contract, she gets up like she ready. I shut that bitch off real quick; I'm ready to tear her ass apart for having the audacity to be mad after trying to fuck my husband and getting caught. I walked right up on that bitch and dared her ass. I already warned her and I made sure she had ample opportunity. Max ran his ass over like Deangelo gone kill his ass if it went too far, I tried to calm down and work with the slut.

"Now where was I? Oh yeah, so the contract says basically this, you piss me off and you lose everything. That's even if you hit your goal, see." I slid her the documents. "Read this here, matter fact; just hire a lawyer I'll tell yo..." After I finished, that trick was whining like a baby, she realized she messed up. I still don't give a hell. This skank sure wouldn't care if Deangelo left me and our three kids. She can cry all the hell she want, she need to think before she act. I gave that tramp some tissue and told her to shut up.

"I'm sorry Mrs. Joseph what do I need to do to make this right?" Now she wants to get some sense in her damn head. I should hold my ring back up at her ass; see if she knows better now. Slow ho took this long for it all to set in, now she realizes just who I am.

"Max now she knows who I am. I thought she was me?" I spoke in Italian we laughed, I looked at her, "If I'm qualified to have this conversation with you now, just be quiet." She didn't say anything so me and Max laughed again. I don't know why I'm messing with this girl. I guess the thought of her running off with Deangelo and her messing with me and my babies kept popping in my head. I figured it was time to stop playing around with her and tell her what I was after. "You don't have to do shit but your job! Don't piss me..." I went on but when I brought up the Bronx, it was like I told the deepest darkest secret ever.

She back crying when I brought up her previous employment, I actually felt a little bad for that. "Mr. Joseph," Max said. I had to drop my head; I wasted all my time messing with this bitch. I couldn't even get ready to surprise my baby. Damn! "What's this T? What you doing..." I know I'm about to hear it for this little stunt. I looked at my baby and was hoping that bitch looked up. I was going to call the game on her ass and be done with it.

He started to go over to her, I spoke in Italian again and so did he. "So you don't see me right here? You just gone run to Essence?" He looked at me and came over. "Baby why you doing this to her? I told you that this was going to be a problem from the beginning. Now you have her crying and shit." I smiled and pecked his lips. "I didn't bring her here; she was in here waiting for you when I got here. You can ask Max, I know you gone ask him anyway. I'm just trying to help her the right way before I kill her ass." He thought the shit was funny.

"T that's enough. You shouldn't have given her your key anyway." He started to walk over to her.

"Really Max? So it's like that husband? You really want me to kill yo' ass." He stopped and laughed hard. She still didn't know what was being said so she cried. "Look Ms. Donahue I see you met my wife and by the way you cr..." he was talking to her. I really do want to see her succeed but not if she just gone fuck her way by. Hell I could've easily lived the life but I know my journey and it damn sho' wasn't handed to my ass. Maybe it was, either way by now, with all the shit I been through, I earned it plus benefits if you ask me. I'm ready to check out and go home, he taking too long.

Once he finished talking she cried more and like I said I'm ready for her to go. I told her to get out then Deangelo had to say I'm being hard on her. I told his ass the legitimacy of what was happening. I had to snap that bitch into reality too. I snapped my fingers in the front of her face thinking maybe this ho is sleep. She finally looked up. "That's right bitch, look at me. That's my husband and you can cry all you want. His word maybe final but my ass is queen and like I said, stay away! Do what the fuck you have to and that will be that!"

She was on fire; she jumped the hell up like I thumped her ass or something. Deangelo know I'm not about to play with her ass, he don't even want to watch. I warned her again and told her to take her best shot, she laughed like the shit was funny. Hell I had to laugh with everybody else when I realized the letter T shit was so funny. She apologized and I told her to leave. Max followed her out; his ass just didn't want to be in the middle of what was going on.

"T I told you this shit was going to happen baby." He still has his head in his hands like he tired.

"It's cool baby, she'll be alright. I'll bet you she takes care of her shit on her own now."

"I don't care what she do T, I don't want to be in this shit." I walked in the room and picked up my stuff.

"Where you going T?" I turned and looked at him. "Where we going? Whatchu thought you were staying here and this trick had her stank ass all up and thru here with nothing on?" He laughed and grabbed his shit we went the hell home.

22 ESSENCE

"Hey Tammy, how we looking today?"

"Essence you have someone in your office." She walked off fast before I could ask her who so I went in. I opened the door and damn near fell to my knees when I saw who it was. "Hello Ms. Donahue, you mind if I call you Essence, I like that name?" Fuck I hate this bitch, she sitting in my chair like she own the fucking place.

"What did I do now? Do I need to leave the state because I can be on the next flight out?" She laughed and came around to the edge of my desk.

"Look Essence, I know you mad at me but hell, you would do the same thing with a man as fine as my husband. I have a family to look after and I'll do whatever I have to do to keep it together." I can't knock this bitch for that.

"You have to be here for a reason Mrs. Joseph so what is it?" She sat in the chair so I walked and sat behind my desk. "I'm just here to say you're doing great. You really should let me sign you up for the seminars that I keep sending Tammy and she keeps saying you're booked for." I just looked at her. "I'm busy; I need to do what I have to do just in case Mrs. Joseph." She thought that was funny.

"Hear me out, I can help you. I don't like you but I can help you. Don't let your pride stop you Essence, it'll only hurt you in the end. Hell, you can't have that much pride, you was popping yo' ass in the strip club." That was it, she'd said enough and I'm done with the insults. I stood up and headed for the door.

"I wouldn't do that if I were you!" I stopped, turned around and held my head back like this bitch had a knife to my throat. She stood up and came forward, I mugged her ass hard. "You look like you want to fight!" "That's the most interesting thing you've said since you been here." This bitch smiled like that was what she wanted to hear.

"Come on Essence, you have a clear schedule." I shook my head and walked behind her. We made it downstairs, Max opened the door for us and we got in. She told him to head to the recreation center, she was on her phone during the ride with nothing said between us we pulled up and got out. We walked in and she headed up the steps, she opened the door and the smell that came out the room smacked me in the face it was so rank. This must be what this ho pussy smell like, she act like it don't bother her.

"What's up Treasure, what you doing here? I thought you were too tired." Some old guy came out and hugged her. He don't look that old actually, it's the way he spoke and held his cigarette that tells me he's old. He has that back in the day slang and his cigarette is hanging out the side of his mouth but it's not even lit. When she asked him why he was smoking he said he don't smoke it's just a habit he hasn't broken yet. I heard her tell him we needed some gear so we could go a couple rounds, I smiled at the thought. "NO! Hell no Treasure, Pandillero is not gone kill me behind this shit!" Who the hell is Pandillero?

He better be worried because I'm about to beat the shit out this bitch once and for all. She walked away to talk to the old guy, I stood around, hell I wanted to stretch. Then she came from the back, tossed a bag at me and told me where I could change. I flew in there, put on the clothes in the bag and was putting on the gloves as I walked back out the locker room.

When I came out she had already changed and was standing around talking to the old guy and Max. Max came over and gave me a form and told me to sign it. "Mrs. Joseph you're not getting me again, I'm not signing shit without a lawyer!" They started laughing, she tried to tell me some bullshit I still wasn't signing it.

"Well here take this, you write on here you won't sue anyone and you're willing to participate for sport and sign and so will I. Max can do his thing and that will be done." That was all I needed to hear before I signed. She saw how fast I was writing so I can beat the shit out of her, I thought this bitch had a change of heart.

"Now before you sign this, these are the rules." Yeah, now this bitch wants to try and not get her ass kicked. "If I win, you let me help you and come to me if you need help. If you win, I'll back off and never see you again." I signed that shit and gave it to Max. The old guy was begging her not to do it and he should've been trying harder because the bitch is about to get a beat down.

We got in the ring and it was on, I'm ready, I went right for her ass. She moving around, I'm swinging but she gone before I can hit her. "Stop running bitch!" She came forward and I went towards her again, she hit me two times but I started swinging and she moved. "Why you ru—" This bitch hit me in the mouth, I'm too mad. I rushed her ass, she held my arms but I can still hit her sides so I did. Then the guy broke us up and she started laughing. "You mad now huh Essence?"

I went back at her. I hit her in the chest a couple times, she moved back to the ropes so I started swinging. I can hear her laugh like I'm not hurting her so I started giving it my all. I'm tired as hell, she pushed me back and I tried to hold my arms up but these gloves feel like they weigh a million pounds. I'm not about to let her hit me though she coming forward fast. I'm moving around to catch my breath. "You tired Essence; you want to call it a loss?"

I shook my head no and that bitch came in, she hit me in my ribs. I thought I would throw up, she hit me again and I'm trying to move. I'm up against the ropes and she's moving from side to side hammering on my ribs. I tried to swing back but she won't stop, then she moved back, "You finished yet Essence?" I shook my head no and walked back up to her ass, I'm not about to go out like a punk.

I don't know why I did because she was on my ass again. This time she's hitting me in the chest and my titties feel like they're about to explode. She asked me if I was done. "Fuck you bitch!" Why did I say that? This slut's hitting me in the face like I'm a got damn punching bag. I move back and I'm back on the ropes. I'm so tired I can barely cover my face; it's hard as hell trying to keep my hands up. When I did, she starts hitting me on both sides of my head like she's trying to knock my brain out.

She stopped again and moved back, I'm not giving up, we turned around and I see Mr. Joseph. He looks like he's trying to figure out who's in the ring, not that he didn't know, I guess he in shock. It's not like she has on gear like I do, she's only wearing gloves. Maybe that's why she gave me all this shit and didn't put this heavy shit on.

"Don't worry, I'm not going to count that look against you bu..." This bitch comes up and hits my ass two times in the face, my ass start counting sheep. I woke up and the old guy had some shit under my nose. My body is aching and I can't move a muscle for shit. She came over and sat beside me, "Essence I won, so like I said, that's that. Sorry about knocking you out but you did look at my husband; I won't hold that against you. I'll be in touch Essence, Max will take you back, and I'm going with my husband." Damn I hate that bitch!

A couple days later Sammy called and said she signed me up for all kinds of shit. I'm working harder than I have in my life. I learned a lot though and I used it every chance I could. She even signed me up to train over at the recreation center and I'm determined to learn so I can kick her ass.

Then it was like she disappeared. No more calls, visits, nothing. Even Mr. Taylor changed numbers and I wouldn't dare try to call Mr. Joseph so it worked out for the best. I continued to work on my business, gained majority control and I never heard from them again. I guess I learned a lot, I even found me a single man and plan on getting married. He knows all my secrets and I hope I know all of his. I'm happy with the way things turned out. I learned a lot from Mrs. Joseph after all.

23 TREASURE

I gave Essence sometime to see what she would do and when I realized that she was moving on, I was getting my faith back in her. I headed to Memphis to get some ideas for a boxing program for Deangelo. I didn't know that Tone was working in the gym. Tone's an older guy from the hood who was a professional boxer. He came in a couple times to teach me some shit when I was working with Rook back in the day.

As soon as we got in Memphis Max ass was on me about heading to the gym and working out first so we did. Tone was surprised to see me and Max couldn't wait for me to show him how well I was doing. They had me doing all kind of shit, I was worn out by the time I drug my ass out of there.

I damn near slept the next day away, Max still had me train but I didn't head back to the gym like I said. Of course Deangelo called to find out why; it's good though, I already have what I need. I'm really here to see Essence anyway, Deangelo taunted me about it but I don't care.

The next morning I went in her office and her secretary is acting like she has a stick up her ass. I had to let her ass have it, "I'm sorry Mrs. Joseph I didn't know who you were." I had to laugh at that bitch. "So you treat everybody that comes in here like that?"

"It's been a rough morning Mrs. Joseph."

"The office opened twenty minutes ago, how the hell you have a rough morning when you just started working? Not to mention the fact that you actually have a job. You know how many people don't have a job right now?"

"I apologize again Mrs. Joseph; it's been a rough morning. I'm aware of that and I didn't mean to come off as having an attitude."

"Rough morning or not, yo' ass have a job and it's so many others out there that would love to have yo' job its crazy. Check this though, one complaint and I'll personally come here and throw yo' ass out in the streets." Her eyes were big.

"Excuse me?"

"I said one complaint and I will personally fire you by throwing yo' ass out that door onto the streets."

"Is that a threat?" I laughed at her ass.

"It's a promise, guarantee, final answer or whatever else you wanna call it. You have by the end of the day to send me the tracking number on the video and all its copies. If not I'll be here first thing in the morning to make good on what I said."

"I don't appreciate your threats and I don't know what video you're talking about. If you'll excuse me, Ms. Donahue is not in and I have work to do," she said and sat behind her desk. I walked around and sat on the edge of her desk and she looked at me like I was crazy.

"Does Ms. Donahue know about the video? Don't act like you don't know what I'm talking about or you can get ready for me to pull you up right now and throw you out!"

"Can you explain exactly what you're talking about?"

"Damn, it's more out there? I want them all to be on their way to Sammy by the end of the day. When Ms. Donahue comes in you need to find yo' way where ever you hid them and get them off to me."

"Is there anything else?"

"Yeah, last I checked Sammy don't get down like that so if I were you, I would stop coming on to her."

"I've never come on to her Mrs. Joseph." I shook my head and told her I would be waiting in Essence office and to not tell her who I was. This bitch won't tell the truth for shit. She said okay and I waited on Essence to come in.

She looks like she wants to die seeing me in here, I'm not even mad with her either. I just want to talk to her, see how she's doing. She keeps acting like she wants to fight so I'll give her ass an invitation. "You look like you want to fight!" "That's the most interesting thing you've said since you been here." She's too happy to take me up on my offer, I just laughed at the thought of putting it on her ass.

"What's up Treasure, what you doing here?"

"Nothing, we came to get out some aggression in the ring that's all." Tone looked at me and told me flat out no and Deangelo wasn't going to kill him for me fighting in his gym. I'm not having it, he tried to walk away but I'm right behind his ass. I told him that I'm grown and Deangelo can't tell me what the hell to do.

He said he would tell him if I did. I walked past him, grabbed some gloves, clothes, told him to tell and walked off. I gave her the shit and she changed. I'm not about to get into anything legal with this bitch so I gave her one of the center waivers. When she told me she wouldn't sign it, I knew she learned her lesson. I was cool with it.

I told her to write some shit out and sign it; she was in a hurry to get in the ring. I tried to warn her again to let her back out but she not having it. This girl really doesn't like me, hell, not too many girls like me so I'm use to it.

"Treasure please don't do this, you know Pandillero will be mad if you do. Come on Treasure it's not worth it."

"Tone what you worried for; he won't even be here 'til late tonight."

"That's it Treasure, I'm calling Pandillero on yo' ass!" I didn't even look back at Tone crazy ass. We got in the ring and this bitch was going crazy, she thought I was going to straight street fight with her ass. She doesn't want that either but I have to show out. I'm fucking with her and I can see Tone is about to lose his mind. He act like this bitch gone knock me out or something. He has the phone up to his ear like he can't wait to reach Deangelo. He knows if she does knock me out, Deangelo gon' probably kill him and Max ass too for letting me do this stupid shit.

She start talking shit about me moving, I hit her ass in the mouth to shut that shit up and she come straight for me swinging hard as hell. I don't care, her hits not fazing me because she can't fight. Plus I can clearly see she tired and she using the last little burst of energy she can muster. She has a nice shape but once again, thick and fit are too different things. Her ass got tired quick and I let that trick have it. They broke us up and I asked her if she was mad. She came at me again; I took a couple hits and let her get some more off.

I laughed at the sound of her losing her breathe, I know what time it is. "You tired Essence; you want to call it a loss?" She said no so I started with the body work and I'm getting her ass good. I back off when I see she's filling it and asked her again if she wanted to stop. She still mad though and want some more.

I returned the favor and let that bitch get a taste of how it feels to be hit in the chest. Then she said fuck me and I went at her face, I don't know why I did that to her. I know she just mad but hell, she did ask for it. I backed off because she didn't even have her hands up after a while. Then I see Deangelo walk in and I want to jump my ass out the ring. I know if I do she'll win so I turn so I won't see his ass. I see her look at him and I clocked her ass good and it was done. I hear Deangelo say, "Come on T." I had to laugh, he looks so disappointed in me but she had it coming.

Tone woke her ass up; I walked over, told her what I had to say and apologized for knocking her out. I know she didn't stand a chance and I really shouldn't have even took it this far but it's too late to change that. I couldn't even change; Deangelo had already grabbed my shit and was walking me to the damn office. Then in came Corey, Tone, and Max, I sat in the chair with a big ass grin on my face, Deangelo hot.

I'm trying to play crazy as hell; I jump on the computer and start playing Solitary. Corey come over and turn the screen off on my ass, I'm bugging up laughing at his ass. He doesn't think it's funny at all though. His crazy ass looks at me like I'm married to him or something. He's so upset with me I stopped laughing and looked down.

"What the fuck wrong with you niggas?" Corey said as they stood waiting on them to respond.

"Pandillero I told her not to do it," Tone said. Deangelo was on fire and he didn't want to hear shit.

"What the hell you mean you told my fucking wife not to do something? Who the fuck are you nigga to tell my wife any damn thing?" Tone stepped back as Deangelo moved closer to him.

"Mr. Joseph, this is my fault I should've taken Ms. Donahue away." Corey walked closer to Max and they were chest to chest.

"Yo' dumb ass means you shouldn't have ever let Essence get in the fucking car!" Deangelo pushed them apart, Corey sat on the desk.

"Let me get this straight, you two niggas just let my wife, the mother of my three kids get into some boxing match? Neither one of you niggas thought for one second to stop Essence ass from coming in the gym?" They didn't respond.

"TALK NIGGAS!" They both started looking around as Corey yelled and jumped back up. "I guess ya'll forgot how to talk," Deangelo said as he walked back over standing in front of both of them.

They both looked away I couldn't let this go on any further; I looked down at the floor. "You can't stop me!" I looked back up and it was like I pulled a string and turned all their heads at one time towards me. "Look, no sense in fussing over spilled milk. This my fault and I knew you would be mad but I'm grown. None of you can stop me from doing anything that I want to do, when I want to do it. Get over it!" Deangelo turned towards me; they all started to back out the

107

room. I hear the door close and they all started to laugh.

"You sure T? That's yo' word, I couldn't have stopped you?" I stood up out the chair and walked to the door, he stood there watching me. "You damn straight!" I took off out the door; he came flying behind my ass. I couldn't even make it out the gym before he pulled my ass up. I'm laughing too hard; he had me on the car tickling the shit out of me.

"T I thought I couldn't stop you? Talk that shit now tough girl! I can't hear you T."

"P-pleeeease, o-okay, okay. I can'..." I'm done, I have tears falling so hard he had to stop and see if I'm hurt. I laughed even more at how protective he really is with me. I pulled him in between my legs and kissed my baby so he would stop worrying.

They all came out and we were in the car, we stopped long enough for him to punish my ass real good in the shower and change. He didn't say shit the entire way to the airport, he was on fire still and I know it. I don't care though, I feel good. He's sitting looking out the window like he doesn't want to look at me. I walked over and sat on his lap.

"That's it T, no more of this Essence shit! You went too far and you have kids at home who need you."

"Okay Deangelo, my pleasure." He smiled and I kissed him.

"Why you knock her out like that T?"

"She did it to herself." He grabbed my thigh and I jumped.

"See T, this is what the hell I'm talking about! What the hell is wrong with you? Did you get hurt?" He all over me checking to see if I'm bruised.

"I'm fine Deangelo, who acting crazy now?" We laughed and I slept on my baby chest all the way back.

"You ready to go T?" I walked over to Deangelo and grabbed his hand.

"Nope! I have something to give you first." He looked at me and licked his lips.

"Not that silly, get yo' mind out the gutter!" I pulled out a box and handed it to him, he opened it and I headed for the door.

"Tell me you didn't T!" He opened the door and looked out.

"You like?" He kissed me and hit the locks on the car.

"Damn I missed my car. What did you do to it?"

"Nothing, I had it cleaned up that's about it."

"Come on T, you did more than clean it up." He popped the hood and was jumping up and down when he saw it was still in its original condition.

"Thank you baby! I should've known something was up when Bateador told me it was stolen but I didn't have to worry about it."

"I'm surprised his ass didn't tell you." Deangelo too happy that I had his white 1971 Plymouth 'Cuda convertible sent over. I know he love this car and hates that it sits in the garage at the lake house. I couldn't wait for it to be delivered and when it was I knew he would be happy with what they did to it.

We headed out for dinner and had a ball laughing and spending time together. "You ready to go dancing baby?" He shook his head no, it didn't matter though, and I grabbed his hand and pulled him out. "What Max doing here?" I thought he said we would be alone but I see that was a lie. He tried to tell me that he was there to switch cars because he doesn't want his old school getting dirty. He doesn't drive the thing already because he claims it's not a car you put miles on. What kinda shit is that?

I knew that was a lie too when Max was standing around outside the club after we went in. I'm not going to let that bother me; we don't even have a table but I pulled him on the floor, we danced and I'm all over him. I don't even like the songs but it don't matter, I love feeling his body against mine.

Once we found a table we sat back still taking in each other's company and I have no problems with it. "I'll be right back; I have to go to the restroom." He let me out and smacked my ass; I backed it right up on him.

"You better stop before you are following me in here."

"You say the word and it's going down T." I laughed and walked away. On my way back I stopped by the bar to get another drink, I realize Deangelo probably already ordered so I changed my mind. I see my baby smiling as I walked towards him, and then I thought I saw someone who looked familiar. I moved a little faster to get a better view. My mind flicking back through all the people I've met in my life. By the time I had a clear view my mind stopped on the day Deangelo took me out to Minnesota. Instantly every angle of that face started moving around in my head, I still don't know the name; all I remember is the face.

It started to hit me the way she's looking at me in some of the different images I've stored away. She looked pissed off in some, and then angry, then I saw a look that told me she was upset with Deangelo. I know that look, it said he slept with her and she was jealous that I was the one with him.

I can read every thought in her head with the images. She hated that she wasn't the one that he chose. Each page that she saw my name, she slammed her stamp down with more hatred and anger. I didn't realize that I never picked up on how she was reacting that day. At the time I was more terrified for Deangelo and the whole situation, I couldn't think about her.

I see something in her hand and it made me want to walk faster to see what it is. I know she has to come past me in order to reach him. I see her hand come up and I move quicker and push her arm down. I look at her, take a still shot of her face, as I place it in my memory bank I hear a shot. I feel a chill then I feel like I put on some Icy Hot. I hear two more shots then all of a sudden I can't hear shit, did this bitch make me go deaf? I looked in her eyes as we both dropped to our knees.

I'm still uploading this bitch face, I'm not going to miss a single detail, it's a scary quiet now. I see Deangelo come closer, he standing over her his gun is empty. In slow motion I hear the clip tear through the wind and hit the ground. I hear him pull another clip and the click when he reloaded. That shit was loud as fuck in my ears; maybe I'm not deaf after all. I fell back as his gun went empty again. My baby came over and caught my head before it touched the ground. I'm tired from capturing that bitch face; I had to close my eyes.

24 DEANGELO

After the twins first birthday I wanted to take T out for a night on the town, it will be her first since having the babies. We made our way to a night club after dinner. We were having a cool night; the place was packed wall to wall with people. T's making her way back to the table and I watched her, she stands out like a light moving her way through the crowd.

I smiled at the site of her, T was no longer looking at me though, and I followed her eyes. That's when I saw her, I jumped up and before I could get out the booth I hear three shots. I'm steaming; I sent four rounds to that bitch side. The closer I came to her the more I sent her way. Before I know it I'm out, I drop the clip, reloaded and emptied everything I have on Loretta.

She's not going to get away this time. I walk over to T as she closes her eyes.

There's no way in hell she's going to die on me, I pick her up and Max speeds to the hospital. I'm covered in blood by the time we make it. They came out; put her on the bed rolling T away. They won't let me go back with her. I want to fight with them but I know I can't slow them down or distract them from helping her.

My hearts on the floor, I'm dying once I realize that I have T blood on my hands again. I feel hopeless; my entire universe is closing in on me with T being here. It's not long before the nurse came and took me to overlook the surgery. The doctor said she was hit in the stomach, the lung, three ribs are shattered and there's major internal damage. That bitch hit my baby five times and if I could kill her again I would make sure I took my time to make her pay. Before he can say anything else alarms went off and he runs back into the room.

I can't take the site of her on that table; I cried and called out to her just hoping she could hear me. Her head rolled over towards me and hurt me even more. The nurse came and took me back out to the waiting area. My phone going crazy, I launched it across the room almost hitting someone that was sitting in here.

Max came and walked me out the hospital; I sat there 'til the sun came up lost and dying. Not a word about how T was doing. Max walked over and told me that Bateador would be here shortly and our parents were on their way. The thought of facing them sent me back out of control. All I had to do was take care of T and I didn't. I know Kathy's going to kill me for letting this happen. I know she blames me for Washington even if she never said it, I know she does. The thought of my princess having to suffer as much as she has sent a chill over my body. I'm paralyzed at the thought of my babies' loss if anything were to happen to T.

The afternoon came and went, all I know is she's stable and that's pretty much it. "Pandillero, man," was all that Bateador said. He jumped out the car coming towards me. We both broke down and tried to comfort each other. "I'm sorry man, I almost had her in Athens but——"

He couldn't finish, I'm not mad at him about this shit though, I can only blame myself. By night fall T was out of surgery and I'm feeling a little better. I know our family will be arriving in the morning, the thought still troubles me. Max picked up some clothes for me from the house and told me everyone was fine. Bateador has already sent over a team to make sure it's locked down.

Early the next morning they said we could go in and see T, the moment I opened the door we both were back at it. I went to T hand as Bateador fell back into a chair in the corner of the room. It took us a minute to pull ourselves together before we could face her. The site of all the tubes, wires and noise sent me right back to Washington. The shit is crazy to see and the sound of all those damn machines is another nuclear explosion to my heart.

Bateador pushed me a chair as I held onto T hand and continued to sob. Every time I look up I see that damn machine pumping air in my baby it's reminding me that she's in pain. All I want to do is make the shit go away, it's a nightmare that I'm watching and I'm beyond scared I'm petrified. If I could kill that bitch again every second of every day that I live it still won't be enough. It was then I decided her death didn't justify what she did to my T. I need to wipe out everybody in that bitch bloodline for this, real slow and painful.

I can hear outside the door as our family came closer, our mothers were already crying when they opened the door. Once they saw T, they only got louder. I can't let go of T, all I want to do is hold on.

"My baby! She on life support. Look at my baby!" was all I hear Kathy say over and over again.

"Treasure baby, wake up! Come on Treasure, wake up baby you have too much to live for baby wake up," my mother said as she spoke into T ear. My father put his hand on my shoulder and I broke down even more. I kissed T hand over and over again begging her to get up out that damn bed. I'd do anything to switch spots with her. We all stood around taking everything in and trying to coax T to wake up in our own different ways.

"You were supposed to take care of her! Why didn't you take care of her," Kathy said as she came over and started hitting me. I sat there and took it while they pulled her out the room. Seem like the days came and went, the only time I let go of T hand was to use the bathroom and change. The only time I was completely alone with T was when I showered in her bathroom. I cried every time I looked out the door at her lying there.

25 TREASURE

Washington eight years ago.

"Come on Terentia, you talk all that stuff like you know how to hoop, let's see what you can do on this here court."

"Xavier stop playing, you don't want none of this. You good but baby I hate to tell you, I'm better." He checked the ball and my poor baby could barely protect the damn thing. I let him come down then I put the pressure on him. He started turning like I couldn't keep up, he shot the jumper and it went in. "Yo' ball! Come on baby, I'm not gone go easy on you." That was all I needed to hear, I checked the ball and came down fast, he was stumbling back, and his defense is the worst.

I slowed down, "You alright, you need me to take it slow?"

"Come on now, you not doing much." I put the ball through my leg and went the other way.

"I'm over here Xavier, you need to keep up." He came over. "You got me but I bet you can't do it again!" I looked at him, backed up and smiled.

"I'm gone crossover again; this time to the left then put it through my legs and fake like I'm going right. The moment you move I'm going in for the layup."

"Yeah wha——" I did everything I told him I would and when I hit the layup he said it was a lucky call.

After the game we walked back to the barracks. "Xavier, why you so quiet? I don't hear you talking anymore." I laughed and he grabbed me and took me to the ground right in the middle of the plaza. He was grabbing my thighs and I was crying laughing. "What you say Terentia, I don't hear you talking anymore. Say something now Terentia." I can't say shit, I can barely breathe from laughing so hard, and my sides are starting to hurt.

He stopped and I put my arms around his neck and we kissed. "You got skills Terentia; I almost had you though baby."

"Yeah, tell me anything Dominic. You need to pick up yo' defense if you want to beat me." He put his hand on my thigh and I bit down on my lip hoping he wouldn't tickle me again.

"Yeah that's what I thought. Come on so we can get in the shower and I can work on my defense." I kissed him again as he helped me up.

What is going on, why are all these people standing around me? This big bitch needs to get the hell off of me. Stop pushing on my chest, would they get this bitch off, feel like she about to crack my rib cage.

Why is my baby out there crying? "Terentia, Terentia, no!" I hear Deangelo say. I want to tell him I'm alright but this bitch won't get off me.

"What's wrong Deangelo, I hear you, what's wrong?" Damn I feel tired, let me close my eyes, I need to rest. I'll talk with him when I wake up.

Nevada seven years ago.

"Terentia Treasure Waters do you take Dominic August Xavier to be you..." After the ceremony we were back at the house going at it. Harmony and Monroe had to head back and I'm not about to waste any of the short amount of time I have with my husband messing around with them. The only time we came up for air was to eat and use the restroom and hell; even then we were going at it. I was so sad when Dominic had to go back to Washington.

I wanted to beg his ass to go AWOL and stay with me but I couldn't do that to him. I went with him to the airport and I was crying like a fool because I had to let his ass go. He kept kissing over my face telling me to calm down; I couldn't though I wanted him to stay. "Wife I know you'll miss me because I'll miss you more, just know I'll be back sooner than what you think. I love you."

"What's up Dominic?" I kissed him and he put his arms around me.

"Come on Terentia let me show you something."

"Dominic let me explain!"

"Terentia you don't have to explain baby. Just watch this."

"Dominic what's wrong with them, why are they crying like that?" I went over to Deangelo.

"Dominic who is that in the bed?" He didn't say anything he just stood there and smiled, I asked him again.

"Terentia why don't you go closer and see." I walked over closer in the room; I can't take my eyes off Deangelo. I tried to kiss him but he didn't move, they were crying so loud he didn't hear me talking to him. I looked over in the bed and ran back to Dominic once I saw myself. He held me in his arms and I cried hard, I can't believe I'm in the bed. I looked over at Corey and saw him folded over in the chair. All I wanted to do was tell them I'm okay. They didn't hear me they just kept crying.

Colorado six years ago.

"Terentia you know were out of here in a week right?"

"Yes Dominic I know, off to the dirty south. You know you not going to those stank strip clubs you and Monroe used to hang out at right?" He smiled and I went over towards him but he ran around the couch.

"Why not, I know a couple strippers who told me to come thru whenever I was in town." I went right over the couch on his ass, he tried to run but I grabbed his ax so he sat back on the couch.

"What was that?"

"I'm just playing Mrs. Xavier, I have everything I could ever want right here." He kissed me and we were rolling around getting sweaty in no time.

As soon as I saw Dominic I was running fast as hell, I jumped in his arms and we kissed as he spun my ass in circles. "I missed you Dominic!" "I missed you too Terentia, come on I want to show you something." I see my mother hitting on Deangelo. I ran over and told her ass to leave him alone but she wasn't listening to a word I'm saying.

After they pulled her off I went over to check on him but he kept his head down and wouldn't look up at me. I'm hot that she attacked him like that. I see Pam and dad sitting in the chair across the room. I tried to tell Pam to kick my momma ass but she won't listen to me. I'm too mad at the way she was hitting on him. I went to Corey and told him to do his job and kick the shit out of her. I mean don't hurt her but kick her straight in the ass.

Two weeks after Dominic left I did the same, I was sick without him being around all I can do is talk to him on the phone. Most of the time we can't do that because the building I'm working in has a block on the cell phones once you're on our floor. I hated that shit, I couldn't wait to leave out and call Dominic. When he said he was getting shipped to me I thought I would explode I was so happy, I went to sick call and played sick on their ass. Dumb ass doctor gave me two days and since it's a holiday weekend, I ended up with damn near a week off; I'm ready for Dominic to show up.

I'm walking back and forth at the gate looking at the people getting off the plane. I know Dominic's coming and I can't wait. I ran to him when I saw him coming up the ramp.

"Terentia, you missed me?"

"Dominic, I miss you so much, Shay is doing well. How are you doing?"

"I'm fine Terentia, I see you not though."

"What? Why you say that?"

"Baby you've been with me for almost five months."

"Dominic you just came back, what are you talking about?"

"Terentia you need to get back, our family needs you. Make sure you look after August close because he's going to remind you the most of me."

"I love you Dominic!"

"I love you too Terentia, now get back and kiss my baby for me."

26 DEANGELO

Weeks past and I haven't seen my babies and T hasn't budged. I'm getting more and more angry and ready for T to get up. "Come here baby! I'm sorry for what I said," Kathy said as I stood up and we hugged. Then I heard a cry that cut my heart wide open. I turned and it was Shay, the twins were right behind her. "Daddy what's wrong with mommy?" I picked her up and I can't help but cry, next thing I know the whole room crying. I kissed my babies as everyone left out the room.

"Daddy, can I give mommy a kiss?" Shay said as she ran back in the room, I held her up; she leaned over and kissed T. She was back out the door just as fast as she came. Time was passing by at the speed of light; I rented out four rooms to make our stay comfortable for everyone. I didn't want the kids to see T laid up in pain day after day but I wanted them to be close to her. Princess had a million and one questions and I wasn't ready to answer them just yet.

T twenty sixth birthday came and went, they wanted to celebrate but I wasn't having it. I told them I was spending the day with her alone and whoever didn't like it was shit outta luck. Jacked up that T missed Princess sixth birthday, and the boys will be two in a couple months. I need my wife to wake the hell up and enjoy life with me; I also need her to remind me why I shouldn't just kill her evil ass mother. I meant what I said about not having fuckin' parties while T is laid the hell up. She must've thought I would change my mind, I bet she knows now that my word is my word.

I know Kathy's upset but I really don't give a shit, that woman knows she can hold a grudge. Her and my mom's are constantly going back and forth about Kathy making comments about either me or T. Seems like every day I'm putting them both out when they start fussing. The only thing that makes the time pass is having the kids close and being near T. Months have passed; T's breathing on her own but still hasn't moved or made a sound. After the kids went to bed I sat next to T and tried my best to get her to wake up.

"T, please T wake up. I need you to wake up T. We have a family that all need you, I need you, T I can't do this without you. I don't know how much longer I can go without tellin' yo' moms she needs to be on the first thing smoking back to the states. She pushing my nerves T, now I see why you said you can only do a couple days at a time around her. You need to get up before yo' moms be in a bed down the hall." I looked up trying to stop the anger in my heart.

"DAMN IT T! For once in your life just do what the hell I said do and stop fucking with me. I can't do this without you T, I can't." I pulled her hand to me and let my tears go.

I felt T squeeze my hand, must be her reflexes I continued to cry. "Shhhhh!" I look up and damn near fell out the chair, I think I'm losing my mind. I held on to her hand while the chair I was sitting in fell back, I moved closer to her. "T, do you hear me?" She didn't say anything; I was starting to realize that I'm really going insane. I felt a squeeze on my hand again so I looked down.

"Shhh!" I looked back up and can see T eyes moving around. They're still closed but they're moving. "Squeeze my hand T if you can hear me." She did it again; I kissed all over her and called everyone to the room. I showed them what she was doing and we all were instantly feeling better. The doctor came in and did some test and we were even happier. A week later Shay, Deangelo and August came in the room to see us. I'm too happy to show them that T's feeling a little better.

I let them all kiss T and as I leaned August down to kiss her, her eyes opened. I damn near dropped my baby; I was shocked to see her eyes. I gave him to my mother and moved in while they called for the doctor. "T, hey baby can you see me? T baby, can you talk?" She continued to blink and those long ass lashes look like they're stuck together. I grabbed a towel, wet it, and then went back over to clean her eyes out.

The doctor walked in and stopped me, the nurse came in, did some shit and put drops in her eyes. He moved a light around and some other shit, I was ready to push they asses the hell out the way. I wanted to talk to T and they were taking too long with the bull. Once they pulled that mess out her nose and mouth the doctor came back in.

"Mrs. Joseph you've been shot and are in the hospital, can you hear me?" T blinked her eyes more. "Mrs. Joseph how do you feel?" I was on blades waiting to hear her voice. She didn't say anything, she closed her eyes and went back to sleep. The doctor kept trying to get her to respond but she wouldn't so they left back out. I asked everyone to give me a minute with T and they did.

I closed the door and went back over to T and whispered in her ear. "So T how long you gone sit around here? I know you have to be ready to go home by now?" I watched as she smiled. "T stop messing around, you know you heard that man talking to you. Why you not saying anything?" I kissed her forehead and looked back down to see those big eyes wide open. "I only wanted to talk to you. That's why," she struggled to say just above a whisper. I'm too excited, I gave her as much of a hug that I could and kissed all over her.

"Why you in here making all that noise anyway?" She tried to clear her throat, "You and Corey cried harder than our mamas," she said as she grumbled out a weak laugh. "T I love you baby, and you know he do too. Seeing you like this is the last thing any of us want. You know we've done everything in our power not to see you like this. He feels the same way I do, like we failed you."

She moved her hand so I helped her lift it; she put it on my face. My tears rolled down the side of her hand. "Stop that, you can never fail me and Corey can't either." She pulled my head onto her so I can hear her heartbeat. Every day she getting stronger and the more the kids are around the stronger she gets.

27 TREASURE

Look at my babies their all so cute, no Shay don't cry boo I'm right here, mommy okay stop crying. Really, she can't hear me either? This some bullshit, I'm sick and tired of people ignoring me like this. Somebody need to take this mess out my nose, this crap in my throat has my neck on fire. "...the hell I said do and stop fucking with me. I can't do this without you T, I can't." Maybe if I do this, I felt that, I can feel my baby hand thank you, I can feel his hand. That shit made me tired, let me rest a minute then I'll try and talk to him.

When I woke up I tried to talk but nothing really came out with this damn tube or should I say pipe. Stop asking me if I can hear you and give me some water, maybe I can say something. Ah hell, "Shhh!" He heard that, really? After all the talking I've been doing I barely squeeze out a sh and he hears that.

Why do I hate when people wake me up? Get this damn light out my eyes. I'm tired and when I can move my foot I'm gone kick the shit out of whoever keeps poking me. I can hear Deangelo but I can't get my damn eyes open, I keep trying and I can't. Then I remembered what Dominic said about August. I opened my eyes and Frat was drooling all over me, his wet kiss made my insides warm.

I can mess Deangelo up for almost dropping my baby, why the hell is he looking at me like that? Yeah stop Deangelo because he must not see all this damn crust that he missing in my eye. Oh shit it's bright as hell; it's hard for me to focus. Only thing I see is this white man big ass mustache all in my face. Man I don't want to talk to you, get the hell out of here. It seems like they're just messing with me just to make me mad.

"...Why you not saying anything?" I wanted to tell him because my breath must smell like hell in a hand basket. I know it has to because my eyes crusted over and no one thought to keep them clean. I don't have the energy so I told him I only wanted to talk to him. Then I teased him about all that crying they were doing. I was getting tired though so I went back to sleep. I was feeling better overtime, I was happy as hell to go home.

Everybody came to see me; I had to run my mama and daddy off because she kept the shit face on like she had a problem with my husband. I'm still mad at her for beating on him the way she did, I didn't speak on it though. Physical therapy was kicking my ass; I thought they tried to kill me. I was happy that I lost the weight I'd picked up; I was in that damn hospital way too long. I was back down to my fighting weight and it took what seemed like hellas. Max thought I needed to lose more though, he had me on a diet and even after therapy he worked the shit out my ass in the gym.

"Corey comes help me outside so I can see Ethan. They should be here in a minute." He came over and walked me to the door. I heard arguing outside and it look like they're about to fight. "STOP!" What the hell, my dumb ass would fall down three freaking steps. All I can do is cry; I landed right on my funny bone and scraped the shit out of my shin. I have to talk with Deangelo, I don't have the strength to have him going at it with Ethan, and this shit has to end. He still thinks we have a thing for each other. No matter how many times I tell him we don't, he still gives Ethan a hard time like that's going to help.

I talked to him and called Ethan to the room, I'm so happy to see him I'm not about to let Deangelo ruin my time. He all surprised to hear what Ethan has accomplished, hell I don't know why he surprised. Like I said, none of us are dummies. Ethan went to school on a boxing scholarship after I left. He realized that wasn't what he wanted to do and worked his way through school. Deangelo still act like he has and attitude and not really wanting to hear shit. Ethan isn't about to beg his ass! I'll tell Ethan to carry me downstairs and just stay out of Deangelo way before I hurt Ethan. Deangelo got over it though and we had a blast together.

28 DEANGELO

It took weeks until I was able to get her home, a full staff came throughout the day to care for her. In no time after that T was up. She was still weak but she was better and I was ecstatic for her. On my way out to pick up some stuff for T I see her brother getting out of the car so I go over to meet him. Then I see City get out. "What's up man, how you been? What's up City, how you doing?" I dapped her brother off as City turned away without saying anything.

I know this nigga ain't come to my house and play me like that. "Damn man you got something you want to say?" He looked at me and I can feel the heat coming off this nigga. "Fuck you nigga!" That's more than enough for me, I move in as Tony steps in between us. "Chill out," Tony said as I continue to make my way to his ass. "Fuck you nigga, Treasure always the one who pay for yo' bullshit. I'm tired of her always in the fucking hospital or heartbroken because of yo' ass. So fuck you nigga!" I'm not gone let this nigga talk to me any kind of way. I push Tony out the way and was ready to put some bricks to his dome.

"STOP!" I hear T say as she came out the door. "What's up Pandillero, we have a problem here?" Bateador said as he ran over. I look over at T trying to come down the steps then she stumbled so I ran over to help her up while everyone came over. I picked her up and carried her in, she cried as I took her to the room. I locked the door; as soon as I'm finished with her I'm goin' make sure I damage that nigga. Somebody needs to get beat down, why not make that slick ass nigga feel my wrath.

Who he think he playing with bringing his ass all the way over here to my house and talking to me like he forgot who he talking too. I can't wait to get my hands on his punk ass. I've been waiting to get at him since back in the day. I never did because the nigga was young and dumb but that ain't gone stop me today. Let's see this nigga man up in a grown man's world since he thinks he ready.

"Deangelo, what is going on?" I tried to pay her no attention; I went in the bathroom to get some towels to wipe off her legs. "Deangelo why are you doing that to him?" Me, this nigga came in my house talking shit, why I have to be doing something to him? She better not be taking that nigga side on this shit, she can't keep trying to save his punk ass. "T I'm not doing anything to him, I was cool until he started running off at the mouth." She stopped me and pulled my head up. "You remember Cindy?" I have no clue where this conversation is going. "Yeah why? What does Cindy have to do with anything?" She smiled.

"That's the same thing you said the last time I asked you that. Do you remember asking me if I was fighting her over something meaningless?"

"Yeah because I told you they would start talking shit if they saw me with you." She smiled, then it hit me what she was saying.

"T I hear you but you kno—"

"The question is do you know Deangelo?"

"Know what T?"

"Do you know better? Because I know you do but do you know better Deangelo? That's my friend, not to mention my family and he's only looking out for me. So you should know better than to attack him for doing the same thing you would do or say."

"T I can ask you the same question."

"What, do I know better? Please tell me what you thinking." She giggled like she know exactly what I'm about to say to her.

"Yes, do you know better? You can try and play like he just your friend and family all you want. That nigga want what he can't have, so do you know better? I hope you know better T, that nigga can't have you I don't give a fuck what the circumstances are."

"I know that Deangelo, for the millionth time there's nothing going on with us. Baby you have my body, heart, mind and soul. Stop with all the madness."

I shook my head and decided to let it go. "Can you ask Ethan to come up here?" T looked over at me while she called downstairs to Max.

"I think you pushing it too far T, let me get a minute to breathe before that nigga come in here."

"Look, unlock the door and sit right here." She patted on the bed beside her;

I walked over, unlocked the door and sat facing the window away from the door. "Huh big baby," she said as she threw the pillow hitting me in the back. "What's up Treasure, how you doing?" This nigga lucky as fuck! I can hear him as he walks over and hugs her.

"Ethan you remember my husband Deangelo don't you?" I'm not even going to look back.

"Yeah Treasure, my bad about that though. Aye Pandillero, my bad for that shit but this my sister that's all. I just had to get some shit off my chest. No hard feelings from me though."

I stood up off the bed looked over and nodded. "Deangelo really? That's it? What the hell you want him to beg? You need to suck it up tough guy because like my brother just said, we come as a package deal, all of us together. Besides, Ethan will be working on those community outreach programs and you Mr. Man gone need to get over it. That is if you want him to incorporate the boxing program into it!"

What she just say? This who she hooked up with? "Yeah right, you are not trying to tell me this nigga the District Attorney who started that program over there?" I laughed as he came around the bed. I still wasn't sure if I wanted to fuck him up so I faced him as he moved closer. He handed me a card.

"If you want, we can take it out in the ring anytime."

"Come on man, don't let the age fool you boy. I still hit the ring on a regular. Hell I'm better than what I was in my hay day."

"Shit me too!" he said as we both started to laugh.

We were all good from there, we spent the next couple days chilling out and going over everything. Since T was running the show we were legit. I let Bateador takeover the street shit a minute ago so the little percentage I was getting off of that-well I shouldn't say little. To anyone else that monthly mil plus would be a hard thing to let go. To me it wasn't worth messing up what we have so I cut that line off.

It took me a while to convince Bateador to move the hell out the states but when he did I could see that it was the change he needed. He found a nice girl and they moved in together. T was trying her best to get him to give up the street shit completely but I don't think he's ready just yet.

Every day T would be on me about talking to Bateador and showing him that he had an easier way. It's not like I didn't try but he not ready, he a hitter, that's all he's ever known. There's nothing that's going to change that. Nothing that I could say to make him change his mind and let that shit go. Not right now anyway.

29 TREASURE

"What's up Sammy girl, I been waiting on yo' ass all morning to get here." She put her bag down and looked at me. "Well if you brought yo' ass home once in a while then you wouldn't be sitting around here by yoself waiting for me." "Girl shut up and give me a hug!" We walked into the house I couldn't wait to tell her where we were going for the week that she would be over. We sat around laughing like we had lost our minds and we had no cares in the world.

We walked out on the patio and enjoyed our breakfast talking about how well our partnership was turning out. "Treasure for real, we need to go international because business is booming right now. Plus I have more than a few people asking about the expansion." I don't know why she keeps telling me that. "I know Sammy but my husband said it's a risk and we need to slow down before making such a big commitment." She looked behind me and turned her head, I have a feeling who she's looking at. "Yep! I sure did say that!"

After we all said hello and took our seats again I sat there listening to her and Deangelo go back and forth with their angles on what needed to be done. All I'm waiting for is one of them to pull out some spreadsheets and roll out a damn projector. I feel like I'm sitting in on major corporation meeting. These two will not let it go, I went inside the house, come back and they still going at it like it's something that has to be addressed now.

Corey laughed; Sammy asked him what he thinks about it. He started breaking shit down to Sammy that neither of us had even thought about. A fly could've landed on her tongue by the time he finished. "Wow Bateador, I didn't know you knew so much about the topic." Deangelo thought that was too funny. "So what, you think I'm dumb?" He looked over at her and she dropped her head slightly trying not to make eye contact with him.

"Leave my girl alone Corey, she's not saying that." Deangelo put his arms on the table and leaned in towards Sammy. "Naw T, I wanna hear the answer to his question." They both sat there waiting for her to say something. "Sammy its cool, you don't have to answer them. Corey is well qualified; he has several degrees in too much shit. They're just messing with you girl." She looked at me and sent me an instant message that said, "Bitch why yo' ass didn't tell me that first?"

Corey still looking at her, "Look Ma, if you want I can send a proposal over to your house and—"

She looked at him with shock in her eyes. "How you know where I live?" Deangelo cracking up.

"I know where yo' parents live and a lot of other shit about you and others. What does that have to do with anything? You need to catch up baby girl."

I stood up. "Alright Corey, spit out what the hell you have to say and leave her alone!" Deangelo pulled me over to him so I sat on his lap. Corey pulled his chair around and slid Sammy facing him. She tried not to look at him but he waved his hand in front of her and like magic she locked eyes with him.

"Like I said I can send it wherever, you look it over and if you like it then use it. Give it a minute and if Pandillero don't back you I will." She smiled. "Really?" "Look I know you scared of me and you should be! But if I say something then that's what I mean. I would back the whole thing now but like I said, you have some holes that need to be looked at."

Sammy must not have been that scared of him because she jumped up out her seat and hugged him. Then he jumped up and acted like he didn't want to touch her. We laughed at the look on his face; he was the one that was uncomfortable now. We all headed out for Paris, we shopped and walked the whole time we were there.

After Sammy left I was starting to really miss home, it's been a minute since I ran the hell away from there with Deangelo. The thought of not being around my family is hard. I decided to put together a family reunion; I want everyone to be there so I started planning it. I planned the reunion for two months then I decided to ask Deangelo. I really don't care if he has a problem with me doing it.

I know he don't want me nowhere near the Lou that's why he always run off there without asking me to go with him. I asked him, he's cool with the reunion. I can tell he's upset with the sudden need for us to stay two weeks at the lake house though. I think he wanted me to say we would be in and out. Hell, I don't want my babies to take that trip back to back like that.

30 DEANGELO

"Deangelo what you think about having a family reunion?" I don't know where this coming from but the thought of it made me feel good. "I'm cool with it T, where though, you know everybody pretty much in the Lou it won't be right if we had it here." She came over and sat in front of me. "Yeah I know I was thinking set it up and head over with the kids. Then we can stay out at the house for a couple weeks once I can put it together." I took her hand and walked her up to the bedroom.

When we were inside I turned on the shower and got in. "Deangelo? What you think?" I turned up the radio in the bathroom then I hear her come in behind me. She pressed her body up against me as the water poured down on us. I hit the surround and she hit me because the water sprayed her drenching her hair. "Deangelo why you do that, I just had my hair done?" I turned around and laughed at the site of all her long straight hair falling onto her face.

"Stop crying, you not going anywhere anyway." She stared me down. I moved her around and sat on the bench letting the water clear my head of all my thoughts. T watched me and moved closer, I kissed the scar on her stomach as she rubbed my head. "It's that bad of an idea?" I still didn't reply, she sat on me and eased me inside of her. I felt like I was trying to force a plug in a flat tire using tweezers she so tight. I watched in agony as she crept further down my mans. I know what she doing, even though I'm loving every second of it; I have to end it.

I lifted her up and she laughed, I slid off the bench more and turned her around. She tried to lean forward but I sat that ass up straight. I held my man so I can make sure it's going straight in. The moment my head touched her I felt even more pressure around it. She started to make it tighter every inch then she slammed her ass all the way down. "Fuuuuuuck!" I hear her giggle at what I said. She rose back up slow without locking my man in her. Then she gripped me even more and bounced up and down, I'm in pain. This the best pain I've felt in my life. I'm holding on to the side of the bench trying my best to hold out.

I wanted to help her squeeze on her big ass titties, she moaning and holding her head back. I know she feeling it just as much as I am. I wanna pull her all the way down my man but I can't move for shit. She got up and I can see her juices wash away from my man with the water. She turned and started to suck me. I can't take my eyes off the way her back is dipped and her ass is up in the air. T licked the front of her teeth then tilted her head sideways. I was ready to nut all over her shit and make them whiter than they already are. She pressed the flat of her teeth against my man, running them up and down the length.

The feeling is so intense I can't look away for nothing. She trying to get me off and I'm not about to let her win. I sat up, put her on the bench and peeled her open, I know just what to do to get her to cum. T biting her lip and breathing hard, her first nut came with ease, I have her where I want her, now she going back to back. She leaking juices bad, I put her leg on my shoulder and hit it. I can feel her try and tighten up, I hit it harder and she yelled out and loosened up.

I'm on to her and she knows it, I bent her over and put her hands on the wall, I'm murdering that ass now. All she can do is scream out and try to get low. And when she does I'll grind that ass forcing her to get up. She got tighter but I smacked her on her ass and she had to let go.

I put my foot up on the bench, pulled both her arms back and long stroked the kitty. I can't do what I want, it's too wet and I'm not about to hurt her. I can see her ice cream every time she cum on my man. I'm winning this battle, it ain't shit she can do now. I let her drop her arms down and she holding on again but she opened her legs up more. The shit feel out of this world, I'm back in beating the coochie up.

She crossed her legs mid pump and I feel like I have six thousand pounds of weight on my man. I can't move, all I can do is throw my head back and bust my nut. T let go and sat on the bench. "You alright husband?" I opened my eyes and looked down at her smiling face.

I move over to sit down and put her on my lap. She damn near slid off from all the juices leaking from her. I can barely hold my head up I'm exhausted, I rested my head back on the wall and closed my eyes. "What the fuck T, how are you doing that? Feel like a vice grip inside yo' ass." She stood up and started to wash me off then did herself. We headed to the bed and she rolled over on me.

"So since I won the debate we can head out in what, a couple weeks?" I really don't want to talk about it; I still need time to think about that shit. Seem like St. Louis is the last place I want my family to be lately. There are too many memories and problems there for me to take them back there. It's not like the kids haven't been to our parents and I've been back several times but not T. She been here and a couple other state side places ever since we left and this the first time she's talked about going back.

I thought I could buy sometime. "Only if you tell me how you do that." She rolled over away from me so I did the same and put her in my arms. The feel of her ass pressed against my man was waking me up, not to mention holding her breast and the feel of her nipples hardening. "Now you quiet." I kissed her neck and closed my eyes. "I just don't want to tell you, if I did yo—" I opened my eyes and pulled her back over in my arms onto my chest. "I what? Why you crying, we can go to St. Louis T if that's what you want to do. But tell me what these tears about, I hate when you cry." I kissed her eyes and wiped her tears away.

"It's just after—" She stopped talking and started to cry more. I squeezed her into my chest tighter. "T come on baby, it can't be that hard, that's some good good right there. I just want to know how you put it on me like that. That's all. If you don't wanna tell me then that's fine." I know a lot of niggas throw that shit out there but T cat is by far the best cat I've ever had. I've been with more chicks then I can count and if any of them had the cat T has my ass would've been in a world of trouble.

She opened her eyes. "It's just after you know." What? I don't know what the hell she talking about. "I know what T, after what?" "After I was raped." My heart sank and I wanted to take back everything I just said and asked her, damn why did I have to ask her that? I felt my man fall between my legs like a dog with his tail between his legs. "You don't have to tell me T, stop all that crying." "It's just, I was so messed up——" I don't want to hear anymore, I'm about to scream at the thought of it. I'm actually trying not to tell her to shut up and walk out the room. I can't do that to her, I should've kept my damn mouth shut from the beginning. "T its cool, you don't have to tell me."

"I want to Deangelo; after they patched me back together I found out I had more control that's all. I probably could always do it but I never had a reason to. The doctor said it's like losing your vision your other senses pick up. It's not like you never had those senses before but they become more aware and sensitive.

So I learned overtime how to do it that's all." I didn't say anything, I just thought about what she said. "You don't want to touch me again now huh?" She tried to turn back over but I locked her in my arms and kissed her. I rolled her on her back and kissed my way down her body. I stopped before I headed in. "Let's see if you can do it to my tongue." I went in and tore her ass up; we went another round and fell asleep.

31 TREASURE

In the end I won the argument so he was good to go and we were back at home. I was feeling like shit from the time we touched down. I didn't have time to worry about it though; I needed to get a ton of shit done in between site seeing like tourist with the family. The kids wanted to go to the Zoo so we spent the day there. Deangelo took the kids to feed the animals in the kids Zoo while I waited outside for them to come out. I turned around and was shocked to see Sebastian. The moment he walked over I couldn't believe he was in front of me. He just stood there looking at me not knowing what to say. I guess we both had a moment of uncertainty; we must've been trying to make sure we were seeing clearly.

"Hello Sebastian." That was all I could think to say to his ass after damn near three years.

"Hey Treasure, how you doing?"

"I'm alright." Damn here he comes, he did not have to do that, and Deangelo know he is something else. After they spoke Sebastian started chatting like we were cool or something.

"Yeah man, had to bring my wife out with the family, good da..." Deangelo know he is too much.

"Yeah I was actually looking for my wife and son myself. I know you don't know Treasure but I got back with Deanne and my lil man couldn't be happier. I hope your wedding was beautiful, you deserve it Treasure."

"Our wedding was just what T wanted it to be any and everything she wanted was what she had. But you and I both know all she wanted was me and I her. You probably don't know, but it's been that way since she was eleven. Matter fact, I remember getting an invite for you to fly over to Paris for the wedding. What happened to his invite T?" Deangelo looked over at me, I stared at him like he insane. He started to laugh as he looked back at Sebastian.

"That's right, she thru that bitch in the fireplace." He really got a kick out of the frown on Sebastian face after he said that. I thought he was about to double over laughing in his face.

"Damn, that hurt! Treasure I'm really sorry," Sebastian said as Deangelo stopped laughing like he just remembered the reason why Sebastian said he was sorry.

Here comes everybody, the last thing I want is for his ass to meet my boys. I waited while he spoke to Shay, and then her grown, spoiled ass had to get beyond herself. "Shay!" I'm gone pop the shit out her smart mouth ass,

Deangelo think the shit funny. Sebastian started telling me about his son and how he got back with his wife. I can really care less and the way Deangelo looking, I know he don't give a fuck. Then Sebastian asked to speak with me, the look in his eyes said he had something he wanted to get off his chest.

Hell, I was about to marry his ass, maybe I need to hear what he has to say. Deangelo not having it though, he tried to shut that shit down. I don't know who the hell he thinks I am. I tried to talk to him in private but he wouldn't move. I know Sebastian won't know what the hell I'm saying if I speak Italian to him.

"Let me talk with him. Why you acting like you have something to lose?" Really, that's how he wants to play it and speak that Greek shit back like he has the upper hand. Well he must not know that I understand everything he said. "What if I don't want you to hear what he has to say?"

He ignored the shit out of me; I can't believe he just did that to me. Let me stop because yes I can, that's all he has ever done to me here. Sebastian said what he wanted to say, I really couldn't pay attention I'm so pissed with Deangelo. "...that happened. The whole time that I was with you physically..." When he walked away I went to the car. I sat there the whole time thinking of all the times Deangelo treated me like I was his puppet and he pulled my strings. The more I thought about it, it seemed like he was in more control of my life at times than I was. The only real time I had free was after the Washington shit.

He came out and of course ordered me in the house. I need a break and I'm about to go to one of my favorite spots but who am I kidding. "...T stop playing with me and sit yo' ass down so we can talk!" Daddy said I can't go out and play. I tried to push his damn head off his shoulder, I walked in the room.

144

My body feeling like hell, I really don't have the energy to argue with him about the shit. It's not like he'll listen no how. "Let's talk T. Last I checked you were my wife and we're in this together. Now this nigga show up and you flip the switch on me." Now he wanna make it seem like I still have feelings for his ass. "...Your wife Deangelo, not your child!" I feel like I'm about to throw up he making me so mad.

I don't know why Deangelo always try and do me. I don't want to argue about this shit anyway because like I said, it won't matter. I'm glad he apologized and said he'll stop doing the shit. Even though I know he won't, it's the fake ass thought that counts. He won't let me cuff his ass so I have to make sure I torture the shit out of him. I started counting his hits then I shut him off and he came. I wouldn't let him pullout, I kept him inside making his ass stand right back up. Each time I did he was making all kinds of noise; I'm surprised the kids didn't run in the room thinking something was wrong with him.

32 DEANGELO

After I helped the kids out the car they all took off to the house and ran inside, I walked over and let T out.

"Welcome home baby."

"Do you know how much I love this place Deangelo? I lost my virginity in this house."

"Yeah, tell me anything T." She hit me then walked faster to the door. I stopped her before she walked in and picked her up.

"You know I hate those kinds of jokes right?"

"T I know and you know I'm just fucking with you. I have a surprise for you." Her eyes lit up as I carried her in the door.

"Deangelo what did you do?" I looked around because I know my surprise not inside. But the way she looking I don't know what she's talking about.

I put her down as she walked over to the portrait on the wall. I walked over and held her while she stared at it. "When did you get this?" I looked up at it, we looked happy; I honestly forgot all about it.

"T this not your surprise. This has been here since we had the boys."

"I can see that but I didn't know you had this done."

"My mom had this done; remember she took the picture of us? The only reason I know it's here is because she sent me a picture of it. This was before you went in the hospital, I forgot all about it once that happened."

"So what's my surprise then?" I turned her around facing the back porch; she jumped up and down, kissed me and ran outside. I walked out after her as she took a seat on the dock and dropped her legs into the water.

"How you gone get a boat in here now with the dock like this?"

"You didn't need that boat anyway so I sold it. Besides, I know you always hated that you couldn't put your feet in the water."

"Thank you baby I love it! Baby can you take me in?" T crazy if she think I'm about to get wet. If anything I'm ready to get my man wet but that's about it.

"No T that's not goin' happen, maybe later." She stood up and walked over to me. I'm not worried, there's no way in hell she's going to push me in. "You sure you don't want to take me in now because I was planning on doing something else with you later." I smiled as she bit down on the corner of her lip and ran her tongue across it.

"Look at you T!" I pulled the stuff out my pockets and dropped it in the chair; I picked her up and jumped in. We splashed around then she put her legs around my waist as we kissed. The kids came over and I had to stop August, he look like he ready to jump in. The boys started pulling off their clothes; all I can think of is them not wanting to get the hell out. "See what you started T?" We both laughed as T told them they couldn't get in. They cried and I sat T up on the dock and got out, we all sat out until the sun went down.

Seemed like all we did waiting for the reunion was bounce around St. Louis like we had never been here before. It was kinda strange that T kept running off for a couple hours, I figured she was doing something for the reunion. So many things had changed and there were so many places that the kids wanted to go. I'm being pulled away not able to focus on T, then she'd pop up right on time to spend time with us. Time was moving faster than what we thought. We headed to the Zoo and walked around, Shay took the boys to feed the animals. I saw Deangelo trying to eat the food so I went over to stop him.

I turned to walk back and instantly went to Mars when I realized who T was talking to. I walked over and bumped into his shoulder and put my arm around T. "What's up wifey, you ready? I think your sons ready to eat." I looked back at the nigga, "What's up Seabas, didn't know you were here." Look at this punk ass nigga here.

"What's up Pandillero, I was saying hello to Treasure that's all. I see ya'll two having a good time out here at the Zoo huh?" I looked at T as she nodded her head and smiled at me. "Yeah man, had to bring my wife out with the family, good day to let the kids run around." I smirked at the stunned look on the nigga face. He getting on my nerve with all the small talk I have to get under his skin. "Daddy, Frick and Frat dropped all their food out on the ground," Shay said as she walked the boys over. I reached down and picked up Frat while T did the same with Frick, Shay stood in front of me.

"Is this Shay? She's so big now, how are you doing Shay?" "I'm well, how are you asshole," Shay said in Italian. "Shay," T said. I told him what she said, the edited version and laughed at what my Princess did. She knows I don't like this nigga so she only speaking to be polite but that asshole was a nice touch. "This is Deangelo and that's August, my sons. Everyone say hello, Shay speak English and don't get hurt," T said then they all said hello. He tried to make small talk again and not look at me. I'm burning more with each second of my life this nigga wasting standing here.

"Do you mind if I talk to Treasure for a minute?" I can't believe this fool just asked me that shit. I put Frat down and sent them all to get Dip in Dots before he can say anything else. "Hell yeah I mind so no!" "Look man I just wanted to talk to Treasure for a minute that's all, no disrespect." I still remember when this nigga put her in the car. I should've told his ass then he could let go, but I know he knows I got her now.

"Like I said, hell yeah I mind! Now what?" I mugged the nigga, I'm beyond playing with his ass and the thought of him asking me again is about to tip the scales. "Deangelo!" I look over at T. She tries to pull me away but I'm not budging, she speaks in Italian at me. Yeah, at me!

"Let me talk with him. Why you acting like you have something to lose?" I changed it up and spoke Greek back to her ass. "Love, whatever he has to say to my heart he can say in front of me." Yeah she wants to change languages, hell; we can do this all day.

I turned and let him know what I told her. "Look, whatever it is spit it out because you can't talk to my wife without me hearing it." This nigga had a dumb look on his face like he surprised we speak English. I know he don't think

Shay's the only one that speaks another language. It don't matter what this punk bitch ass nigga think. He should be thinking how his life's about to end if he don't walk the fuck away. "What if I don't want you to hear what he has to say?" T said. I'm not about to argue with her and I know he don't understand shit she just said so I focused in on him.

"I can respect that." You don't have a choice, Bitch! He turned and looked at T. "I just wanted to tell you that I was sorry about everything that happened. The whole time that I was with you physically..." I can feel my jaw clinch up. "I shut that part of me off, I was only with you and no one else. I hate that I hurt you the way that I did and I truly am sorry for any pain that I caused you. I hope someday we can get our friendship back or close to it, I never lost the love I have for you Treasure. You have a beautiful family and it was good seeing you." He turned and walked away.

I looked over at T and she was already heading in the opposite direction. I grabbed the kids and we walked to the car. T didn't say a word even when we stopped to eat, she was silent even on the way home from the restaurant. All she did was stare out the window like she in deep thought about something. I opened the door for her and picked up the boys who were sleeping in the back as Shay stumbled against my leg into the house.

After everyone was in their beds I'm walking around looking for T. I look out in the garage and she's still sitting there with the door opened. "T you gone sit here all day or you coming in?" She didn't say anything she got out and walked past me avoiding touching me. "Really T?" I slammed the door and followed behind her.

She stood by the door like she contemplating leaving. This some Grade A bullshit right here and it can't be all about that bitch ass nigga Seabas.

"What's wrong T?"

"You back on that bullshit Deangelo." What did I do now?

"T what are you talking about." She didn't say anything so I moved over to her but she moved back.

"What's all this here about? You mad about that nigga T, really?" She looked up at me and that look is all too familiar.

"I need to get out of here for a minute." She turned and grabbed the keys I stopped her.

"What the hell you think this is? T stop playing with me and sit yo' ass down so we can talk!" I'm trying to be as patient as I can but she's pushing my buttons. She dropped the keys on the floor, turned and put her finger right up to my face.

"See, that's the shit I'm talking about right there!" She pushed my head back and headed to the bedroom. She knows she sexy as hell when she mad and the way that ass moving down the hall makes me wanna spank that mufucka.

Now I'm standing here debating on going after her or not but fuck it, I know better so I'm right behind her. I lock the door and turned up the radio. I watch her walk around slinging her shit off onto the dresser; she tried not to look up at me the whole time. The more she tries to avoid me the more she turning me on. That shit made me want her to lock my man up in her until I explode inside her.

"What T, you want to fight me over this or something?" She walked into the bathroom but before she can close the door I pick her up and put her on the bed.

"Let's talk T. Last I checked you were my wife and we were in this together. Now this nigga show up and you flip the switch on me."

"Don't do me Deangelo, I am your wife. Your wife Deangelo, not your child!" I'm not about to attempt to figure out what that mean.

"I know you not my child T." If she was my child she damn sho' wouldn't be acting like she is right now. Since she my wife this shit only getting my man hard.

"Why is it that when we in St. Louis you treat me like your child? If I say give me a minute, why you can't do that? Why you have to be in control all the time like I have to follow your orders or I can't do shit?" Aw hell here she go, fuck this, I'm about to run this shit right past her tough ass. I sat up off of her, pulled her up and got down on my knees in between her legs.

"T I'm sorry. I know how much he put you through and I didn't want you to go through that. I'll listen to you from now on I promise, you're right and I'm wrong. I love you, do you forgive me?" I watched as she rolled her eyes, I bit her thigh as she giggled.

"I see what you doing Mr. Man, don't think you slick." I smiled and hugged her, we made love and she had me about to howl the way she was putting it on my ass. She been holding back big time.

33 TREASURE

The next morning we head to breakfast and Deangelo being pulled from table to table by his family. He made sure to drag all of us right along with him. I felt honored every time he introduced me as his wife. The more he said it, the more I wanted to hear it be said. "Angelo, why has it been almost ten years and I haven't seen you baby?" his great-great grandmother said as he kneeled down to speak with her.

"I'm sorry Ma'; I should've come out to see you. As you can see my gorgeous wife and three beautiful kids need me to be with them. It's not an excuse; I should've been more considerate and come to see you. Ma' please understand that my T has a spell over my soul that has bound me to stay put with her and my babies. I hope you accept my apology," he said then kissed her.

"Angelo baby, anyone with eyes can see the love your stunning wife has cloaked you in. Baby I'm one hundred and sixteen years young and can see the love she has cast over you. I saw it the moment you walked in here Angelo. She has protected you with love better than Fort Knox could ever do. I see you though Angelo, you still my smooth talking baby. Just remember I have excellent eye sight and, I's Tell All baby! I's Tell All." She looked over at me, winked and reached up for August so Deangelo put him on her lap. She in tears looking at them all, Shay went over and kissed her. "It's okay, I cry too," Shay said as his grandmother kissed her and held on to the two of them. He wasn't about to get away though, I returned the favor and did the same to him with my family.

I even took him over to the table where Barbie crack head ass was sitting and introduced him to her. He looked like he wanted to throw up once he saw how fucked up she looked. Back in the day; don't get me wrong, they didn't call her Barbie for nothing. The streets can lock you in and it ain't no way in hell you can get out without losing something. I don't feel bad for her ass at all either. As soon as I left that bitch stole all my shit from my momma house. My mom's said it started coming in by carrier and she put all the boxes in my room. She found her and beat the shit out of her for it too. I never even had a chance to see the stuff.

We stopped by Pam house and sat around then we headed to the reunion, we were busy before the doors closed on the car. We had fun; I had to make sure we all made it to each station. Then we sat and watched Deangelo show out in the softball game. I don't know how much shit I ate; I know when I get home Max gone kick my ass in the gym. Deangelo headed to pickup ice so I watched the boys while they jumped around in the bounce house. Shay wasn't too far away making baby dolls with the other little girls.

Aw hell, I know that ain't who I think it is, I watched as the black on black hummer parked. And just like I was thinking I see Stacy get out the back. Stacy was the only one back in the day that gave Deangelo a run for his money. They were complete opposites traveling the same paths. Stacy rocked black on black, Deangelo white on white, Deangelo only drank water, and Stacy only drank milk.

Deangelo didn't have any tattoos but Stacy did. He's damn near covered on his neck, chest and back. I can't forget about the one on his hand. I mean the shit was crazy; they played on all the same teams and even trained with Rook. You could still tell that they were competing against each other even then. As far as the lifestyle go, they started at the same time and took off, Deangelo was hands on but Stacy was brutal.

He didn't take shit and everyone knew it, whenever Stacy would come around me Deangelo would send me away. When I asked him about it, all he would say was stay away from him. The way Stacy looked at me; I wasn't trying to find out why. I remember when he walked up and blew Big Red head off in front of hella people right as the clock hit midnight on Christmas day. Still it was hard as hell to keep away; this brother is fine.

They're the same age, Stacy is probably an inch taller than Deangelo but they built the same. Stacy's really light skinned; he can pass as a white guy but he far from it. Back in the day his hair was long and wavy. I see he cut it low now; I'm getting sea sick all the way over here from the waves in his damn head.

He reminds me of Christian Keys, I mean Stacy has it going on. Oh, I can't

155

forget about his hazel eyes and we all know what hazel eyes do to my ass. He even has thick, full, long curly eye lashes and he keeps his face clean shaved. Only thing he had on it was a thin line under his lip and you know what they say about that. The last I heard he was getting back to his old ways, that bad boy fuck the world shit.

They were supposed to go pro together but Deangelo pulled out at the last minute. He said he was making more money and was young and dumb so he didn't take the opportunity. Stacy did though; he played six years and won two rings. I guess Deangelo didn't want to miss out, that's why he went overseas to play. Once again he was distracted from that; I can only blame myself for it.

"Damn Treasure, it's been way too long since I seen you." Why do fine men always smell so fucking good? "Hey Stacy, how you doing?" Let me make this quick, the last thing I need is Corey coming over here. Hell, I need to be worried about Deangelo; I know he still would tell me to stay the fuck away from him.

"Girl give me a hug. I see you lost the contacts. I'm a little hurt, they were sexy as hell." I hugged Stacy and got the hell back. The boys came running over, Stacy jumped back like he was scared I just laughed. "This is Deangelo and August my sons. Say hello boys." I looked down at them and they both said, "Hello asshole." in Italian. "What the fuck?" I let it out without even realizing that the words came out my mouth.

Stacy laughed and squatted down in front of them. "Now I know your mother taught you two not to be rude to..." he said in Italian and they both put up their fist and took their stance. Before I knew it, they were dancing around Stacy and he thought it was too funny. They started boxing and Stacy was still laughing weaving around with them. I can't help but laugh at the site of my babies trying to fight his big ass for me.

I told them to apologize and they did, I sent them to look for their sister. "So you here to talk with Deangelo?" He looked at me then gave me a once over like he trying to see something he missed. "I actually heard you're the one I need to talk to." I looked at his ass like he crazy. "Why would you think that and who in the hell would tell you that? What could you possibly need to track me down to talk about?"

He started laughing like I told a joke; he moved forward then leaned down in my ear. "It ain't what you think." He backed up. "How would you know what I'm thinking?" He held his chin with his fist showing me the back of his hand and smiled. The way his third arm trying to break out I know what the hell he thinking.

"I see you Treasure. Like I said it's not what you think, I wish it was though. You want to come for a ride real quick?" I can't believe he asked me that. "Yeah you wish Stacy!" He laughed and turned around. "Thought I could run you to get those contacts real quick that's all. I'll be at you soon Treasure, tell Pandillero I said what's up." Stacy walked back to his car, jumped back in and pulled off.

"Come on Treasure; let's get in this game before it starts." I laughed right in Ethan face. "I guess you didn't notice that I have on all white now did you?" He put his arm around my shoulder. "Yeah I did notice, you always wearing all white. Why you the only one without a t-shirt and who the hell wears all white to a reunion anyway. You planned it so I know you were fully aware that you would get dirty." We laughed. "Ethan I've changed three times already, I'm done with the dress changes. Besides, I don't feel too well anyway so I'll shoot with you but

I can't do anything more than that." We shot around and he decided that I was going to play something with his ass so we played horse.

I was beat, every chance I had I was sitting down. "Treasure you don't look too hot, you sure you okay?" Ethan came and sat down beside me. "Nope, I feel like shit for real, I'm trying to hang in there, and I left my medicine at home." He looked around in my face. "At home-home or here in St. Louis? It's going to be hard to get a refill if you left it at home." I told him it was here so he decided to get me something to drink. After I sat down and chilled for a minute I was feeling better.

We were back up shooting again, that's until Deangelo told me that he overruled my ass again. Of course he told the kids they could go with my mother. Then he thought he was funny and carried me to the car like I'm a duffle bag or some shit. I was in tears, my stomach was churning too hard by the time he put me down.

I went off on his ass and realized I really don't feel like hearing crying ass kids anyway. I sho' didn't tell him that though. He took me home and soon as I walked in I grabbed my bag and took my medicine. That must've been what I needed because I was feeling better.

34 STACY

"What's good Drag, how you been boy?"

"Superstar is in the building! Look at this nigga here ya'll. What's good wit' chu Stacy?"

"You know how it is. Let me holla at you for a second man." We walked outside and sat at a table on Washington Avenue, its bumping. I can't believe what they've done with the place since I been gone.

"Look here man; I've been trying to reach out to Pandillero, errbody in the streets say that nigga long gone and shit." He looked over at me and then away like he doesn't know who the hell I'm talking about.

"Damn Drag, it's like that man?" He stood up so I did to. He looked around like he trying to check if I'm being followed or something.

"I don't know man, he long gone from this shit here, been like that for a minute. Check this though, if I do run into him or his people, I'll let 'em know you trying to holla at him." I can't believe he doing this shit, I know this nigga don't think I'm with them alphabet boys.

"Here man take this, let him know I say no to illegal shit I'm just trying to invest these here. I put my number on it so can you at least give it to that nigga Bateador, I know he around somewhere." He took the dollar out of my hand and put it in his pocket. "Man you been gone way too long, I ain't seen either one of them niggas. But I'll let them know if I run into their people." We laughed, he walked off, and I jumped in the whip and burnt out.

I see this gone be harder than I thought, seem like everybody I grew up with then cut all ties with my ass. Hell, I don't really care because when I played ball them niggas didn't reach out to me and I damn sho' didn't reach out to them. I had too much money on the line to be fucking with that shit. The last thing I needed was to get caught up on some bullshit. I've had my fair share of the life; I'm in no hurry to turn back.

After I tore my ACL I decided it was time to stop blowing through my dough. Them ho's out in LA were getting old. I had to make my way back to the Lou and man it feel good to be back. I can't stand around waiting on Pandillero ass to pop up and get me in on his connections. I might as well move on and wait for the call from that nigga.

Found me a secluded spot out in Ballwin and I been buying up more shit than I can keep track of in this bitch. That nigga need to stop playing and come out of hiding. I know he can reach out to some of these stuck up mufuckas downtown so they can stop giving me a hard time. Seem like every time I turn around I'm getting fined or they threaten to shut my shit down. I had two fucking walkouts already from these union mufuckas and I spent damn near half a mil to fix that shit.

"What's good man, see yo' ass got it crackin' in nis bitch boy."

"What's good Lil C, Drag, Mike, Tubb, Johnny 'bout time ya'll asses came out to one of my grand openings. Welcome to Club Paradise." I showed them around then we headed to the VIP section and chilled out. Before we could even sit down the ho's started coming over. The club bumping that Rico shit so hard the floors shaking, we got loose! Damn, that looks like Peaches. I told them I would be back and went over to see if it was her or not and of course it was.

"Damn Peaches, yo' name says it all baby." She turned around, poked out her lips and snapped her neck to the side.

"Stop playing with me Stacy, last I saw, yo' ass wuz all up in Treasure face on the low." The mention of Treasure name made my pipe move.

"What? You know damn well I'm not studding no fucking Treasure." She grabbed my hand so I looked at what she was looking at, we laughed as she let go shaking her head. She put her empty glass down on the bar; I already know what that mean. Hell, as soon as she saw me she took that shit back in one sip from the straw. I called the bartender over to get her another drink and to give me one.

"I see you still drinking dat nasty ass milk huh Stacy?"

"How you been? How's the family doing?"

"Yeah okay Stacy, I already know why you came over herrre. So if you want da nine-one-one you know you shouldn't waste yo' time playing wit' me." Never fails with St. Louis chicks, big mouths, proudly ghetto but so fucking thick and sexy you can't help but give their ass what they want. Most of 'em anyway.

"Why you think I want information from you Peaches? I thought we were better than that?" She looked me up and down then turned to walk away. I grabbed her arm and walked her into my office. Once I closed the door and looked at her she looked like she ready to go.

I walked around the desk and asked her to have a seat; she chose to sit her thick ass on the desk in front of me. I'm debating on waxing her ass all in this bitch. I need to get what I want and if I do that I'll most definitely not get it. "So what chu want Stacy?" I want yo' ass to go sit down before you get fucked! I can't even tell her that though, I know she'll do the opposite. Next thing I know her mouth, neck and chest would be filled with my pipe.

"Nothing Peaches; I just wanna know what's up with Pandillero for real. Seem like that nigga went ghost or some shit." She laughed then got off the desk and sat in the chair. The only thing she said was, "Um!"

"What that mean girl? What the hell is wrong with errbody acting like I'm talking about some top secret UFO shit. All I want to know is what's up with Pandillero." She opened up her purse and looked down in it. Her silly ass takes the purse flipping it over on the desk. The only thing that came out was a blunt, some keys to her apartment maybe, and not even a car key because she doesn't have a car. I was hollan; this girl is still something else.

I stood up and put a hundred down on the desk, she just looked at me. I dropped another one and sat back down; she reached over and picked it up. "He out da game!"

I couldn't help but laugh. "Peaches you just took me for two hundred dollars just to tell me some shit I already know?"

She laughed. "You need way more den dat Mr. Superstar."

"Damn Peaches, how much?" She sat back on the desk and leaned in.

"How much you need to know?" Why in the hell am I playing with her? I should just bend this trick over and bang her ass 'til she tells me everything she ever knew in her fucking life. Which probably won't be much.

"How about this, I'll put two grand on the table, you tell me. If you tell me enough then I'll give you two more." Her eyes lit up at the sound of what I told her. She watched me count out both stacks then she sat back in the chair.

"Well like I said he out, him and Bateador, dey long gone from herrre overseas. Drag top dog now and from what I herrre, don't none of dem come close to shit. Dey all on dat drug free shit now. Even though dey out, word is dey doing better den dey ever have befo'."

See, this why I always fucked with that nigga. He always was smart and knew how to handle money so I have to get in with this shit. Fuck Drag and that dope game I need this legal shit, I can't afford to be headline news.

I passed her the two grand and rolled the rest up. "Dere's more!" I put the money back down. "Dey have a bunch of businesses all over da Lou and da country. If you give me yo' number I can pass it to dis girl I know at da hotel and she'll send it to dem." Now we talking, that's all I need I'm good now. I passed her the rest with my number, she stood up and walked around in front of me and leaned in. Her hands held her up on the arms of the chair. I can see clean down her shirt to the belly ring she has on.

"I got more but it'll cost you five grand. You don't want to miss out on dis because it has to do wit' my lil cousin. You know the one yo' ass always checking fo'."

There go my pipe again, I pulled out the money and she started laughing so hard she dropped her head to the ground.

"Dat's fucked up Stacy, all dis time and you still tryin' to get at Treasure? Yo' ass willing to pay five stacks just to know about her? I don't know what ya'll see in her ass. She stuck up and always mad about something."

"Man stop playing with me Peaches, you gone tell me or not?"

"Give me my money first, ain't like yo' ass gone miss it no how." I gave her the money.

"Well yo' precious Treasure is da one you really need to talk to if you not tryin' to get back in the game." Oh really, I can't wait for her to tell me why.

"I know you don't know it but she has a little girl and twin boys."

I didn't see that coming but okay. "From what I herrre she has major shit going on that's pulling in some heavy dough fo' huh husband." I damn near fell back out the chair when she said husband. She thought that shit was hilarious, she look weak cackling at my ass.

"Yeah nigga huh husband, now dis probably gone really fuck you up." She stopped talking and looked at me. "Damn Peaches you already have my money spit the shit out."

"She married to Pandillero. Dat bitch had da nerve to invite us to da damn wedding. Den she had a funky ass attitude." I'm wondering why the fuck she stopped telling me the good shit for this but I figure she wanted me to ask why so I did.

"What's wrong wit' inviting ya'll to her wedding, ya'll are cousins right? Ya'll didn't go? Why she get an attitude?"

"You know we cousins, our moms are sisters. Neway, me, my sister, and

164

other cousin went. Had the nerve to send us commercial all the way over to Paris, but her moms and nem flew private. She only invited us to throw it in our faces! So when we got dere dey gave errbody a grand to spend errday until da wedding. Had us waiting around for damn near a week just so she can get married.

Den she get mad because we is too wasted to make it to da' wedding. I mean we showed up in time for the reception, she shoulda been happy we came neway. Can you believe dat shit?" Did this bitch just sit here and say that shit? I guess she think what they did was right. If it was my wedding to Treasure I would've bodied all dem ho's for pulling some shit like that on her.

"Fuck all dat, finish tellin' me Peaches." I don't have time for her hatin' bullshit. I'm ready to smack her simple ass now and I don't have shit to do with it.

"Yeah dey been married fo' a minute now and dose his boys. Dey live somewhere in Greece and so do Bateador. She haven't been back since she ran'd off. If you wanna know when she'll be herrre it's gone cost you another lil grand. If you wanna get in touch with herrre now dat's gone cost you another two grand." This girl knows she can rip a mufucka off; I pull out the money while she laughed again. She came and wrote down a date, address and email address then handed it to me.

35 DEANGELO

The next morning it was time for the reunion so we headed to the hotel not far from the airport for the family breakfast. From the moment we walked in I can see T managed to get everyone all together for this. It's strange because some of my great greats are in the building.

Its people here that I haven't seen in years, with all of her family and extended family the place is jammed packed. We still have people coming in from out of town so I know the reunion is going to be off the chain. After breakfast we went to my mom's house and sat around laughing and joking.

I know something's up, my father pulled me aside. "I wanted to give you this later but I figured I'd give it to you now." He pulled out a piece of paper, I read over it as Bateador came over. "I see you told him huh?" I looked up at Bateador.

"Man you always been my brother, I don't need this to prove it."

I hugged him as my father hugged the both of us. I wasn't surprised at all with the news, we been together since preschool. We never even had a fight with each other unless it was in the ring. We stood around and talked about everything then we all made our way back outside to enjoy the day.

"So I guess yo' cheating ass father told you that Corey is your brother," my mother said as I walked over and kissed her on the temple.

"Yeah he did, just came over here to see how you're holding up." She looked at me and put her arms around me.

"Baby I been knew, I was there when he was born. You don't have to worry about me, just make sure you don't do that shit to my baby over there." We both looked over at T as she turned and made her way over.

"Ma' you don't have to worry about that."

I went over to T and put my arms around her. "What's all that about? I know ya'll were talking about me."

"Nothing." She pulled back and squinted her eyes.

"She was telling me not to have any kids outside of my marriage like my father. That's all." T kissed me.

"I'll kill you and the bitch if you do! Then I'll adopt the baby and raise it to make sure it won't do the same dumb shit it's daddy did." I watched her hold a straight face.

"Where you hear that at T? I like that?" We both laughed. I walked her in the house and took her downstairs; about an hour later we came back and sat around with everyone else.

We all headed out to Bellefontaine Park for the reunion and the whole park is covered with all kinds of shit. Rides, games, food and people everywhere. After the softball game we ate and laughed at the old head dance off. T was having a good time and so were the kids. I took the boys on the four wheelers then bounced around in the bounce house with Shay. T signed use up for the three leg race, we were booed because we laid there kissing after we fell. We did everything there was to do and the kids loved all of it, I know they'll be tired as hell later on.

I watched T and the kids as they made their way around while I sat with my people. "So when you gone let me get my nephews in the ring Pandillero?" I looked over at Rook, he already know what I'm thinking. "Never unless you plan on moving. We out of here in two days, so if you plan on moving let me know." Rook stood up and walked over. "You ain't said nothing but a word young blood. I can be over next month to start training."

We all laughed at the thought of Rook leaving St. Louis. "Stop playing Rook, you know yo' old ass not leaving the Lou!" Cap said as everybody started to laugh harder. "Whatever man, I already have an invite and my word is my word! It ain't nothing holding me to this place. They tore down the towers so I don't have the kids coming in the Center anymore. I would love to pass on what I know to my nephews."

I didn't say anything; we all sat quite at the thought of what Rook said. Made me realize that he's getting older and he won't be here that much longer. Shit, it'll be nothing to let him stay at the old villa; Bateador was staying there until he found him a spot.

"Daddy can we stay with Granny tonight?" Shay said as the boys came running behind her. "What did your mother say?" She looked down; I already know T must've said no. "But Daddy we won't be here that much longer," she said as the boys started to cry. I squatted down and pulled their heads up.

"Man up! Wipe those tears from your eyes and man up." They stopped crying and did what I said, I looked up at Shay and she started to cry. "Princess you need to stop the waterworks, T said no. Why you doing this to me Princess?" She put on her puppy dog eyes and her lip started to tremble.

"Go 'head, I'll tell T I said yeah but you all better not let T see you until I tell her. Okay!" They all said yes. "Now go find Kathy and tell her I said ya'll can go." They all took off. I walked around forever to find T, this woman know she can blend in when she really want too. Even with all white on I still don't see her ass. After I made a run for ice I walked about six laps around looking for her. Then I see her, she shooting buckets with City while everyone else playing a game on the other court.

"What's good man; you came to get in the game?"

"Naw City man, I just came to holla at T for a minute that's all. Why ya'll not playing in the game though?" T turned and looked at me.

"Man Treasure lost it, she don't know what to do on this here court no more." We both laughed as I put my arm around her.

"Whatever Ethan, I just don't want to play that's all."

We sat on the bleachers and I sat her on my lap, I really don't feel like hearing her mouth about what I'm going to tell her. "Don't tell me you think I lost it too." I looked up at her. "Naw, I don't think you lost anything T, I did tell the kids they could go over Kathy house." She stood up and crossed her arms. "Here you go again!" she said as she tried to leave. I picked her up, put her over my shoulder and carried her all the way to the car. I put her in the back and got in behind her.

"You hurt my stomach Deangelo."

"I'm sorry T I didn't mean to hurt you, you know that right?" I kissed her and rubbed her stomach trying to make her feel better.

I reached in the front and turned the air on. "T what is it about St. Louis that make you act like this?" She looked at me and before I know it her eyes glistening and she breathing hard. I always knew T was crazy but her mood swings always seem to take me for a loop. I didn't say anything, I let her finish.

"I'm tired Deangelo, can we get out of here?"

"You sure T?"

"Yeah, everyone's leaving anyway and I need a break, I been feeling like crap since this morning."

"Only if you promise to tell me what's up when we get home." She rolled her eyes and cocked her head to the side. We went around letting everyone know that we were heading out and kissed the kids before they left with Kathy.

36 STACY

The second we pulled up at the reunion all I could do was shake my fucking head. The thought of Peaches scamming my ass out of twelve large had me rolling. She gave me more than enough info so I was cool with that. Had I known the family reunion shit was going to be announced on the radio, I could've saved that last five grand. At least one, the email was worth more than that alone. We drove around until I saw Treasure. The moment I saw her ass made me realize that I would've paid Peaches ass twenty large to get her alone with me for a minute.

After I saw Pandillero and Bateador pull off we swung around where she was at. I wanted to holla at her first before I saw those niggas anyway. Pandillero made sure to keep her ass hidden back then and that nigga Bateador was so far up his ass I couldn't even get close. When I did though, boy-o-boy, I realized exactly why that nigga kept the treasure on a lost island.

I ain't mad at his ass for it. The closer I walked to her my pipe's throbbing harder. I know I just had some pussy last night so that can't be the problem. Now that I think about it, I had some pussy and mouth service about an hour ago.

"Damn Treasure, it's been way too long since I seen you." This girl still bad as fuck, she look like she's only gotten finer and thicker since the last time I saw her. I need to calm down, hugging her only make me want to snatch her ass away with me and take care of Pandillero ass for good. She changed her hair up and the way it's pulling her eyes up on the sides more making my ass sweat. I hate like hell she not rocking the contacts anymore, those set her ass off to the extreme.

She acts like she looking for somebody but I know I saw his ass get ghost. She just gone have to keep playing like she scared of me for now. Her sons came over and they think they talking to a dummy. Trying to speak Italian to me, let me show them I understand what the hell they saying. "Now I know your mother taught you not to be rude to a friend? I see ya'll tough like ya'll daddy though. What ya'll want to fight?"

I see they working with Rook old ass, I haven't seen him since I been back. They said he didn't even work at the Center anymore. Shit, by the looks of things over there that bitch a ghost town. Let me hurry up, I have a meeting in an hour all the way on the other side of town. After I told her that I needed to talk with her, she tried to play me like she doesn't want to hear it but its all good. She can play like she doesn't want to hear me. I know she do, I jump back

172

in the whip and head out.

37 TREASURE

I was exhausted by the time we left the reunion, all that running around was kicking my ass. I walked in and took my medicine; I was feeling better just waiting on it to kick in. I need to hurry up and get home. Because if I didn't know any better, I would think shit was all good and I wasn't pregnant. Hell, with as much nut that I've swallowed I wouldn't be surprised if I'm carrying in my damn stomach. I had to laugh at the thought of that.

As soon as we made it in the house all I wanted to do was fall asleep on my baby chest. The last thing I want to do is argue with him about something he has been doing all my fucking life. It hasn't stopped him in the past so why would he stop doing the shit now?

"So talk to me T, what's going on?" Here he goes, maybe if I play like I'm sleep he'll leave it alone. Of course not, the moment I feel him raise up I just sat up. I know he's going to make me face this shit head on. Why the hell am I so ticklish? It never fails, all he has to do is touch me there and I laugh so hard my cheeks hurt.

I don't know what it is about St. Louis that takes me down memory lane. I guess this is where I had the most pain and heartache. It don't help that Deangelo was the cause of most of it or should I say the center of it all.

The more I think back about all the girls and standing on the side watching him do his thing it made me self conscious or insecure. He could've been with anyone he wanted to be with and here he is married to me. It's cool when we're away from here. I feel like the one and only, no chick out there can have my husband and he wouldn't dare step out with them ho's.

We come to St. Louis and reality sets in, ain't no telling how many of these ho's he been with. I know if he ran past them sluts they would do whatever they could to make it happen. Hell, I couldn't stop him then, I don't feel like I can stop him now, I hate that shit. Not to mention all the dirt he's done here. All the bodies and drugs, I don't know why but I just don't want to let him out of my site.

For him to send the kids away with us all being in town just makes me even more afraid. I think if we all together nothing will happen. Plus I know when the kids are around he keeps four or five extra guys not far. I don't want to tell him that though, he'll have a battalion of niggas following our every move. That's one thing I don't want or need to make the moves I need to make before we go home.

Now he wants to lie and say he wanted to be alone for a minute. He cool as a fan, at least he think he is. I can't wait to get in here; I turned the shower on good and hot. After we washed off I'm ready to go and he about to feel it. I don't have time for the four play, I'm ready and my man's standing strong so I know he's good. I put my right leg up across his right shoulder; he didn't know I'm this flexible.

"You sure you can handle that Lil Mama?"

"Question is, can you Big Poppa?" He slid his finger in and bit down on his bottom lip closing his eyes.

"Hell, naw!" I giggled as he moved my leg onto his left shoulder easing inside of me as his mouth consumed mine.

I let him in and gave him time to get me good and wet. He backed me up against the wall and put both his hands around my thigh. I made it ripple on his ass. I can feel my walls as they wave over his stick with each stroke he put in me. I know he's feeling it, his eyes closed; he's concentrating hard on what's happening. I did it a little harder and he slowed down. I figure he wants to enjoy each move of my walls as he smashed.

I watched as his legs buckled, I kissed him and slowly pulled my leg down. "Something wrong with your legs baby?" He smiled and licked his lips; I went down sucking him in. Pulling away I showed him what I was doing. He tightened his lips together; I put his man on my forehead while slurping on his balls. Even with all the heat in the room I can tell he getting hotter.

Standing up after cleaning my honey off of him I turned around. I crossed my legs and bent over, he shook his head no and I uncrossed my legs. He smacked me on the ass. "Not yet T, I like where this going." I shook my head as he pulls my hair and before I can get ready he came in. I'm not hurt but the length is something I have to prepare myself for. I yelled out, he thought it was funny; he sent some long deep strokes in me that made me cum.

Okay, I see. I'm already against the wall so I bent all the way over and touched my toes and locked down on him. He started stomping his foot like he in pain so I eased off and started pulsating my walls around his stick. "Oh shit T! Got Damn! Hold up T! Hold up!" I stopped and stood back up pushing my ass back slamming him back inside and it was a wrap. I can feel him shoot in me as he licked my back and grabbed my throat.

His body uncontrollable, he's on his tip toes jerking. I started to grind back on him and the more I grind the more he came. "Damn T, why you do that?" I turned around and smiled then kissed him. He turned off the water and picked me up putting his man right back inside. He was going down so I started pulsating again, this time harder and in no time his stick was hard.

He laid me on the bed and damn near begged me to let him out, I laughed and let go. He got my ass back though; he played with my walls with his tongue and was hitting my G spot in a matter of minutes. He flipped me over and licked all over my back, I felt like he was torturing me. I wanted to feel him inside of me so bad I started beggin' him to put his man in. He was licking my ass and then back to my coochie, I was cumin' like a faucet.

My ass sloppy wet, I came so many times I lost count. The sheets were soaked. I didn't have the energy to fuck with him anymore so he gave it back to me just as I had given it to him. We were wore the hell out and both needed to get back in the shower with all the sweating we've done. I was beat though, I didn't want to move an inch. I put my rump up against my stick and was out like a light.

38 DEANGELO

We sat on the couch and T laid on my chest while the music played. "So talk to me T, what's going on?" She didn't say anything; I thought maybe she was sleep. I leaned up which caused her to sit up then she turned and looked away. "So you not talking?" I squeezed her thighs and she started to laugh. I told her I wouldn't stop until she talked to me so she finally gave in.

"I don't know what it is about being here. It reminds me of all the shit I went through with you. All the times you pulled me aside chastising me, the skanks and all the drama." Girls, you would think after all this time T would be over this but I guess she not.

"T you don't have anything to worry about I promise you that! Stop fucking with me, I love you, stop with all this crazy talk."

"Deangelo whenever we're here it's like you don't take me serious. We just talked about this and here it is a day later and your selective amnesia has kicked back in." What she expect for me to do when my princess sad? I know she don't think I'm gone tell her no when it really ain't a reason to tell her that.

"T I know you said the kids couldn't go with Kathy and Shay told me that. I really just wanted to spend a little time alone with you."

T turned and smiled, "Why you didn't tell me that first? Never mind, I already know why."

"Why T?"

"Deangelo you not slick, you're just saying that now but I got something for yo' ass so come on Mr. Man." She started toward the bedroom, I'm right behind her. T was right, she put it on me from the time we hit the shower all the way 'til we finished in the bed. I was worn out. After T was good and sleep I woke up and went to the kitchen to get some water.

As I closed the door to the refrigerator I felt something hit me in the back of my head. I'm dazed but still standing. I turned as the bat came back across my arm. I grabbed the nigga by the throat, I went ape shit on his ass. I'm hitting this nigga with rounds that any other mufucka would've died from. Something about his style reminds me of someone. I feel someone else come behind me and try to put something around my neck.

I tried to stop it but the nigga I have is getting free from the thunder I'm dropping on his ass. We're fighting all around the damn kitchen. I'm not about to let these niggas go after T so this goin' be a hell of a fight. These unlucky bastards are in for some shit they don't really want to be a part of. My mind moving showing me all the outcomes of how this will turn out. My hands are

180

hitting the mark; I need this shit away from my neck so I can really go at it with these bitches.

All I can think about is T, begging she's not in the room and she got the hell out of here. I don't know if she can hear what's going on. I pushed the nigga on my back up against the door and hit the panic button on the lip of the table. That should get her up and out of here; the alarms went off as the table fell over. I'm still fighting for my family; I kicked the nigga in front of me off then I hear a shot, it's T. I still have the other nigga on my back with this shit around my neck.

"Let him the fuck go," she said, we were still going at it. "LET HIM GO," she screamed. As soon as I felt him loosen his grip I pulled it from around my neck as he stepped back. Before I can turn, T shot him in the head. She kept shooting until she was empty, I went over to her but she pulled away. She walked over to the couch and picked up another gun and shot the first bitch again until it was empty.

I moved closer to her, she turned and pointed the gun at me, I put my hands up, "T it's me baby, put the gun down, T it's empty love." I took another step she dropped the gun; I looked down trying to catch my breath and back up when I hear her hit the chamber. All I see is a Tec Nine.

I always knew T was crazy but she can't be this crazy to kill me. I can't say the shit enough, her fucking mood swings always throw me for a loop. "T what are you doing?" I see the tears roll down her face, I watched as she pulled the trigger. I grabbed my ear from the pain and moved the hell out the way. I hear something behind me fall; T reloaded and grabbed my arm.

"Deangelo they all around the house, we have to get out of here." Before we can make it out the back someone came around the corner. I took the gun from T and turned in their direction. They ducked back around so we went back inside. I pulled T into the back room of the basement, gave her my shirt and opened the door to the box. "T stay in here, don't open it for anyone!" She looked at me then opened the cabinet and grabbed the AR and extra clips.

"Go T, put this shit back! I don't have time to argue with you about this!"

"You den lost yo' damn mind if you think I'm going in there without you! Now shut up and man the fuck up!"

As much as I want to push her ass inside I know if I do she'll shoot me and go at this alone. She kissed me as we made our way to watch what's coming down the steps. I feel like eternity is passing waiting on this shit to pop off. I'm starting to think that maybe they left, and then I hear a full blown war of shots go on and on. The alarm stopped and Bateador came over the speakers throughout the house.

"Pandillero, Five-O around the corner dump what you have we out." I went in the box.

"Alright man good looking, see you in a minute." We watched as they pulled off, I took the guns leaving us with two and dropped the rest in the hole in the box. I closed it back up and we waited in the back room for the police to come down the steps.

"So you're telling me that you only shot three people inside and you don't know how we found ten other people dead outside of your property." We both looked at each other then at him with straight faces and said, "No!" He shook his head like he in disbelief of what we said. Fuck him, he gets paid to figure this shit out so he need to do his fucking job and tell us.

"Ma'am I need to speak with you alone." Like hell he does! I stood up in front of her blocking his view as T sat on the couch.

"Anything you have to say to my wife you can say in front of me. Matter fact, you can contact our attorney if you have anything else to say to either one of us."

"Your wife?" He looked around me; I can see T holding her hand up. He looked back at me like he can't believe we're married.

"I didn't know that was your wife. I thou..." This pig crazy, he takes one more look at her the wrong way and he gone find out how all them niggas died.

"It don't matter what the hell you thought! Like I said my wife!" He turned around and walked off.

I watch as he walks over to where a group of them bitches are lurking. They all start glancing over at T, these bitches lucky as fuck! I stopped one of the medics and watch the bastards all trying to see thru me. Disrespectful, punk ass bitches, hiding behind a badge ass niggas keep it up and they gone find out that badge don't mean shit.

T still behind me, the wife beater ripped but she holding it together. I waited for the medic to come back with a blanket. I put it around T making sure them bitches can't see shit. At that moment I wanted to cover T from head to toe and get her the fuck out of here. I wonder if I can get her ass to wear an abaya or a burqa, I need to make a mental note to try and make that happen. It took everything out of me to stop myself from checking these soft ass cats. After the police released us we headed to my mother house and sat in the driveway.

39 TREASURE

My mind is clear, no dreams, no worries, nothing; I'm at peace and loving it. "Get up Terentia!" Dominic? I jumped up out of my sleep, what the hell is that? I reach over thinking maybe Deangelo on the other side of this big ass bed but he gone. The more I came into reality the more noise I hear from downstairs. I turned on the TV above the bed and watched as people climb over the fence and head up the driveway.

I ran across the bed to the cabinet where he keeps his guns, it's locked; I don't have time to look for a key so I pushed it over. Why did I do that, this thing heavy as hell. I jump on the back of it as hard as I can and broke the back off it. This loud as alarm came on, it sound like Deangelo Sr. I listened as he told Deangelo what's going on.

I grabbed the bag of clips and shoved a couple guns in then ran out the room down the hall. I damn near tumbled down the steps; I recovered and ran into the living room. I'm trying to get a clear shot but they're going at it too close. Then my baby kicked the guy in front of him off and I didn't waste any time shooting his ass. He fell back, he still in front of me so it don't matter if he alive or not.

"Let him the fuck go!" I'm trying to buy Deangelo sometime to kick his ass. He acts like he doesn't hear me so I screamed at his ass and he stopped. The second Deangelo head out of the way I sent a bulls eye to his ass. I'm infuriated; I go over and hit that bastard with everything that's left in the clip.

I go back over, put in another clip and finish off the first bitch that I hit. Like I said, it doesn't matter if he's dead or not. Then I see a shadow come around the corner but Deangelo's standing in front of me like he wants me to shoot him. "T it's me baby, put the gun down, T its empty love." He reminded me that the damn gun empty, I hurried up and grabbed another one. I made sure it was ready for whatever's coming around that corner. Then I see my shot, I let his ass have it, my eyes go big as hell because I damn near shot Deangelo. My arms tired as fuck trying to control that thing.

All of a sudden I remember that there's more of them coming, I pulled Deangelo up, "Deangelo they all around the house, we have to get out of here." We ran out the backdoor, that's when I realize I'm porn star naked. That air came across me and all I can think is fuck! Deangelo took the gun because somebody coming around the corner. We went back inside and headed for the basement. He gave me his shirt and tried to make me go into the panic room. I don't know what the hell he's thinking. If anything I'll shoot his ass and we're both going in that bitch together. He got me fucked up if he thinks it's going down any other way.

I grabbed a gun that I know I can work with and told his ass to man up. He likes to tell my babies that shit, let's see how he likes it. I kissed my husband not knowing if I will ever kiss him again, I'm ready to go as long as we're together. Made me think about Bonnie and Clyde. I don't have room in me to laugh about it, the thought of him dying starting to set in.

I just know they'll be coming down but it's taking them hellas to get here. It made me wonder if they found whatever they came for. I'm hoping they have what they want and are going to leave us the hell alone. I can't believe Tree punk ass straight tried to kill my baby, I know Smalls is behind this shit. Smalls has been acting like a bitch ever since he robbed my girl at the hotel a couple months back.

All of a sudden it sounds like I'm back in Basic Training going through the live arms course. That shit so loud I have to cover my ears. I'm wondering when the house will explode from all the fucking grenades somebody's dropping. I mean it went on so long; the only thing I can really compare it to is the fireworks display at the Arch on the fourth. Only difference is, we were sitting on the barge they use to shoot the shit off of. I'm too happy to hear Corey; with all the noise I'm not surprised the police are coming.

After Deangelo dropped that shit and closed up that fucked up room I don't want to let his ass go. I'm all over him; I kissed my baby and looked everywhere to make sure he's not really hurt. Hell, I would've given him a head job if I didn't think somebody watching us.

I'm immediately embarrassed when I thought about who all can see us. I know that his parents had to see what was going on. This means they most definitely saw my naked ass running around here. The thought of it is front and center the entire time the police talked to us. I'm so ready to get the hell out of here; I called my brother and told him to call Ethan. It seem like these bastards are trying their hardest to find something to blame on Deangelo.

They finally let us go about an hour later; I hadn't even realized we had been talking with them for three hours. I was glad to go though, these fools kept asking us if we wanted to go back through the house to get some of our belongings. Deangelo told 'em hell naw! I damn near died laughing at the look on the officers faces. I didn't though; I know I have to face his parents.

My stomach in knots, I'm starting to feel sick as hell all over again. I hope I'm not pregnant because the pain I feel now can't be anything good. We sat in the driveway and Deangelo asked me to not blah, blah, blah. I climbed over in his lap and told him how I felt. I enjoyed being able to be with my husband alive and well.

Dad hugged me and thanked me, I'm really uncomfortable. I still only have on Deangelo ripped up ass wife beater. I'm trying to cover myself up but it seemed like no one is tripping off what the hell I have on. I know Corey not the way he slung me around, I can feel my ass cheeks come from out of hiding. We all laughed at what happened, I guess we all have a sick sense of humor.

The way Deangelo's looking at me, I feel something. It's a different vibe he's sending me, almost like the dominate Deangelo's showing. He started to look different; stronger, wider, taller, dangerous, and angry as fuck. I don't know what it is but it's changing me. Bruce Banner keeps coming to mind. It's like I'm about to morph into a werewolf and the full moon is right in front of me. I'm trying to shake it off but the look he's giving me and the thought of my babies is only helping it along.

"T you have to change and leave with them." I didn't hear anything else after Deangelo said that shit to me. Here we are going through all this and he back to demanding me to do shit. Let's not forget, he didn't say WE, he said I need to leave. Ain't this a bitch! I tried to play it off before I released Taz, I want to make my way out of here as fast as possible. Maybe if I get away from here I'll shake this shit off. I'm borderline, I have everything except my claws, and then Deangelo slammed the door back shut.

"Why in the fuck you stopping me from leaving? Ain't this what chu want me to do, or should I say you ordering me to do Deangelo?" Fuck this shit. I have my claws; I'm tired of him always doing this to me. AND we in the Lou? He right back in his games.

Cindy, flaunting that bitch in my face and the head job yo' ass got from my cousin Barbie. Is all I'm thinking as I hit his ass three times. Thinking I was on drugs, breaking my heart, and leaving me by myself in the first place. I got two of those off on his ass but he grabbed me and he has my arms good.

I put a front kick right to his stomach when I thought about him fucking with Dominic. When Xavier came into my head, I wanted to knock the mother fucking living daylights out of Deangelo ass. I moved around a bit to get the right angel on his ass. I swung with everything I had left in me, trying to take his fucking head off his shoulders.

He thinks he got me but he doesn't because I still remember when he told me. "T, I have a lot of shit going on with me right now and I want to do what's best for you. I just don't know what that is right now. I can't lie to you T; I need to take a step back. I'm not saying I regret anything but I need to work some shit out and I don't want you to wait around on me."

I slung my head back at the pain I felt when I heard him tell me that shit. He mad and I don't care. He forced me on the ground hard knocking the wind out of me. "What the fuck is wrong with you Terentia? Look at what the fuck you doing?"

I know next time you'll think twice about fucking with me. "Get off of me! I'm tired of yo' shit Deangelo! You just gone pick this shit over me and your kids! What about us huh? If you're here doing what the fuck you want what are we supposed to do when you never bring yo' ass home. Or end up in jail, but who you think you fooling? You'll die before you do any time locked up, that don't matter though! I'm not sitting on the sidelines and watching you do whatever anymore. Fuck you Deangelo!"

All I can do is cry after they pushed him off of me, I'm starting to feel that demon get off my shoulders. I rolled over onto Pam and held on. I need to feel loved and my own fucking husband doesn't understand that.

"We been through hell tonight and the first thing he wants to do is get rid of me. Of us! Why Pam? Why would he run back to these fucked up ass streets instead of taking care of us?"

"Treasure calm down baby, ya'll just need to take a minute and breathe baby!" his father said.

"You heard him, both of you did, he said I need to leave with the kids! He didn't say anything about coming with us or when he will be coming home. I'm not stupid; I know these streets always calling him. I know the only reason he's stayed away is because we all the way over there." I stood up.

"Ya'll can't tell me that if we lived here we would still be together or he wouldn't be dead or worse in jail!"

I sat on the hood of the car and told them to give me a minute so they walked off into the house. The moment I lifted my head it's like I'm freed from all of the shit I wanted to tell him. The crying is from the guilt of me using my hands to tell him instead of talking to my husband like I have some common sense. The more I sat there the more I realize I need to say my peace and go.

He was in the shower so I went in, I don't know if he wants me in here with him or not. When I asked him he sounded like he pissed so I was about to leave. He called me back so I got in, I can tell he doesn't want to talk. Shit, he doesn't even want to look at me. I talked with him and got out, I can't face him no how after what I just did to him. I know if he would've did some shit like that to me he would be dead.

I put on some clothes and Corey said he'll drive me. "Corey I'm sorry for the way I behaved, I hope you can forgive me even if Deangelo won't." Corey put his arm around my shoulder as we walked to the car.

"He a'ight, nothing like a good match to clear yo' head. Besides lil sis, you earned it after all we've put you through." We laughed; he helped me in the car.

"Corey who all can see in the house?" He looked over at me and started cracking up at my question.

"Don't worry, we all could see yo' naked ass running around." I pushed his shoulder and sank down in the seat.

"So who?"

"Just Pops nem and me. See." He put his phone into the slot and it showed the house cameras on the screen in the car.

"All the time?" I hope he don't say all the time because we've done shit all over that house.

"Naw, Pandillero always turn the inside cameras off whenever ya'll there. But we can still see what's going on outside. At all the houses, even mine and pops nem." I looked over at him as he stopped at the light.

"So what the hell took ya'll so long?" He put his head back on the head rest and looked like he was disappointed with the thought of my question.

"We were headed out when we got the call from Pops; he said a silent alarm went off at the gate. I already knew that and was on my way; I was in the middle of handlin' some other shit. Once Deangelo hit the alarm all the cameras kicked back on inside, that's how we were able to see you." I'm mortified because I know they saw everything, literally everything.

"Don't worry Treasure, I don't find you attractive and I hope Pops don't!" I can smack the shit out of him.

"Thanks for the boost of self esteem Corey." He thought that shit was just too funny.

"So where you goin'?" He stopped laughing and looked over at me.

"You're going to the airport like your husband is expecting you to do, where your kids are waiting on you." I turned watching out the window.

"Do we have a problem Treasure? If we do, save us all the trouble and tell me so I don't have to go through the bullshit. I have enough on my plate." I continued looking out the window; he pulled over turning my head towards him.

"Can I have a hug?"

"No, leave me alone Corey." I got out the car slamming the door shut. He came around pulling me into his arms hugging me so tight I begged him to put me down and stop. He walked me in and told the kids he'll see them later and was back out the door. I sat with my babies and called Ethan to tell him about Tree and Smalls. I needed to handle something's, by the time I calmed down almost four hours had flown pass.

I looked down at my kids knowing it will only be us for a minute. The thought of it is making my head spin, I can only hope Deangelo's safe. I pray they don't call me saying he's dead or in prison for the rest of his life. Then I felt so much fucking pain come over me I just broke down crying. I scared the shit out of them, they all started to cry, and I have to get my shit together.

40 DEANGELO

"T please don't ever do that again. If something happen to you I won't be able to live with myself." She climbed over onto my lap and put her arms around my neck.

"What do you think I would do if something happened to you? Have you ever considered how I would feel?" My father came out and knocked on the window, we got out he hugged us.

"Damn Treasure yo' ass was on fire tonight. This was some fucked up shit but I'm sho' glad yo' ass was there baby." We all laugh as my mother came running out the house.

"What in the world Deangelo, why you didn't answer the phone? What took you so fucking long to hit the damn alarm?" She let us go and held on to T as she started to cry.

"Treasure baby, I didn't know you had it in you. I am so glad my babies are okay." Bateador pulled up and we watched as he walked over, we hugged then he picked up T and spun her around.

"Really, all of ya'll just gone play me like I'm weak," I said as they all laughed harder.

"Treasure I owe you my life for saving my brother ass the way you did," Bateador said as we headed into the house.

"We need to go get the kids!" T said then turned back around to leave out.

"Baby their on their way to the airport with Ms. Jackson," my mother said.

"T you have to change and leave with them. I want you all in the air within the hour, so hurry up so you can go." She turned back around and shot me like she held a fifty caliber to my chest with her gaze.

"Treasure he's right, you need to go back with them," Bateador said.

"Don't you mean all of you need to go back," my mother said as she stood by T side and helped her fuck me up with their stares. T kissed everybody, reloaded the fifty, shot me again and grabbed the keys off the counter. She stomped past me headed back out the door without saying a word. I followed behind her as she stormed to the car.

She pulled the door open and I slammed it shut. "Why in the fuck you stopping me from leaving? Ain't this what you want me to do, or should I say you ordering me to do Deangelo?"

"T it's not like that you—" She dropped the keys and hit me three times in the face and stepped back. I can't believe she did it, I grabbed my face she hit me two more times. Before she can move I grab her arms but she kicked me in the

194

stomach. I wasn't expecting that or anything else she doing. I let her go; she shifted around and swung on me like she really wants to put me the fuck to sleep. I caught her and I'm pissed about the amount of force she tried to hit me with.

I snatched her hands locking 'em behind her back turning her around into my chest. I'm not about to take another hit or kick from her ass again. I put her up against the side of the car and held her under my weight. She throws her head back catching me in the nose, I'm boiling. I put her on the ground and sat on top of her. "What the fuck is wrong with you Terentia? Look at what the fuck you doing?" She starts to scream at me as everyone came running back out the house telling me to stop.

Bateador and my father pulled me off of her; she rolled over and began to cry. I'm still dazed from the ass kicking she put on me so I get up and push them off of me. I walk in the house leaving T with my mother consoling her.

"What the hell is wrong with you Pandillero," Bateador screamed at me as we made it in the house.

"Man that's her, I didn't put my hands on T you know that, she losing her damn mind. Matter fact, you in her yelling at me, you need to be yelling at her crazy ass, she the one went Sho'nuff on my ass."

We looked at each other and both started cracking up laughing. "She fucked you up didn't she?"

"Man she just beat the shit out of me. Hell, if she was working with them niggas earlier I wouldn't be standing here." We laughed even harder. T must've been wanting to do that shit for a minute. She quick as hell I have to give that to her and her hits have a sting to 'em.

I didn't bother to go back out and face them or T; I went in the room and jumped in the shower. I feel like hell and I need a break from T putting her foot in my ass. I sat there for a minute then I hear someone come in the door. I know it's T, she'll be the only one to come in the bathroom with me. I can hear her as she walks back and forth like she's trying to get the words together before she says anything.

"Can I join you?"

"Why so you can beat my ass some more?" I didn't look up at her; she turned and started to walk away. I stood up and told her to come here, she stopped took off the wife beater she had on and came in with me.

We stood there quite; I moved back, closed my eyes and let her wash up. When she was finished I let the water run down my face as she put her arms around my waist. "I'm sorry Deangelo. I truly am sorry for what I did to you." I didn't respond, I put my hands on the wall and leaned closer to the showerhead drowning out her voice. She came around me and pulled my chin down so I could look at her.

"I was wrong for what I did to you; I hope you can forgive me. After I get out the shower I'll head straight to the airport and back home like you told me. I hope you come home Deangelo, I won't go through losing you like I did with Dominic. I can't! I won't! So just know that if you die I will too, the kids will go to our parents. As much as I would hate to do it, I will Deangelo. I love you!" She kissed me and got out the shower.

By the time I came out the room T long gone. My mother came down and sat beside me on the couch. I put my head in her lap while we looked into the fire place.

196

"Baby I know you two have been through a lot but if you don't go home you'll lose your family baby."

"Ma T crazy, one minute she like the perfect day, next she like a hurricane just out of control. I can't figure her out. With all this shit going on you would think she wouldn't fight me as much as she is. I mean she kicked my ass out there for no fucking reason. I heard ya'll replaying the tape laughing at the shit so I know you seen it."

After my mother finished laughing she hit me on the shoulder and told me to watch my mouth. "Deangelo you know why she did it right?" I can't believe she taking T side.

"What? You think it's okay that she put her hands on me?" I can't believe my mother even asked me that shit.

"No son it's not okay what she did. You have to look at it from her side; she was fighting for her family. You about to be right back in these streets behind all of this. She knows if you stay here you will have the only two options you started with. So she wasn't right. Think about this, do you remember when I beat yo' ass when I found out what you had been doing? I wasn't right for doing that but I was trying to get you to understand that the streets are not worth your life." We sat there in silence.

My father came out the back and sat on the table. "Deangelo get up!" I sat up and looked at my pops.

"I heard enough and I've held my tongue long enough. You hear me?"

"Yeah pops what's up?"

"Look son, any woman that will kill three fucking people that are trying to kill you is worth fighting for. Do you understand me? Of course she kicked yo' ass out there today, you know why she did it don't you?"

I don't know if he wants me to answer or not. Something telling me it's a rhetorical question so I just looked at him. Plus I know he heard my mom's ask the same dumb ass question. "She did it because you not thinking about your fucking family, that's why?" Hold the fuck up! I know he didn't just go there because I think about my family every second of the day. "What chu mean Pops? That's all I ever think about. My family!" He stood up, the tone in my voice was disrespectful and he's not about to have it.

"No you not! You're thinking about these streets and how you would handle this situation if you did NOT have a family to take care of. But guess what, you do have a family and they need you to worry about them right now. Yo' dumb ass sitting her getting babied by your mother. Your wife is sitting at the damn airport with three kids waiting on a flight that won't be there until noon. Do you realize that's five hours from now?

Why you not with her and those kids? You know damn well you not sticking around to talk to the police. I'm done son, you can let them leave without you if you want and you gone regret it for the rest of your life. I should call her back over here so she can beat the shit out yo' ass again." He started to go back down the hall.

"Pops you trippin', T already gone, she took the jet o..." He turned and walked back over so I stood up.

"You not that naive son! I held the flight so you could get some sense in your head and get the fuck out of here! Do you remember when you told her you knew better and it was time for you to do better? Act like it now and show her. MAN THE FUCK UP! Come on Pam, leave this fool right here if that's where he want to be. Hell, we about to burn copies of that ass kicking and pass 'em out if he stays here." He grabbed my mom hand and continued to go off as they walked out the room.

The more 1 thought about what my father said, the more 1 realize I'm making a mistake by staying here. 1 can't decide how 1 feel about the situation with T, especially after she did what she did. If she was anyone else 1 don't think 1 would've been able to control myself after that kick she landed on my ass. All 1 know is that my heart is saying to let St. Louis go and deal with this another day. My family needs me and 1 need to make sure they're alright. 1 called Bateador and he said he was too far away, 1 jumped in the whip.

"I'm headed back from meeting up with Cargo, Ghost got out in time."

"Put Cargo on it man, 1 don't think Ghost will be very effective with the situation. We don't need this shit sloppy or fucked up."

"Come on Pandillero; give Ghost a little more credit than that. We need to find out the deal and you know Ghost can get it done."

"1 hear you Bateador but has Ghost even told you about that secret yet? 1 mean Ghost may need a minute alone to figure this shit out given the facts behind that secret."

"Shit! 1 told you 1 hated this shit involved that punk ass nigga, 1 should've told Ghost but 1 know Cargo probably already let Ghost know by now. 1 can send Ghost with Prime for a minute at least until this shit die down. If Ghost not willing to go with Prime I'm dragging Ghost ass back to the house. Either way Ghost gotta get the hell out of the Lou for a while."

"Let me know what's up either way. Let Cap and Flight know what the deal is if you send Ghost with Prime. 1 know they gon' want to double up on Prime security if that's the case." I hang up with Bateador and called my father back, thanked him and my moms and told him to send the plane. I walked into the hanger and watched as my babies all ran into my arms. "Daddy what took you so long?" August said, I looked down at Shay, she crying, I picked her up. "What's wrong Princess?"

"Mommy sad, she won't stop crying and you leaving us and I don't want you to leave and I don't want her to cry." She put her arms around me as the boys cried on my legs. I shuffled them all over to the waiting area.

"Look, you all need to stop crying, Mommy's sad but she's alright. I'm not leaving, we all going home together, we all will be just like we always have been. I need everybody to stay here while I talk to Mommy okay? Shay you watch your brothers until I get back."

I kissed them and made my way over to T, I put my arms around her as she stared out the window. She put her head back against my chest. We didn't say a word, then we saw the plane so we boarded. The kids were all sleep in no time and T sat looking out the window. After I helped Frick I went back into the bathroom, I looked in the mirror trying to figure out what the hell I need to do. I walked back out and noticed T changed seats out of view from where I'm sitting, I sat back down. "Come here T." She came over and sat on my lap, the whole ride back we barely said two words to each other.

41 TREASURE

I cleaned up my face trying to hold on. "Shay, watch them for a second I have to use the bathroom." She still has tears rolling down her face but I have to get out of here. I pulled myself along the walls to the bathroom. I found the first stall I can reach, got out of my clothes and sat my ass right on that damn stool. I don't care at this point.

All I can do is bare down, I'm feeling better so I wiped and saw nothing but blood. I look in the toilet and there's a ton of blood. I'm not on my monthly so I know this a problem. I'm ballin' at the thought of what's happing to me. I hear Shay come in and I scream at her to go back with her brothers. I know Ms. Jackson's not far so I sat there crying my eyes out.

I come out and I'm numb, my bodies still in pain but I'm too hurt that my husband's not there to take care of me. I stared out the window and felt him wrap his arms around me. I don't know if I should be happy that he here or sad about all the shit that has happened.

Plus the thought of what I'm thinking just happened in the bathroom fucked my head up. We barely said anything on the ride back, I'm good just being in his arms, it gave me a chance to really think. I can't sleep a wink, I tried my best but when I close my eyes all I can see is blood. That shit's killing me to hold it in.

As soon as we made it home I call the doctor, all I can think about are my babies and how short life really is. I put them all in the guest bed with me and I'm starting to feel at peace with the situation. I woke up early; I don't want Deangelo asking me where I'm going so I ran out the door as quick as I can. I'm not quick enough because Corey's coming in when I'm heading out.

"Where you going Treasure?"

"Nowhere!" I tried to lie but the look on his face telling me he doesn't believe me.

"Pandillero never told me about a place you go called nowhere." I smiled but I don't have time to mess around with Corey.

"I'm late so I'll be back soon." He grabbed the keys from me and headed to the passenger door opening it for me.

"Well let me take you to nowhere, that way I know where it is the next time you have to go there." I sat in the car and closed my eyes contemplating if I should tell him where I'm going or not. I know they won't have another appointment for two weeks but damn, should I tell Corey snitchin' ass or not.

"Treasure, you remember the last time you tried to ditch Pandillero and we stopped the bus and got yo' ass off." I smiled at the thought of all the people being mad. The bus driver was hot until Deangelo put some money in his fat ass hands.

"So stop with the games, where you going? I know you not going to see Harlem right." I almost jumped out the seat, he started to laugh.

"No I'm not Corey and that shit ain't funny so stop laughing! Just take me to my damn doctor and shut up!"

"Calm down Treasure I already know where you going anyway see." I looked up and he was pulling up right outside the office. We went in and I tried to get Corey to wait outside but he insisted on sitting in. I cried the whole ride back home, he took me to his house while I cried some more.

"Treasure I'm sorry but this does not mean you can't have any more kids. You heard the doctor say it was the stress so you just need to take it easy." I held my head up off the arm of the couch and looked at him.

"How am I going to tell Deangelo, he already wants to leave me. He'll never forgive me for this Corey." He pulled me up straight.

"It was a miscarriage Treasure, no one's fault but those punk ass niggas and I handled that so he won't blame you. Think of it this way, that baby's now in heaven and no one can hurt it now. You have another angel looking over you and the rest of us." I started to cry more.

"I, I can't tell him Corey!" He let me cry until I couldn't anymore then he took me home. I tried my best to hide from Deangelo. I'm surprised it's as easy as it is; I went back into the room with my babies. I cried all fucking night. I'm exhausted by the time they woke up the next morning.

I'm moving around the house barely able to keep my shit together, every time one of them walks pass I burst into tears. My head pounding, I need to calm down and relax so I went and took a bath. When the water wasn't helping I made my way to the shower. The longer I sat there letting the water clear my head the better I felt.

I was starting to think I can face my family without crying. I have to get as many of my tears out first. I hear Deangelo come in, he just stood there so I don't know if he wants to get in or not. I've been in here for hours; I need to get out anyway. Before I can pass him he made me feel better and pulled me close. I really don't want to talk but I need to clear this shit up.

42 DEANGELO

Once we were home I was happy that my family safe but my mind still on what happened and T. For days I found myself sleeping alone. T sleeping with the kids in the guest room like she doesn't want to be bothered. I want to fix whatever it is but my mind racing in so many directions I don't know where to start. I watched as T stayed busy with the kids and kept away from me as much as she could. Whenever I come in she leaves out.

I sat on the porch trying to figure out what's happening, I see Shay as she heads for the swings. I listened as she cried; I went down to see what the problem was.

"Princess what's wrong with you?" She put her arms around me and cried more. "Tell me Princess, what's wrong?" She looked up at me.

"You and mommy getting a divorce and I won't see you or my brothers anymore. Then I won't have any daddy because Dominic is dead. I don't want you to die daddy; I don't want to lose my brothers. Mommy is sad all the time, all she do is cry. Why don't you love me and mommy anymore daddy? What did we do? I won't ask to stay over Granny house anymore daddy I promise." She put her head back into my chest and cried.

"Princess I love you, your brothers and mommy, I would never divorce mommy. Where you hear that at anyway? What do you know about a divorce?" I pulled her chin up.

"My daddy Dominic died and mommy divorced him and she cried like she cries now. I don't want you to die and divorce mommy." I don't know how she put that together. But hell, I didn't think she would remember how T was when Dominic died. I carried her to her room and told her I would talk with her later. This shit is crazy, I can't take this here anymore, and my house has to get back right and fast.

I walked into the bedroom, I need to talk to T and end this before I lose my family for good. I walked in and didn't see her. I hear the radio going so I walk into the bathroom. I can hear her crying in the shower, I sat on the sink listening. When she realized I was in the room she finished up and got out.

Before she can pass me I pulled her into my arms trying to see if she's going to pull away. "Terentia can I talk to you?" She shook her head and walked into the room, I waited as she got dressed and sat on the bed. "T how long are we going to do this? We need to talk and deal with this before it gets out of hand. I know we can make it through this, we have to talk and get it all out." That wasn't that bad but by the look on her face maybe it's about to turn in a whole other direction.

She looked up at me long and hard. "Deangelo, I don't know where to start. You wanted to stick me in some room while you risked your life. Then you try and send me and your kids away not knowing if you would come back alive. I put my hands on you and I wish I could take it back but I can't. You're ready to leave me and I deserve it for what I did. I need to get used to you not being around because I know where this is heading." Tears started running down her face.

"T all I want to do is protect you. Why can't you understand that?" She stood up and walked around to me.

"Why can't you understand that we need to protect each other? I know you can protect us but if we in this together then you need to understand that I have your back no matter what. I told you before I'm not one of those weak bitches you then fucked with back in the day. If yo' damn life on the line then mine is too." She sat on the side of the bed.

"T I understand that and like I told you before, I would never compare you to anyone I've been with. Stop saying that shit." I pulled her on top of me.

"T what made you do it?" She cleaned her face and laid beside me.

"Do what?"

"First, what made you come downstairs? I know you saw what was going on on the screen why didn't you run?" She shook her head and rolled her eyes.

"I heard something break but I thought I was tripping. I turned on the cameras and the alarm went off. It took me so long to get down there because you locked the case. I didn't know where the key was. But if I had to fight them off of you I would have." She laid down on me.

"All you needed to do was use your ring it would have opened the case. I should have told you that when we first made it to the house but I didn't remember. I thought yo' ass was trying to kill me for a second there." She lifted up and kissed my chin.

"Never! I saw him peeking around the corner but I didn't have time to explain it to you before I set the damn gun. I'm sorry; I shouldn't have fired that close to you."

"You know my ears been ringing ever since T. Now why did you want to fight me? Or should I say, why did you kick my ass?" She sat all the way up and pulled me up with her.

"Deangelo I was mad that you were picking St. Louis over us. I know that if you would've stayed there you would go after Small and Bunk—"

"What? How you know it was them T?"

"I saw Tree, Small brother; he was the one that was trying to choke the shit out of you. I know they're close nit. Plus they've been trying to reach out for months now to get in. I told my girl down there not to deal with them. You remember about three months ago the hotel was robbed right? Ethan said there was an investigation that was leading to Small.

When I saw Tree I knew it was them, plus I called Ethan after I left from with you and told him what happened. He said give him a couple hours. Then he called back and said he was taking care of it we could leave. I spoke with him after we made it back and he told me that they had already taken them in."

"T your life has been on the line far too many times because of me not protecting you. I'm tired of fighting you about letting me do what I have to do to make sure you're okay. I don't want you to ever talk about the kids going with our parents again. I don't care what happens to me if you're okay then you make sure you take care of our kids." She stood up and looked at me.

"Deangelo I can't take another loss baby! I can't lose you like I did Dominic, that shit hurt me to the bone, why can't you see that?"

I pulled her in my arms. "Terentia I understand that but you have to understand me. I will never leave you or the kids you know that. Promise me this, look at me T. If anything ever happens to me that you will make sure, you! No one else but you take care of our kids Terentia. I mean it so just make me this one promise." She wiped her face.

"Okay I promise, but only if you promise to let me do what I can to help you. Even if that means killing anybody trying to hurt us."

"Didn't you tell me you wanted me to stop killing these niggas? You sound like a hypocrite T." I smiled and kissed her.

"T I know you can hold your own but if the shit hit the fan and I tell you to go just go and make sure you keep our kids safe okay." I wanted to make love to her but she said she wasn't feeling well. Which was kind of weird, that always made her feel better in the past. I was cool with that so I just held her until we fell asleep. The next morning I sat everyone down at the table.

"Now Deangelo, August, you two are getting too big to be walking around here crying all the time. So in a couple weeks Rook is going to be working with both of you." They smiled and clapped.

"Princess I want you to understand that we are not getting a divorc—"

"Where that come from Deangelo," T said as she walked over to me.

"What? Shay been crying about us getting a divorce since we been back. She thinks that when someone dies it means they get divorced." T walked over to

Shay.

"Shay death is not the same as a divorce, you don't know that already?" Shay shook her head no.

"Well what happened to your daddy was he died Shay. We didn't get a divorce he died. There was nothing that could have stopped that from happening, I don't think. When you get a divorce that means two people go in there own direction and move on without each other." She wiped the tears from Shay face.

"Princess we will never get a divorce, Kathy will kill me first baby girl."

"Deangelo," T said as she looked back at me.

"Princess I'm fine and Mommy's fine, we will never get a divorce and we are not going anywhere any time soon okay?" They all ran out leaving me and T alone.

"T you need to stop with the mood swings in front of them baby. The boys and Shay are picking up on it, she's afraid for you and so am I." She sat up on the table.

"I'll work on it Deangelo, these last couple days have been a nightmare without you to talk to. I have so much shit on me right now. Reminds me of how I felt when you left and I signed up. I guess you can expect a hefty bill from the doctor, I think we all need to have a sit down." I can't respond because I know it's my fault in the first place. I slid her off the table onto me and held her.

A couple weeks had past and I was getting worried about T, we still hadn't had sex and I know she had to be feeling better by now. I tried to ignore it so me and Bateador went to the gym to go a couple rounds in the ring. When we were done we sat around taking in all that Rook had done with the small gym and just how many people he was able to bring in.

"Hey Pandillero man, have you talked to Treasure yet?" What he mean why wouldn't I talk to her?

"Yeah why?" Why the hell he think I wouldn't talk to T, what this nigga got on his mind?

"I mean talk to her talk to her?" Okay, now he's starting to piss me off with this.

"Spit it out Bateador, I don't have all day to sit her playing twenty questions with you." He looked down; I know this has to be something big.

"Well she didn't ask me not to say anything to you. But I think, or I should say I know why she not having sex with you." That was enough I stood up and walked right in his face.

"So you telling me that you know why my wife, my wife, not having sex with me? Her husband! Is that right? What make you think that shit anyway?" I'm ready to go heads up with his ass bare knuckle style if he about to tell me some bullshit. Brother or not, it ain't that type of party. He moved back then sat down on the bench; I stood there looking at his ass waiting to kill him.

"Look man, not too long after we came back she was trying to creep out the hous—" I heard enough, I picked his ass up by his shirt; all he did was put his hands up.

"Hear me out man; it's not what you think!" He doesn't know what the fuck I think right now. If he says the wrong thing his ass won't have to worry about what I'm thinking, he gone feel it.

"Tell me Bateador!" I'm too hot to yell at his ass.

"Just let me go man!"

"Fuck that, tell me Bateador!"

"She had a miscarriage!"

I looked at him not believing what he said, I let go and stepped back. I felt like he hit me with a gut punch and knocked all the wind out of me.

"What did you say?" I fell back into the chair and almost flipped over.

"She was trying to sneak and go to the doctor by herself a couple days after we came back. Jazell told me what she was going in for. I was headed over to the house to see if ya'll wanted me to go with ya'll but she tried to play it off. I didn't want her to go alone and I didn't know if you told her you didn't want to go or not."

"WHAT THE FUCK YOU MEAN?" Now I'm ready to yell at his ass, what kind of dumb shit is that? All the noise in the gym went quite, all eyes were on us. Rook said something and they went back to doing what they were doing.

"Look, ya'll were going at it, I didn't know what was up so I went with her. The doctor said the stress caused her to lose the baby. That's why she's been acting the way she has. I know you banging your head about all the crying and shit so I had to tell you."

I'm pissed, "You felt so fucking bad for me it took you this long to tell me? What kind of shit is that? You my brother and you don't tell me I lost my child? That's fucked up nigga!" I snatched up my bag and jetted to the house. I know the kids are all gone for the next two days and I'm goin' take both of these days going the fuck off on T.

"Terentia! Where the fuck you at?" I'm yelling over and over, I started looking around the house for her ass. I'm looking high and low. I go out back and see her; I'm running over to her ass full speed ahead. I slowed down and watch as she sat rocking back and forth. She crying so hard she don't hear me.

She lit a candle and put it in some balloon thing while she held onto a piece of cloth in her hand. "T! What are you doing?" She jumped and stood up leaving the stuff on the ground. "I'm saying goodbye; I was asking Dominic for his help." The tears came pouring down as she dropped down and held onto her legs. I walked over, all I can do is wrap her legs around my waist and sit with her.

"Why didn't you tell me T? I was so pissed when Bateador just told me. You should've told me T, we could've handled this together." I'm too hurt, I let my tears go.

"I'm sorry baby but I couldn't tell you. I thought if you found out you would blame me for not listening to you and leave us." I cleaned my face.

"T how many times do I have to tell you I'm not going anywhere? Since you not listening just know the only way you getting rid of me is if I kill yo' ass." She giggled and I hugged her.

"What's all this about?" I helped her dry her eyes.

"Jazell said that in some cultures they take something of a passed love one and ask for their help with whatever you need. Then you put it in this here with the candle and let the wind deliver the message."

We sent the message off and headed in the house when we couldn't see it anymore. T went in and got on the phone then she came into the living room with me. We talked about everything I'm still a little upset that I was the last to find out but I understand where she's coming from with it.

"Deangelo please don't be mad at Corey, he knows that I wanted to tell you, I just didn't know how. It's my fault that I was holding it from you." I wasn't mad

213

at Bateador at all, I was mad with myself if anything.

"T I'm not mad at him or you." She laid on my chest and we watched TV, about an hour later the doorbell rang and I opened it.

"What's up man? 'Bout time yo' ass got over here?"

"What's good Pandillero, I was trying to wait on Jazell to pull up but I didn't know if you wanted to kick my ass or not." I laughed and walked outside with him.

"It's all good man, that was my bad back there I just lost it for a second." We dropped our problems and he ran over to help Jazell out the car. I walked over and kissed her as she headed in the door. Before I could make it back on the couch the doorbell rang again so I went back over. I paid the guy and brought the food inside to T. We all sat around and ate dinner with no beefs or secrets between us.

Everything was good after that; Rook had been down for months training the boys. Bateador cleaned up the niggas that were in on that bullshit that went down. I was even able to hook Rook and Ethan up to run the boxing program. Princess and T are both happy and both getting the help they need. I was surprised when she told me they would be seeing a doctor on a regular but I was happy she made the call. Business is booming and there's no stopping us on that front so I have no worries all around.

43 TREASURE

Deangelo and I were moving forward and I was feeling better. I still cried some nights about the baby but when I did I would see Dominic. He didn't say anything, he just smiled and I felt better about the situation.

"T you wanna play a game with me?" My mind was right in the gutter.

"What kind? I hope you talking about something that will have me screaming your name." He laughed and kissed me.

"Not now T, come show me what you got out on this court though."

"If I win you get the cuffs later." He popped me on my ass.

"You crazy as hell if you think I'm letting you cuff my ass again. Fuck that shit!" We laughed and went out to the court.

He kicking my ass, I lost my touch, this shit not as easy as it used to be. I hit a three closing his lead in the game as Bateador came out the back. He told Deangelo that their father was sick, Deangelo ran inside and changed.

"Corey, what's wrong with him?" He opened the door for me as we walked in.

"He has Cancer, I don't know if Pandillero knows or not but Pam said its serious." I don't know what to say. He didn't look sick the last time we saw him, hell who does look sick. You start to look sick when yo' ass gets in the hospital. You look so bad people start to question how they didn't know something was wrong with you.

I talked to Corey for a while then I headed upstairs to check on Deangelo. "Can I go with you baby?" I already know the answer, shit; he didn't say come on T. Besides I know the routine when he in St. Louis; he's the same old Deangelo.

He didn't say anything so I have my answer and I don't want to fight with him about his decision. I guess I'm finally getting broken in. I walked them out and hugged Corey. "Please don't let anything happen to you two while ya'll there. If you don't make the call by the time ya'll land then just know that I will." He didn't say anything he just smiled. He knows that I'll call and have every available officer Ethan can send them and he doesn't want that. I kissed and hugged Deangelo and told him to hurry back.

Corey called me before they landed and said he doubled up on security so I was feeling a little better. I sat around the house trying to play obedient house wife for days. The kids were tired of me trailing behind them. I know Rook loved for me to get his paperwork and books together at the gym. He called before they had practice just to ask me if I'm coming.

"Rook you need to hire someone to do this, if not you gone be in trouble." He came over and threw his fist up.

"Treasure I been doing that stuff since before you were born. I just don't like to sit down and do it because I have to train these kids."

"That's why you need to hire someone to do this. I know you don't think it will get any easier next year when those centers start opening up." He laughed and threw his hand at me.

"Rook I'm serious, I'm hiring someone to do this for you. Yo' old tail don't know anything about a computer anyway." He turned.

"I know about that ring, you wanna spar with my old tail in there?" I shook my head no.

"Well watch your mouth young lady and help me without all the back talk!" He walked off and started yelling at the kids

44 DEANGELO

"Come on, T you know I'm winning, look like you just threw in the towel." She smiled and checked the ball, she came in tried to back me down then pulled up for the jumper but I blocked it. We both went for the ball then I see Bateador come out the house, she grabbed it and hit the three. "You know that's cheating right?" "What she say, all's fair in love and basketball?" We both laughed and walked over to Bateador.

I waited as he hugged and kissed T. "Pandillero I been trying to reach you. Pops is sick, he in the hospital." I ran into the house so I can change, I heard T come in the room. "Can I go with you baby?" I put on my shirt and grabbed up my stuff and headed to the door. T came down and walked with us out to the car. She hugged Bateador and whispered something to him, she kissed and hugged me and said hurry back. I told her not to worry and that I loved her.

We were back in the states and headed to the hospital. My mother hugged us as we came in and walked us up so we can see pops. "What you two doing here," he said then he tried to laugh but coughed. We went over to him, I waited as Bateador told him to get up and stop being lazy. "Whatchu so quiet for son?" He looked over at me. "I'm not, just wondering how long you plan on sitting around in this place that's all."

We all laughed, I know he's in pain and it won't be long before the Cancer takes his last breath. We sat around talking. Days past with us by his side; seem like everyone from the hood made it by to see him and say their final goodbyes. I talked to T and the kid's everyday and everyday she would ask when we were coming home. I avoided her worries and moved onto something else. I don't want to fight with her, all of my energy's with my father.

We decided to chill out at the East Coast to lose our uncertainties before we headed back to the hospital. It felt like old times. I sat chilling with my people while the ho's came flocking over. "What's up Pandillero, you remember me?" She looks familiar, I just looked at her. Umm, is all I can think, boy she's thick and cute.

"Naw I don't, I guess you from the hood though right?" She smiled, licked her lips and came closer to me.

"It's me Mona, Kay Baby is my sister." Now I remember, she a year older than T and stayed in all the parties when she knew she was too young. I remember when I met Kay Baby on Seventh Street; they were trying to jump on T when she was walking back from the mall. She was a little thing last time I saw her but damn, she sure did grow up and out on a nigga. "Yeah now I do, how you been girl?" She came over and hugged me.

We sat back and talked while everyone looked in on what was being said. I can see what she doing, playing around with that straw in her mouth. She keeps laughing grabbing on my leg like I don't know her game. She asked me to dance I told her I was good. That didn't stop her from dancing anyway, I'm enjoying the view.

She moved in front of me bouncing that ass, she popped her hips and dropped down low to the floor. She leaned back enough so she could show me she didn't have on any panties.

"You sure you don't wanna dance Pandillero? If you want we can get out of herrre and I can do somefin' for you that I know you'll like."

"Really? You something else Lil Mona." I laughed as she kept going on dancing and talking shit about what she could do for me.

She doing too much, I need to get my mind right, I head to the tight ass bathroom in the back. After I finished I go to leave out the narrow ass hall she standing in front of the door. She came right up on me; I'm backed up against the wall.

"Damn Pandillero why you act like you don't wanna fuck? I can tell you do so why you fighting it?" She reached down and grabbed my man then she started licking on my neck.

"Can I at least suck yo' dick?"

I know I'm doing too much but damn it feel good. She turned around and put her ass up on me. The way she moved her hips had me standing tall, my mind's all over the place. She giving me a personal dance right here in this little ass hall. She turned back around, put her leg up. I can't help but hold it there while she traced my ear with her tongue. I can feel the heat from her cat and my hand slowly creeping down to take a dip.

The more she move her cat up against me the more I think about taking her up on her offer about my man in her mouth. Damn I need my man sucked and I know I can ram my joint all down her throat without mercy. I can probably get it all the way in until she licking the back of my nuts in her big ass mouth. I'm fighting good and evil in my head. It's like I can't think straight and make my damn mind up either way about what the fuck I'm about to do.

The door swung open and it's Bateador, "My bad man." He closed the door back. I know I'm tripping so I let go of her leg. "You be easy Lil Mona, here, take this and get yoself some water before one of these niggas take advantage of you." I passed her two hundred and made my way out the door. I saw Bateador as he headed out the door, I did the same. After I made it out I started to go back in because I could've sworn I saw someone. I think I'm still tripping, I really don't need to go back in there, and I ran over and got in.

45 TREASURE

I talked to Deangelo every day; I could tell his spirits were down. I decided I sat on the side for long enough, I want to see dad anyway. I need to see Deangelo, whether he like it or not I'm on my way. I made it to the hospital and dad was sleep. Pam said Corey and Deangelo left out. Corey called Pam and said they were headed to the East Coast first; she couldn't stop me from leaving.

I pull up and I'm dreading going in the damn place, the last time I was here is playing back in my mind in slow motion. I sat across the street; I can see Deangelo talking to someone. Then I see her get up and start to dance. I just shook my head at the sight of it. I'm surprised it doesn't bother me. Then I remembered how I was looking at those Greek Gods as they stood displaying all their weapons of mass destruction. Not to mention those Egyptian deities, they were beyond words.

I saw him get up and walk off then she followed behind him. I felt the switch flip in my damn head. Didn't this nigga learn anything from Cindy in this muthafucka? I can't believe this shit. I pushed that raggedy ass door open and Corey looked like he shit a brick. Corey jumped up too fast and ran off; I made my way to the bar. I sat down and got some cranberry juice, I need something to calm my ass down. Corey comes blowing past me trying not to look in my direction then I see Deangelo walkout. By the way my dick's leading the way I'm done. I know that ain't Mona punk ass. I still remember that bitch from back in the day, they thought they had me.

She walked pass me heading out the door; I see Corey and Deangelo turn the corner so I walk out behind her. That bitch look shook when she turned around and saw me. "Hey Treasure, I haven't seen you in a long time." I just looked at the Gnawing Nora looking ass bitch, she tried to go around me but I cut her off. "What Treasure, I know you ain't mad at me over that nigga. Gurl I'm trying to get paid that's all. You know how it is."

I know this bitch didn't just say that. "So let me get this straight, you trying to get paid by my husband?" She looked at me like she praying somebody saw her leave out the club.

"My bad Treasure, gurl you know I didn't know ya'll wuz together. He didn't say he wuz married when we wuz in da bathroom together."

"Bitch you a damn lie, the whole hood know." I should smack her for trying to distract me with that 'in da bathroom together' shit.

"So what Treasure, what chu wanna do? I already got some dough off the nigga, what's done is done, get over it." She tried to get tough when her lil click came out the door. I hit that bitch without even caring who has this skank ass trick back. She fell back and the whole club emptied out. Drag started yelling at me to stop, I see these ho's trying to run up. I up'd my bitch on ney asses and told 'em not to move.

Drag came over I gave him my shit, he told them ho's we would fight one on one. I don't give a fuck, how I'm feeling I'm ready to take all these bitches on. That bitch got up and tried to rush me but I'm too hot for that. I helped her with the ass whooping her crackhead ass momma should've given her. I dog walked that bitch all up Broadway, all she could do was scream. I stopped because she balled up crying pleading for someone to help her. I'm stomping the bitch out so good I started to feel bad. My heart want to end this bitch life but I have to follow my head and stop.

"Stay the fuck away from my husband bitch!" I yelled all in this trick face. I want all these ho's to know not to fuck with my husband anymore. I sat back and let them talk slick for way too long. I only had to fuck up a few of them but after the dish I handed her ass tonight, I think they know the deal.

"Anybody else wanna run up and catch a good old fashion Cochran beat down?" I hear some bitch ask who I'm talking to. I told them bitches loud and clear, anybody!

"Here Treasure, get yo' crazy ass out of here before I call Pandillero." I want to punch Drag ass for letting the shit go down. Then I thought about it and hit his ass anyway.

"Damn Treasure! What was that for?"

"That was for not telling me about Sebastian!" He laughed and put his hands up. I jumped in the car and whipped that bitch around damn near hitting that schmutt and drove back to the hospital hoping Pam wouldn't tell

Deangelo I'm here.

46 DEANGELO

The whole ride back to the hospital Bateador didn't say anything; we rode out to the music. He parked and just sat there as I got out the car. "Aye man, you coming?" He didn't say anything; he stepped out the car and slammed the door. I don't know what his problem is.

As he past me he knocked into my shoulder so I know something's up. "Bateador what the fuck is wrong with you?" He turned around headed for me then pushed me in the chest.

"You my fucking problem!" I'm at a loss.

"What the fuck did I do?" I pushed his ass back.

"What the fuck you thinking, about to fuck that dumb ass girl back there!"

"Fuck you nigga, why don't you mind yo' damn business!" I walk past him; I can't believe he's being a bitch about that shit. He grabbed my arm so I turned around; he came right up in my face.

"Man you know how many niggas I den canceled out for yo' ass for the same shit? I know Treasure your wife but she my sister and my fucking business ever since WE met her. You know how much shit she has been through because of us? Don't tell me you forgot about the gun at her fucking head, in that same fucking club. Fucking with her old dude, sitting in the room with her while she had bullets in her fighting to stay alive. Let's not forget how she saved yo' ass and killed them niggas for you. Oh yeah, I know you didn't forget about the rape and how that nigga ripped her ass open with a broken bottle did you?"

I'm about the break the levees off on his ass after hearing what he said. I hit him and we started to go at it. I'm beyond discussing it with him, we stood there exchanging blows back and forth as people started to gather around screaming for us to stop. Then I hear my mother and he looks over at her but I continue to hit his ass. I don't care if he's not fighting back. I feel my mother hit me and I drew back but Bateador finally hit me and I stopped. I watch as they go inside, I sat there thinking about everything.

I feel someone sit down beside me, when I look over its T. I drop my head in shame. "So I guess St. Louis does something to all of us huh?" She passed me a tissue to wipe the blood from my nose; I sat there and let her do it for me. "So did you fuck her?" I look over at her and shake my head no. "Did you want to?" I didn't look up; she pulled out another tissue and wiped my face. "Husband, did you want to?" she ask as she stared into my eyes, I can't answer because I know she'll be hurt. "I take that as a yes." She finished cleaning me up, kissed the top of my head then stood up and walked away.

Once I went back in the room everyone looked over at me and turned away. My father said he wanted to talk with me so they all left out the room. I walked over. "Son, I know what all this is about, don't be mad at Corey; he's only doing what you would want him to do. You have a great wife son, don't fuck up and lose her like I almost did with your mother. Treasure won't stick around like your mother if you do."

He began to cough. "Give me your word son that you won't lose Treasure. She's the one for you, can't you see that?" I held on and gave him my word. I walked out as they all headed back in. I wrapped T in my arms, "Baby I'm sorry." She smiled and kissed me. "I know you sorry Deangelo that's why Corey kicked yo' ass!"

We both laughed. "What you doing here T?"

"I couldn't sit at home while my dad's in pain, he was there for me. I been here for a minute anyway waiting on you to come back." I looked at her and laughed.

"Yeah I started to beat that bitch ass for popping all in your face like that. But as soon as Corey saw me walk in the door he ran to get yo' ass. Your man was so hard when you came out of there with her you walked right past me." I flashed back and thought about leaving out. If I would've followed my first instinct and looked back in the club I would've seen her. Then I remembered seeing my white Aston Martin DBS parked across the street.

"T I'm sorry, I shouldn't have let it go that far. Hell, I shouldn't have even chilled with her."

"Deangelo just remember that I'm your wife and don't try and pull that shit again. Besides, I don't know if I wanted Harlem to kiss me but I could've prevented it. So I know we all have temptations." I can't believe she tried to slide that shit past me like that.

"T yo' ass think you slick with that, I already know about that shit anyway."

"Corey told you didn't he?" I shook my head.

"Max told me, yo' ass forgot about him didn't you? I talked to that nigga Harlem that same day and he told me what happened. Max called me when the shit was going down.

'Mr. Joseph we had a situation!' I don't know why the hell I didn't go with you that morning. 'What the fuck Max, this was supposed to be a simple fucking task! How in the hell did something happen with you and Bateador there?'

I tried to calm down while Max told me what the hell happened. I was already in the car once he told me it was a problem. I called up Harlem and told him to meet up with me. He tried to talk but I told him where to come and hung up on his ass. I got out the car and waited thinking, 'I know he better hurry the fuck up before I have to go looking,' and he damn sure didn't want that.

I watched as he pulled up and got out, by the looks of that nigga face I could see that Bateador already tagged his ass a couple times. 'Pandillero, it was a mistake this was all my fault and Treasure had nothing to do with it.' I walked over to his ass man to man.

'So you've been fucking around with T behind my back? I already know you feeling T, what straight man wouldn't?' He backed the fuck up. 'Pandillero it was my bad. I've never came at her before but something came over me and I let that shit take over me. Don't let my fuck up ruin the shit we have going. I'll stay the hell away from Treasure this shit was a mistake.'

That nigga was begging for me to keep him on, he did all the renovations at the lofts for free. I understood what the nigga was saying and I know damn well you aren't going anywhere. I let his ass off the hook and took the shit for what it was worth. By the time I made it to the house you still weren't there."

She looked at me and turned her lips up on the side. "So you used me to get free work done?"

"T I don't know if you realize it or not but you fine as hell. A man will do some real fucked up shit without thinking about it. You know better than to think I would use you so don't make me kill that nigga to show you." I smacked her on the ass and held onto her.

Bateador came out, T walked over and hugged him then said something to him and went back in. "Aye man, I apologize. You right and we better—"

"It's cool man we family, all of us. Just keep that shit in check. We can't hurt her; I know you know better than that." That was enough for us; we went back in the room and waited with pops.

47 TREASURE

I pull up and I see a crowd of people outside then I see Corey and Deangelo going at it. I mean they're really going at it hard. I haven't seen them like this in years but this not for sport, this looks real personal. I hear Pam scream and Deangelo look like he wants to hit her for hitting him. All I thought was, 'I'm sure glad he didn't hit me that night'. Then Corey hit his ass real good sending him right on the ground. He sat there and my baby look like he exhausted. He don't look defeated, something saying he's just tired of fighting. I know that feeling all too well.

I sat beside him, he looks surprised to see me, I'm suddenly glad that Max is on vacation. I know if he wasn't then I wouldn't have known about any of this. "So I guess St. Louis does something to all of us huh?" He didn't answer and he stopped cleaning his self up. I gave him a tissue and took over doing it for him. I asked him if he fucked her, he said no and oddly enough I believe him. I asked him if he wanted to and that's the real question I want him to answer.

Hell, I wanted to kiss Harlem, but when he kissed me I had a change of heart. Yeah it sound fucked up but hell, that's the story I'm sticking too. I pushed him off right after he touched my lips so that don't hardly count. "Husband, did you want to?" He still didn't answer so I know he must've wanted to fuck her but that's on him. I can't keep doing this shit with Deangelo anymore.

I finished cleaning him up and went back to the room. I don't care that his parents are here. "Corey thanks for what you did down there but the next time you do that to my husband we gone have a problem. I don't care how many of these skeezas he sleep with that's between us not you!" We all laughed as he came over and hugged me. "I told you we can't hurt you anymore and if I have to kick his ass to get that through his thick head I will." We sat around, I talked to dad and it seemed like any other day with them. Everyone was happy and enjoying each other's company. Deangelo walked in and all the laughing stopped, dad said he wanted to talk with him. We walked to the lunch room.

By the time we came back Deangelo was walking out so they went in and he held me in his arms. My baby still has blood on the side of his nose. "Baby I'm sorry." I'm about to burst out laughing hearing him say that. I'm waiting on the rest of the joke, baby I didn't mean it. Only thing I need to tell his ass after that is to call Tyrone. I'm over it I guess, after beating the shit out of Mona I let all the anger go.

I teased him about the fight and told him that I saw him at the club. He was stunned that he didn't see me. I guess I'm losing my touch. There was a time back in the day if no one else could find me he could. I don't know if it's a good thing or bad thing. All I know is I can't worry about that shit anymore; I have to worry about my babies.

I talked with Deangelo about it and tried to glide the Harlem incident past him since he feeling guilty. He told my ass he knew about the shit the same day. It don't matter because it was nothing to start with. He popped my ass and I'm feeling great. Corey came out and I know they need to talk. Before I went in I whispered to Corey, "Now we even with that Harlem bullshit so we can let that go since yo' ass had Max tell him. Also, I sort of kind of beat the shit out of Mona, if you can stop them from telling Deangelo I'll be very grateful." He shook his head as I went in.

They both came back in shortly after and we were good again, one big happy family. Pam's in the bed with dad, I'm in my favorite spot on Deangelo chest listening to his heartbeat. Corey sat in the chair closer to the door on the side of dad. Pam's getting annoyed with his constant texting, he giggling like he's a teenager. Corey's in love and I'm happy because he let go of his dealing with that street shit once Layla was born. Deangelo said a man will only change when something else is more important to him, either way I'm happy. I know he's talking to Jazell, I can tell by the smile on his face, and then he made a sound that made us all laugh.

"Damn man, she must be saying some freaky stuff over there," Deangelo said as we laughed more.

"Nope! Picture my brother, they worth a thousand words." Dad even laughed at what Corey said, he continued and so did we.

48 DEANGELO

We headed to the house and T was surprised to see the portrait all done up. She walked around checking out the loft we picked up after the shooting. Bateador had a spot in the building down the hall already. We decided to get the top two floors and make it our own. T loved it; she had a clear shot of the water from every room in the house. We sat around doing nothing and chilled out. Bateador came down and T fixed us all something to eat. We laughed about the fight and T thought it was too funny to see us go at it.

"Yo' ass lucky Pam came out. That's the only way you got that shit off," Bateador said as he walked over to the couch.

"Yeah baby, if that was the fight at the games you probably would have taken silver and not gold," T said as she kissed me.

"Everybody have jokes huh, damn wifey you don't have faith in yo' man no more?" She walked over and hugged me.

"Always baby you know that, but you deserved to get that ass kicked." She kissed me and sat on me.

"Hell, I should've let her come in so she could kick yo' ass," Bateador said as we all continued to laugh.

"From what I hear she already did some ass kicking of her own." T looked over at Bateador.

"He didn't have to tell me, I told you the hood talk." T put her head into my shoulder and we all laughed.

At the same moment we both looked down at the sound of our phones ringing. Bateador answered and I gave mine to T. I dropped my head because I know what my mother's going to say. Bateador stood up and walked over to the window, T came back and sat in my lap and hugged me. We didn't say a word after that; you can hear the time tick by as we sat in silence.

My phone began to ring; T answered then started making calls as Bateador headed to the door with me behind him. Before he left out I hugged him and he did the same. I sat on the couch thinking back on all that my father has been to me. T came over and helped me come to terms with his death.

A couple days later I hear Bateador at the door so I go over to answer. Then I realize it wasn't him at all and opened it. All my babies ran in hugging me as Ms. Jackson came in. The boys showed me their moves and Shay ran off to find T. Later that day T and Jazell drug Bateador and I out for a picnic under the Arch. The kids ran around while T looked over at me holding my niece Layla in her arms.

"You know I proposed to Jazell don't you?" I looked over at Bateador and shook my head yes.

"Man who don't know? That big ass rock on her finger, you trying to start some shit with that asteroid." We laughed.

"Go 'head with that Pandillero, I had to make it official though. We not doing anything like ya'll did all big and shit. Just us ya'll and my baby girl, that's it." We chilled out and talked, the more I looked at T and how peaceful she looked holding Layla it made me relax. She looked over at me and told me what she wanted without saying anything. I can't wait to give it to her when we get home.

I took the kids to my mother; she didn't want to be alone before the funeral. I know she has a lot on her mind so I sent Ms. Jackson with her. We all headed to the house and called it a night.

"So Deangelo, I was thinking, maybe we could have another." T stopped and looked up at me.

"Really T! Another what? Car, house, hell a dog?" She laughed and walked into the living room.

"No Mr. Man, another baby, what do you think about that?" I got up from off the couch and walked towards the hall, T came around the corner watching me.

"So we not even gone talk about it," she yelled down the hall at me, I turned around.

"We don't have to talk about it T." I opened the door to the room.

"So what, that's it? Just like yo' ass ca—" I pulled off my shirt.

"T I'm waiting on you." She ran down the hall and we officially christened the house.

49 TREASURE

We headed downtown to go to the loft so we can change and rest before going back out to the hospital. I walk in and can't believe my eyes, it's huge. The windows are wrapped all around the first and second floor. We are high enough that no matter where I'm sitting I can see the Arch. I can also see all the water as it moves past continuing on its journey.

I'm in love with our bedroom, lying in another huge canopy bed. If you lookout the doors leading to the balcony you can see the water. "Deangelo, I know you're tall but why do you always have to get a bed that is so damn big?" He smiled and sat down. "Come on T, you never know how many people you need to get in a bed at one time." I turned and just stared at him, he think the shit's funny. I went over and pushed his ass back on the bed, he grabbed me and started making me laugh.

"So what you trying to say Husband, you gone make me fuck you up or what?"

"Nope, but what if all the kids want to sleep in here with us, we gone need the room."

"Yeah, tell me anything."

Corey came over so I cooked us a small lunch, a salad, baked chicken, and vegetables they had water and I had V8 juice. We just laughed and let loose, Deangelo cleaned the dishes and we found ourselves laughing even more while we sat on the couch. I'm ready to punch Corey in his head for not keeping his damn mouth shut. I should've known that there's no way in hell this fly on the wall husband of mine wouldn't find out.

Later on both of them had a call; Deangelo gave me his phone so I answered. The pain in Pam's words made me remember Dominic. I know Deangelo needed me and I needed him. I felt guilty because the more I sat there with him the more I remembered my time locked in the house while he took care of me. Ms. Mack called about an hour later. Deangelo used Ms. Mack, an older lady who is a retired executive level secretary to do almost all of his personal stuff for him.

I talked with her and went over the details for the funeral she said Pam had already called her. I asked her what she needed me to do so I made the calls and that was that. Ms. Mack had already sent for the kids and I know that will cheer up Deangelo. She sent for Jazell and the baby so I know Corey will be just as happy.

Ms. Jackson called a couple days later, they were all downstairs. I called down so they can get in the building. The second Deangelo opened the door I

239

hear the kids running around like crazy, my baby came flying in the room.

"Mommy I missed you." She ran and jumped on the bed, I'm cracking up. Shay started jumping all across the bed like she found a jungle gym. I hugged her and asked if she saw her room yet, she took off out the door. I walked downstairs and found my little ones shadow boxing with Deangelo and I remembered my first time sparring with him.

Jazell came down and asked if I wanted to go to the Arch for a picnic and I was down. I know she don't want to go alone. Not that she don't want to be alone with Corey or anything. She only speaks Italian so she won't have anyone else to talk to. I wasn't sure if they wanted to go but we were able to convince them to come out, we sat out and enjoyed the view.

Layla's only two months, she's so cute and little, her eyes are so big. Her lashes reminded me of mine, long and curly. I know Corey must've been begging for a boy for those things to be that long. Her hair has tight curls but it's long and full. If you pull one of the curls it's in the middle of her back. She's a sweetheart, I looked over at Deangelo as he smiled and watched what I was doing.

After we dropped off the kids we headed home, I know where my head's at and I want to get it off my chest. When we had the boys it wasn't a surprise but I never did have the chance to ask Deangelo. I'm not about to hear his lame ass jokes so I have to ask. I'm scared to hear what he'll say with the miscarriage and all but I finally asked him. After he tried to play like I was talking about a damn car that is.

He didn't say anything, the look on his face said he had enough to worry about but I'm not finished. I at least thought he'd tell me what the hell he's thinking. He just walked up the steps and headed for the room. I stopped at the top of the steps, I can't believe he just gone go in there like that.

"We don't have to talk about it T." Really, we don't? Hell if I would've known that I wouldn't have asked him the fucking question. "T I'm waiting on you." I was so happy I ran down and jumped into his arms. I let his ass have it for playing with me and for that comment about people being in the bed.

50 DEANGELO

The next day we went to breakfast with the family then the funeral. It was standing room only; everyone came in to say their goodbyes. After the burial we went to the Center for the repast, it looked like the old days people were errwhere. This place has been a ghost town since the towers came down. You'd never know that by the looks of all the people here.

All of us sat at the table, I had August and T had Deangelo while Shay stood in between us. "Hey Treasure and Pandillero baby, how ya'll been?" I turned around and it was Ms. Sherry, I stood up and gave her a hug and T did the same. We talked for a minute then I see a familiar face come up from behind her.

"What's up Pandillero?" I didn't say anything; I put Frat down and moved closer blocking the view of them all.

"Stop that Pandillero, wez family whether you like it or not! Wez may not be blood but wez still family!"

"I'm sorry Ms. Sherry. What's up Myzphyt?" Ms. Sherry turned and looked at him like he was supposed to say something back or something.

"Well Myzphyt, don't chu see Treasure, chu gone speak to herrre?" He looked down then back up at me.

"Is it cool Pandillero?" You bitch ass nigga, fuck naw it ain't cool. Punk ass come all the way over here with yo' momma so you can talk to my wife. Ms. Sherry just stared at me.

"Hey Myzphyt, how are you doing?" T said as she passed me Frick and walked towards him. His punk ass still didn't say shit; T looked back at me like she want to kill my ass.

"Yeah man it's cool, damn!" I tried to sit back down; Ms. Sherry grabbed Frick out my hands so Frat wanted me to pick him up. She sat in my chair watching my ass watch T and this nigga. I just sat back and watched while T talked to the nigga, then she hugged him and they walked away.

"T why you always think I'm just supposed to smile all up in yo' ex niggas face?"

She sat back down. "Deangelo you don't have to be so fucking mean all the time! I'm your wife; you don't have anything to worry about so stop acting like that."

"I'm not being mean, I just don't want to be smiling up in no nigga face that den had my dessert!"

She leaned over and put her lips right by mine. "I can count six bitches at this table you den fucked. If I count the ho's in the building you then fucked or you let suck yo' stick it'll take all night." She kissed me and I laughed as she pushed my chest.

I showed Frat the trophy case and all of the different awards and teams I played on. Bateador and Jazell walked in the backdoors with Layla so we headed over to see them. "BATEADOR!" I yelled as time stood still. His arm was around Jazell's shoulders. It rocked forward as blood splattered all across me and Frat. Layla's in the air, I moved to catch her and was barely able to get a hold of her before she fell. I pushed Frat under the pinball machine and put Layla beside him. I ran to the front door as everyone else headed for the back.

Once I make it out I see the truck come flying around the corner. I can hear the rounds bouncing off the car as it speeds right toward me. I waited and hit the driver three times and watch as the truck jump onto the sidewalk and stop. All of my people come around still firing. One of the niggas gets out the back and tries to run. Before he can get across Cass he's hit with more rounds than his body can take. I walk over to the car as they pull Bunk out from the back, he's leaking. "Fuck ya'll niggas!" he said as blood pours out his mouth.

I fell someone push me aside, I watch as Bateador took the sawed off to create a gestural abstraction all across the wall. Hell, I wish we had a canvas behind this nigga first so I could hang that shit in the entry to da house. Bateador ran back inside. I look around in disbelief at all the people around me putting away their guns jumping in their cars and driving off. Seem like everybody made sure to run the nigga over that's lying in the street as they sped away.

All I'm thinking is, 'Who brings a gun to a damn funeral?' By the looks of it, everybody I know. I put mine back on my waist and went back in; I need to check on August and Layla. I see a crowd of people standing around then I hear my brother yell out. I look in the gym and see T with the kids and she has Layla in her arms.

"Alright errbody, please go out da gym!" Laura said as the crowd broke up. "Help me Pandillero! Please help me wake her up!" Bateador cried but there's nothing we can do. Jazell has blood pouring out of the hole in her forehead; it's nothing anyone can do to save her. I sat next to him then the medics came and I walked over to T and Layla.

"Get away! I'm not leaving her! Baby wake up! Wake up Baby, please wake up!" One of the medics grabbed Bateador's arm and he threw him off with ease. I move over to calm him down as another one reaches for him. Bateador pulled out his strap and told everyone to backup. T walks over in front of Bateador with Layla still in her arms. "Corey, Corey look at me. We have to get her back home bruh. Layla needs you to take Jazell back home!" Bateador put the gun down, T put Layla in his arms, and I helped him up as the medics look after Jazell.

The kids left for home that day and we stayed around so we can take Jazell back with us. T looked after Layla while I consoled Bateador. Since she's not a citizen it took a couple days then we headed home. The only time Bateador slept was after forcing him to take the pain pills they gave him for the bullet that went through his arm.

Even then he tossed and turned, he wouldn't sleep long but it was long enough for the pain to simmer. After we landed Jazell's family met us, he pleaded with her family but they weren't trying to hear it. They didn't want him at the funeral but T convinced them to let him and Layla attend. T never told me how she did it but Max did and I wasn't mad at her for how she handled it.

I'm only three weeks older than Bateador but it's hard to see my little brother go through what he is. I'm feeling like I should've protected him better. All I can think about is all the times he was there for me with T so I was there for him. Layla stayed at the house while I stayed with Bateador at his. Weeks passed by and I was still at a loss with what would take his pain away. T came over and asked if she could speak with Bateador alone so I headed back to the house.

A few hours later they came over and Bateador looked like he was in better spirits. "Hey baby, you feel like heading out tonight?" She put her arms around me. "If you want to I guess." I watched Bateador as he held Layla and played around with the boys while Shay patted him on the back. About an hour later he gave them all hugs and headed over towards us.

"Aye Treasure, thanks for everything, Pandillero I'll see you later man, I need to get Layla home." I walked them out.

"You sure man, you know you can chill out with us tonight if you want."

"Yeah man, good looking though, I've spent enough time and I need to take care of my angel." He closed the door then drove off. Later that night me and T went out and enjoyed our time together.

We sat out on the beach. "Deangelo you never did really answer my question about having another baby." I don't know why she thinks I don't want kids and then she started going to work. I'm lost, my body feeling so fucking good all I can do is lay back and take it. After she finished she sat on me and I sat up. "So you gone answer me now?" I kissed her and filled her up. "T you asking me the wrong question."

She looked at me then tried to stand up but I pulled her hard back down slamming her onto my man. She screamed out. "What you should be asking me is how many kids I want. You may just be surprised with that answer." She smiled so I rocked her hips back and forth.

She bit down on my joint with some force that had me wanna jump my ass to my feet. "Why you playing with me?" I kissed her she started to let go. "T if it was up to me we would have a football team around this bitch. So yes baby, I want as many kids as you will give me." She smiled and put her arms around me. The kids were all sleep by the time we made it home.

51 TREASURE

The funeral and burial were hard to watch, it was over five hundred people crying and giving their condolences. I don't know how Pam did it and kept a smile on her face. Shit, I don't remember who was at Dominic funeral; it was like I was sleepwalking. I didn't know Deangelo was there until he told me. I looked back in the register and his name's the first one in the damn book. He said he was at the church before everyone made it then he sat in the back. He was even at the burial. I remember seeing the envelopes but I didn't know he gave them to them right before they came over.

Everything happened just as planned, by the time we made it to the Center it was jammed packed. I thought the funeral and burial was crazy they had nothing on the Center. It was standing room only, like it was a hood reunion.

People were upstairs and down and it was still standing room only. Ms. Sherry came over and talked with us, I was happy to see her. She was just too blown away about the boys and us not bringing them to meet her.

Then Myzphyt walked over and he looks like he has really changed his ways, he wore a suit and looked very put together. I can tell by the look on his face that the streets and drugs have aged him well beyond his years. Ms. Sherry's trying to get him to speak to me. I can tell by the way Deangelo moved us all behind him that there must've been some unresolved beef there.

"Well Myzphyt, don't chu see Treasure, chu gone speak to herrre?" Ms. Sherry's really pushing it and I'm not about to stand around and watch him be tortured any longer. I moved from behind Deangelo gave him Deangelo Jr. and spoke to Myzphyt.

He still won't say anything; he looks like he don't even want to look at me. My heart sank, I feel so bad for him, I look back at Deangelo and he told him he can talk with me. Ms. Sherry made sure she hung around; I see her playing with Frick.

"How you been Myzphyt?" He looked at me then down; I saw a tear drop from his eye.

"I'm alright now Treasure." His voice crackling and I have a feeling he's hurt.

"Come on Myzphyt, I know you not that surprised that I ran my crazy ass back to Deangelo." He laughed and shook his head.

"Naw, I'm not surprised at all. I been wanting to talk with you for so long and tell you I was sorry about everything that happened. I've been to hell and back trying to get myself together and I'm glad that now I've seen you I'm clean." I smiled.

"I'm happy for you Myzphyt. Cheer up, we have to play the hand we're dealt. Sometimes we don't make the right choices but we have to move on."

He reached for my hand and stopped, and then he looked over at Deangelo who I could feel staring at me. "I'm three years clean Treasure and I have a good job. I even went back to school, got my GED and getting my Associates in a couple months. Seeing you has made me want to keep moving and get my stuff together." He put his head down to stop the tears from falling so I hugged him.

He jumped when I touched him and I could feel him start to put his arms around my waist. Deangelo must've got up when he did because he pulled back away from me. I said goodbye and turned and watched Deangelo try to sit back down like I don't know what the hell he's doing.

I messed with Deangelo for his little smart comment about who the hell I been with, he has his nerves. All these ho's mugging me and my kids because they had some of his ass. He the biggest ho in here to tell the truth. I sat with my babies while Deangelo showed August around, those two are inseparable. At times it worries me when I think back about what Dominic told me. It made me think that maybe August will be the one to follow in Deangelo's footsteps. But I know Deangelo wouldn't have that.

It seemed like everyone all at once stopped talking and glass started breaking. Then I hear the memorable sound of the night at the lake house. I sat Deangelo in Ms. Jackson arms and ran out to the lobby. I know my babies are out there. It's chaos, I see Corey holding Jazell and I freeze but the sound of my baby crying thawed my ass out real quick.

I ran over to him, he's under a machine covered with blood and he's holding Layla in his little arms. I grabbed her and picked him up turning his head.

Corey stopped crying and ran out the front door. I walked back in the gym and Pam took August, she thought he was hurt. I tried to get Layla to calm down, I looked up and I see Deangelo walking past the door.

In no time the medics arrive, I stood watching and crying while they tried to get Corey to let them help. He pulled out his gun and I know he's serious. I'm not about to let him go to jail over some shit he had no way of preventing. I had him point his gun at me; he looks like he's ready to pull the trigger. Shit, maybe I should've thought about this more. I don't care though, "...Layla needs you to take Jazell back home!"

That's the Corey I know, I gave him his baby and held onto him while he let it out. The medics wanted him to ride down because he's shot in the arm so we all headed to the hospital. I was so glad Deangelo took his gun because he's not about to let them take Layla. I told him she needed to be changed so he let me take her.

It was heart breaking to watch the way Jazell family treated Corey; they blamed him for what happened. I'm not about to let them treat him like that. The next day I went over and I tried to reason with them but they so fucking old fashioned. Something's telling me they despised the fact that Jazell was even with Corey so it pissed me off even more. They tried to pull that broken ass Italian shit on me.

I've been over long enough to know how to put that shit together. It's like Ebonics. Some shit you have to hear a couple times to figure out what the hell is being said. I looked her parents both in the eyes and told them off. If he's not completely welcomed to the funeral, I'll make sure that everything they have and any blood relatives have will be taken from them.

251

Her father got up like he ready to attack but Max stood forward and he thought twice about it. "Max pass me that bag please." He did, I pull out the papers and passed them both some. It's a list of all their living relatives and all that they own.

"Don't think I'm bluffing! Now if you take a look at these copies here you will see that there is a clause in your land. I know you don't have the money and everyone else will be easy." I sit back in my seat and watch as her mother cries. I don't give a shit though, these mother fuckers are not about to do my brother any kind of way. They're too old to still be racist!

After her wide, flat booty ass finished crying she ran out the house. "Now I'll send over a check to cover all the expenses and that will be that. All you have to do is make the call to Corey and beg him to come to the damn funeral! You better hope they come because if not I'm coming for your ass!" He red hot, I bet he thinking, 'Who is this nigger bitch to come in my house and talk to me like this?' fuck them though!

It's okay, this 'nigger bitch' mean what the hell I say and wish he make me go there. We left and headed back home.

"Dang Mrs. Joseph, I thought you were about to slap his ass back there."

"You silly Max, you know if I did Deangelo would have yo' ass."

"Yeah I know, I sure thought I was going to have to kill all they're asses if he came any closer. Mr. Joseph would've fired my ass real quick after that."

Her family made good on what was said so I sent over a check to them. I already knew they wouldn't accept it so when it was returned I opened an account for Layla. I wasn't surprised that they sent back Corey check either. She had six million dollars total that I made sure would take care of her for the rest of her life. By the time she's old enough that money will be in the double digits. So in the end fuck them, they don't have to want any contact with her. I watch over her like she my own while Corey's getting his shit together.

Time was passing by and I know Corey don't want to miss the changes with her. Ms. Jackson watched her and I went over to talk with him. "Hey baby, the kids at home but I wanted to talk to Corey for a minute." He kissed me and told me to hurry home and headed out the door. Corey was sitting out back so I pulled a chair up in front of him.

"Corey, I know what you're going through and I know it takes time but Layla really needs her father right now."

I watched tears roll down his face. "You remember what you told me about having another angel watching over us?" He sat back and wiped his face. "Well you have something better; you have an angel here with us watching you. Jazell is with Layla and if you want to be with her you need to take care of Layla now, that's what Jazell would want you to do."

We sat there in silence, I'm not sure if I'm getting through to him or not. He don't have any look on his face to make me think he's listening to what I'm saying. "Let's take a jump Corey!" He looked at me with a baffled look on his face. "Corey if you're going to shut down then I know someone who is dying to join you! So if you keep this up at least throw a bone out and make a move. I'm sure she would love to keep you company right now."

He stood up and held out his hand, I stood up and took it. "Come on Corey let's take that jump. Then after that I know she'll feel relieved and so will you." We headed to the car. "Thanks Treasure, I know what I have to do. Hold up for a minute though. That was cool and all but keep her the fuck away from here!" I hugged him and we headed back to the house.

After we made it to the house he went straight for Layla and I went to find my husband. I asked him if he wanted to go out. "If you want to I guess." "I was just asking to be nice but we're going out Mr. Man!" He smiled and we talked for a minute, Corey walked past and said he was out, Deangelo followed him outside.

We sat out on the beach and talked about all the shit that we have gone through. It seems like some shit that you only read about. To some this would be a hard life to live, but with us it was Just Another Day in the Lou when it all came down to it.

"Deangelo, you never did really answer my question about having another baby." He started to laugh.

"T I did answer your question." He's not about to get off that easy, I turned over and pulled myself out of his arms.

"So that's the lie you gone stick with?" I unzipped his pants and pulled out his natural version of Big Bertha.

"What you gone make me say yes?" I latched on him, his head fell back.

"T what the hell is that?" I massaged the pop rocks all around him without letting him pull out. He fell back off his elbows and grabbed the sand. I let the pop rocks do the job and he was feeding me his load soon after.

52 DEANGELO

Reunion fifteen months ago.

** Superstar made a move**

** Two little Soldiers throwing them hands with his ass**

"Hell naw!"

"What's up Bateador, that nigga got out or what?" He looked over at me and nodded his head.

"You was right man, that nigga was waiting on us to leave. Just got word Deangelo and August are kicking his ass for you." I started to laugh at the thought of my babies holding it down.

"So what you wanna do 'cause now we know he not just checking for you or me. Hell, he been riding around long enough to come holla at us." Stacy always wanted what I had, this shit ain't nothing new. If it wasn't for me his ass wouldn't have ever made it to the league.

"Just stay on his ass, we out of here in a minute anyway. I know I ain't got shit to worry about with T." We loaded the last of the ice and headed back to the reunion.

"Ghost holla at you yet?" I look over at Bateador and can tell by his expression that he's disappointed.

"Nope, not a word yet. I don't know what's going on or why the shit's being kept a secret. I'm happy about the shit, I just hate that it's that punk ass nigga for real."

"T tried to get Marco to come out but the nigga busy as shit so he couldn't make it. What you think about that?" Bateador laughed and shook his head.

"I think Ghost would eat that nigga alive and dip out first time anything goes sour. Even if that was a possibility before, I don't see it happening now. I mean the shit changed and I don't know what Ghost gone do."

"What about Cargo?" Bateador laughed pulling back up at the reunion.

"He still lookin' for Jackie. I think he not really tryin' to find her because she only fifteen. Then again, I don't know if he even knows that much about her.

"What's wrong with that? He only seventeen last I checked. He need to find her so he can get his ass out these streets."

"Nigga you say that like Shay won't be fifteen in a blink of an eye. What the hell you gon' do when a nigga like Cargo come lookin'?"

"If I'm alive that nigga betta save his life and stay the fuck away from mine. If I was Jackie pops, I would dead his ass for taking so fuckin' long to find her." We both laughed and got out.

"What's good Drag?"

"Shit, what's not Pandillero? What's up Bateador, I know ya'll got my messages."

"Yeah, I told Pandillero what you said." We all laughed.

"Check though, he ain't been up to shit like I told you. Mainly working legit. Most of the time he only around his people when they stop by one of his spots. That's not even often, he keep two guardians with his ass at all times though. Did some checks, both of them are former liquidators from N'Djamena, Chad. Weird thing is, they don't look it but they seem to be born and raised there."

"Yeah we know all that already." Bateador said.

"It don't matter one bit to me man. How long that nigga hang around?"

"Not long Pandillero, he hollad at Treasure about something then he was back in his whip. I say five minutes total he was out of here with no problems. Like I said, he didn't take long to get at her after ya'll pulled off," Drag said.

"Shit, I say let me go!" Bateador said.

"Hell, why you? Let me get this one. Shit, that nigga got a stay for my uncle Beanie and my cousin Short," Drag said to Bateador, they continued to go back and forth on all the reasons they should be the one.

"Look, if you nigga's finished telling me ya'll synopsis of Stacy resume and shit let me fill you niggas in. Believe it or not Stacy may have done all the shit ya'll just said, but if he didn't, none of today would be possible. We know what the hell he about and we know he has something up his sleeve. Let's keep it cool so we can find out what the fuck he really wants. Just so I'm clear, nobody, I mean no one gets the go! Stacy like my brother, if anybody will deal with him it'll be me and only me." They both looked around like they didn't want to hear what the hell I said.

"Alright, try and play me crazy! I'm out I need to find T." I walked away as they started to laugh and talk. As I make my way around towards the parking lot I see the youngin's Prime and Cargo heading my way. We all speak and dab each other off.

"Why is it that I've seen both ya'll peoples but not you two?"

"You know how it is Pandillero."

"I guess that hunt you been on not that easy huh? I told you Cargo I can put you in arms reach if you want."

"I'm good, if I need you I'll let you know."

"What about you Prime man, what's yo excuse for showing up to the reunion late?"

"I had that damn examine I couldn't get out of so I had to make that shit happen. But I'm here now so let me show my face before everybody think I ditched." Prime walks off as me and Cargo head over to check out what Princess is up to. When she sees us coming her way she takes off running in our direction jumping into Cargo arms.

"Cousin Tristan I've been thinking about that old warehouse in that bad neighborhood that we talked about you turning into a mini Six Flags. I think you should look into another building because of the security; getting people outside the neighborhood to visit will be hard. Those outsiders will be your bread and butter but if they don't feel safe, they won't come. Maybe get another location and provide transportation to the neighborhoods for a small fee."

"Princess you never cease to amaze me with how smart you are."

"I didn't think about that cousin Shay, maybe your pops here will let me come over in a few weeks and we can go over everything again. That will give us enough time to find some locations and I can look into the transportation, I'm pretty good in that department." We laugh as he puts Princess down.

"Daddy please can cousin Tristan come over? I have a few locations already in mind and I can look for some more just in case cousin Tristan can't afford them." She scratches her head then looks back at me, "If he can't, can you loan me some money? Maybe I can convince cousin Tristan to let me be his partner and make my own money. If he does then I can pay you back!" We both laugh at what Princess is talking about.

"No problem Princess but I'm sure Cargo can afford whatever he needs or wants. I think you need to spend some time on your proposition of becoming a partner instead of worrying about the money. If you need it though, I can make it happen for you without a doubt." Princess thanks me, hugs Cargo telling him not to forget and runs off as we both laugh.

"You better watch out, sound like a hostile takeover to me."

"Yeah, I'ma let a six year old do that, it was really her idea. Look at these niggas here." I look over to see who he talking about. All my peoples chillin' over by the bleachers Damon, Blane, Sam, Flight, James, Rider, Tony, Mackie, Keith, Darrius, T.R, Yoppa, Shane, Cameron and Cap."

53 STACY

Man seeing Treasure at the reunion just made me want to get at her more than ever before. I need to see what's really good with her though. Last time I saw her she was at the Troops Weekend event I was hosting and man it seem like yesterday.

"Aye Stacy, who is that fine ass chick over there?" Clive asked me but when I tried to see who he was talking about I didn't see her. It seem like every nigga on the team was coming back saying they had been turned down by some thick, brown skin, St. Louis chick. I had to show them niggas how it was done.

"Say word, a hometown chick? Ya'll niggas think I can't pull a chick from my hometown? Show me where she at!" Tommy pointed her out and she turned around like she knew we were looking at her.

"Man her? Watch out man." She watched me walk over; she sat her drink down and met me on the dance floor. She didn't say shit; she just started to dance with a nigga. I hear all these niggas behind me hating and shit so I hug her and pick her up.

"Damn Treasure it's good to see you."

"Stop fronting Stacy, yo' ass know you ain't checking for me." I put her back down and let her groove out with me on the floor.

"What yo' ass doing all the way out here anyway, that nigga Pandillero know where you at?" She looked up at me then turned and tried to walk away. My team thought that shit was hilarious, they all walked off.

I grabbed her hand and pulled her ass up against me pressing my chest into her back. "You know you not going no damn where, save that for that nigga." She turned around and stretched to say something in my ear. I lifted her up a little to help her short ass out.

"You know you need to stay out my business if you don't want me to go anywhere." She bit the side of my ear and I had to get her ass alone.

My man was standing tall and without Pandillero blocking I'm about to get at her ass. I let her down and took her back to our section. "You still didn't answer my question Treasure, whatchu doing out here?"

"I see all men from home have memory loss."

"Yeah I know you were helping out at the blood drive but why you out here? They don't have blood drives back in the Lou?"

She started laughing; the girl came over with her pineapple juice. She was trying to get me to fuck with her again, earlier I told her we would hook up when she got off. I didn't look up at her though so she stormed away.

"Why you do her like that Stacy? You know she trying to get at you." I lifted her on my lap.

"I ain't studdin' that girl; I'm waiting on you to answer my question." I took her drink.

"I'm out here for AIT Stacy; can I have my drink back now?" I couldn't believe what she said so I put her drink on the table.

"You telling me that nigga Pandillero let you join this bullshit Army? What the hell is he thinking? I see a lot has changed since a nigga been away."

She tried to stand up but I held onto her so she couldn't move. "I'm not with Deangelo; he has nothing to do with me. You already know I've never been with him like that. So can you stop with all the Deangelo shit?"

"Yeah tell me anything if you think that's gon' work. I see you still have that smart ass mouth." She turned her head and put on the stank face.

"I see you still competing with him." We both had to laugh at that shit, we chilled out and talked. The clubs closed early so we headed to Virginia Beach and her friends came along with us. We sat out catching up and I wasn't about to let her fine ass get away from me again. "You wanna come chill with me tonight? I know you don't want to go back to those cheap ass motels yo' battle said ya'll stay at." She started laughing hard like I told her the funniest joke she had ever heard.

"Stacy you crazy if you think I'm fucking you." Yep, she still got that smart ass mouth that shit won't ever change. I pulled her up to her feet and pulled her in.

"I said chill, I don't want to fuck yo' hostadiddy ass no way."

262

"Yeah, tell me anything Stacy."

"Treasure stop playing with me and come stay the night with me. I know you don't have to be back 'til Tuesday so we can chill and hit the town." She smiled and started to walk away again so I stopped her.

"Stacy I'm not trying to fuck you. Find some other chick it's plenty of them out here right now." I picked her ass up, she started cracking up laughing. Then I realize I hit her spot, it's my hand squeezing her thigh and I had her in tears.

"I'm for real Treasure, no sex, just chill with me." I took her back to my room; she tried to sleep in her clothes because we didn't stop at her room. I called down and told her to gone jump in the shower if she wanted I would be back. I came back and I heard the shower going so I put the clothes on the table and left back out the room.

I opened the door and she was standing there in my jersey. She turned around and we were bugging up at the negligee they gave me. She was holding it by the string off her pinky.

"Really Stacy, this how you gone try and play me?" I took that thing and threw it in the trash.

"Naw Treasure, this look better anyway." I cleaned up and she was sitting on the chair watching TV. "So you want me to sleep on the couch or what because I'm not having sex with you." I found her spot and had her laughing and running around the room. I put her ass in the bed and got on top of her.

"I know but let me sleep here for a minute, then if I get too heavy just push my ass on the floor."

I woke up and she was on my chest knocked out. I didn't move a muscle; I laid there with a stupid ass smile on my face until she woke up on her own. We spent the next day eating, dancing; I took her to every spot we could find. She didn't let me buy her anything she said she didn't need shit and they couldn't take it back with them.

I played it off and whatever she was looking at I shipped it back to her mom's house. I was looking to get another tat to celebrate my trade and I wanted a nugget. I told him to put it in a treasure box, she said I was corny but it didn't matter, I was good.

Saturday we had mad fun together, after we left dinner we went back to the room. "Stacy why you do the shit you do?" I was about to get smart but the way she said it made me have to think about it.

"Just trying to take advantage of the situation I guess. Live each day like it's my last."

"So you surprised too huh?" What the hell?

"About what Treasure?" She walked over to me.

"Surprised that you still alive and out of the hood." I never thought about it, hell I really don't give a fuck either way.

"I guess I am surprised."

"Stacy if you really want to take advantage of whatever has saved yo' crazy ass from meeting your death, don't you think it's time to change? I mean you have to know better by now, why you not trying to do better?"

"I thought you didn't want to talk about Pandillero?" She laughed; I tucked her hair behind her ear so I could see her face.

"Yeah, the last time I talked to his ass he said to remember that if you know better you do better. I told that nigga he needed to tell his self that and drop out of college and join the league. He tried to lie and say he was makin' hella dough in the streets but that nigga was stuntin'. He was on that degree shit so he stayed in school and missed the chance." I wish my dumb ass would've followed his lead now. "Enough of that though, I hear what you saying, I can only do so much." She stared me in my eyes like she was reading my thoughts.

"Whatever you do Stacy, just know that you can't get time back so use it wisely." That nigga Pandillero groomed the hell out of her. She know all his sayings and hearing the shit from her actually make sense the first time. I leaned in and kissed her; once she kissed me back it was on.

I was happy and hating that she had to be back so soon. Monday night we headed to the club, shit was going smooth. I wanted to hurry up and get out but I had to host for two hours. We had fun and I couldn't wait for the last bit of time to go by so we could roll. I went in the back to take care of business. I came back out and the lights were on, the music was off and the club was damn near empty. I go outside and see all these cattle trucks pulling off.

I go in looking for Treasure she was gone; before I could get back out Ted pussy ass stopped me. "Look at this nigga sad and shit about that broke ass Army bitch getting drug up out of here." I walked over to him and asked him to say that shit again, he did so I beat the shit out of him. The security broke us up and within a couple hours we were sitting in coach office. He fined us then said the police were outside the door waiting to arrest us.

I couldn't believe it, after all the niggas I've killed, and all the dirt I did. They charged me with some white bitch death that happened after we left. It took me almost two years to get the charges dropped.

I was blackballed across the league and I knew then that Treasure was right. Hell, Pandillero was right. When you know better you do better. If I would've known better then to fight that nigga maybe I would be married to Treasure right now. Hell, who knows, but now since I got my chance to meet up with her without so many ears around, I can see if that nigga taking care of business like he should be.

54 TREASURE

"Treasure you silly. You know ever since Corey helped me we've been pulling in triple digits." Sammy thinks she really talking to a dummy now.

"Yeah I know, so next time try not to judge a book by its cover, he is my brother trick." After we finished up in her office we were heading out for lunch so I can get back.

"Excuse me Mrs. Joseph; I have a call for you." We looked at each other then around.

"You sure they said Mrs. Joseph Sarah?" Sammy asked her secretary then she started walking towards her, she picked up the phone. She asked who they wanted to speak with and she said it was for me. I asked her who the hell is it because I know damn well nobody I need to speak with would be calling her office. Shit, I keep three phones on me at all times so this can't be a call for me.

"It's some man; he asked for you by name girl, you want me to hang up?" Hell, I'll be the huckleberry, let me see who it is. I walked back towards her and she said she would transfer it in her office.

"Hello." The moment I heard the voice I sat back in the chair.

"Why you acting like that Treasure, I told you I was gone get at you." What the hell does he want? I been ducking his ass since I found out he was at the hotel looking for me.

"How may I help you Mr. Carr?"

"Really Treasure, that's how you doing me? It's all good, I need to see you for a minute so stop staring at the ceiling and come over to the back elevator." He hung up; I'm looking around thinking where the hell is he at. Then it dawned on me that Corey will be coming up in a minute if we don't get our asses downstairs. I walk back out and tell Sammy to go down and stall Corey. Seem like she too happy to do the shit, I don't know why and don't have time to question her, she took off and left. I damn near ran around to the elevator.

"What is it Stacy, I don't have all day to be playing with you!" He still fine as hell but something telling me that I'm about to get my ass in a lot of trouble behind this here meeting. He hugged me then once again I got the hell away, he still smells finger licking good though.

"I'll make this quick because I know yo' ass have more security than the Mayor." He stood there looking me over trying to work his magic on me but I looked away.

"Why you trying to act like you so fucking scared of me? Treasure you sho' wasn't scared of me whe—"

"Okay Stacy, you know damn well I'm not scared of you. Hurry up because I am scared of losing my family so what?" I'm tired of playing with him; he's taken more than enough of a chance by being here.

"I just wanted to hook up with Pandillero; you know I'm not on no drug shit. And I'm not trying to be connected in no way to it. All I'm looking for is some connections back in the Lou to ease some of the bullshit they throwing at me down at City Hall." Really, that's it? He came all the fucking way to New York for that. You fine, dumb ass, soft lips, big stick slinging, insides punishing Neanderthal.

"So why you don't talk to Deangelo instead of coming to me about this shit?" He licked his lips and moved closer to me.

"I told you I heard you was the one I needed to holla at so I am. Besides, I know you can hook me up. Hell, you ain't said shit this long to him so I know you looking out for me."

"Whatever. There was and never has been anything to say to him. But I can let Corey know what you looking for." Yeah, how you like that, trying to blackmail me about some old shit, that's not gone work.

"Cool, either way I'm good. Here, I got these for you. But I'm out, have a good day, I'll see you soon." What the fuck? He den lost his damn mind; he jumped on the elevator and was gone. He gave me a small box; I put it in my purse without looking in it. I turned around and started walking back. As soon as I pass the bathroom I see Corey getting off the elevator.

After we had lunch I was headed to the airport, I'm too ready to see my baby. I already know he gon' put it on me with all the shit he was rappin' about last night. "See you later Corey, be careful and hurry the hell home." He stopped me before I could go up the steps further.

"So you gone tell him or do I have to kill yo' ass?" FUCK! FUCK! FUCK! FUCK! FUCK! It never fails with them; I can't piss without them knowing the exact amount.

"What Corey? Tell him what?" He tugged on my hand like he wants me to come back down the steps so I do. He walks up in my face and leaned right in front of my ass.

"So I take that as a no. You ready to get this over with? No need in boarding if you not breathing." The look in his eyes say he not playing around with me and I don't give a fuck.

"You can save yo' promises Corey you don't scare me. Matter fact, I'll tell him when I get the fuck ready to tell him!" I said it so hard I rolled my eyes pushed my purse and bag down to the ground then leaned to the side. All I need to do is Z snap and pop my tongue; I would've been in full Sheneneh mode.

He picked up my stuff, stood up and started to laugh. "Yeah keep them eyes in check! Okay." He waved his hand towards the steps. I grabbed my stuff and ran up the steps with his ass still laughing and getting back in the car with Sammy. I'm happy as hell once we took off. I closed my eyes; I really need to think about this. Stacy put me in a fucked up position, I don't know if he doing the shit on purpose or if he's suicidal.

"So you ready to tell me now or should I have Bateador?" I don't even bother opening my eyes; I let the seat back on his ass.

"Leave me alone, there's nothing to tell. You didn't say shit when Corey was down there talking all that noise so I don't have shit to say now." He didn't say anything else the entire ride, I walked in the house and went right to the kitchen. We all sat down and ate dinner and all he did was watch me like he annoyed. He talked to the kids but he wouldn't even look at them, he kept his eyes on me.

I got out the shower and climbed in the bed I was out. I woke up the next morning and he was nowhere to be found. The boys were already gone so I sent Shay off to ballet and chilled blasting the radio all over the house. After I cleaned the house I got in the shower and heard my jam come on, "I Wanna Know," by Joe.

I opened the door and dropped the towel I was scared as hell. Not really, but I had to loosen him up and it's nothing like some wet cat to do just that. Deangelo was standing here like he was waiting on my ass to walkout. I don't care if he mad or not, I put my arms around him and started to dance. He smiled at me and moved with me all over the room like nothing was going on but what we were doing. The song went off and he hit the radio off.

"T I thought we were past all the bullshit? You ready to talk to me or what?" I put on my dress and slid on the top of the dresser.

"Do you trust me?" He stood up and pulled the chair over in front of me.

"Of course I trust you, why you think you still breathing?" I giggled and shook my head.

"Why don't you act like you trust me Deangelo? Every second I turn around you have people looking over my shoulder. Any man that comes within two feet of me you act like I can't control myself. You know that's not fair right? You run all over the place and I don't get a full report of every person you talk to." He stood up.

"You right, but I'm not letting anything happen to you. T you just gone have

271

to deal with it. You know how I feel about you being around him. Ain't a damn thing changed about that so why the hell you think it's alright I don't know, but you need to tell me."

I moved forward and put my legs around his waist. "Can we go out tonight, I feel like dancing." We both started laughing at my failed attempt to distract him. Maybe I should've started out with that while I was still butt ass naked and wet.

"Come on T."

"I know how you feel but you have to remember that we in this together and I love you. Stacy asked for some help over there with some business that he has going on. I did the checks and it's all legit. But they running that drain the bank shit on him to slow his silly ass down. I was going to tell you when I came back then Corey tried to check me like he really was gone do something to me and I had to make you sweat."

He looked at me like there was something else I was supposed to tell him. Then he took my friend out and pulled me on it. I was up against the wall while he was holding me in his arms slaying my ass, we went at it. "So that's it T, nothing else." I can't respond or think he's banging my ass so good. We both were tired when we finished.

He sat up and looked down at me so I put my head in his lap and poked my lips up at him. He kissed me and detained my eyes.

"I take it you're asking me about Ft. Lee right?" He raised his eyebrows.

"Stop T, you don't want me to go there with you." I laughed at him.

"So there are something's that you don't know then huh?" He got up off the bed, stick slinging around heading to the other side and grabbed his phone. He came over to me so I sat up and looked at him.

"Tell me now or I make the call T I'm telling you, you don't want me to go there." I laughed harder and fell back on the bed; he wasn't amused one bit. He put the phone up to his ear and I jumped up and tried to grab it from him.

"Deangelo stop!" He hung up the phone and pulled me over to the couch.

"Why you so jealous? You are so fucking cute when you get jealous." I sat back on him he just looked at me.

"Well you remember after you dumped me and I left. Well I was stationed in Ft. Lee after basic." He shaking his head, there's no way I'm missing the opportunity of throwing all that shit in his face first.

"I had a detail and I saw Stacy. He was in town for some bullshit; it's been so long ago I can't remember. Anyway it was a holiday weekend and we had off post passes. Like I said, I had already bumped into Stacy so I ended up seeing him again at the club. One thing led to another and we spent four days together. That's it."

He started cracking up laughing at what I said. "Damn T, yo' ass get a sample and you was on fire after that." I can't believe he just called me a ho.

"So that's what you have to say. You Mr. Man, if I'm not mistaken my record is still at six, now let's hear yours." He stopped laughing and then laughed some more.

"Shit T, you got me there, I den had six in one session." I pushed his ass, I wanted to hit him but I said I would never do that shit again.

"It's cool T, he always had a thing for you but I didn't know you let the nigga hit. That explain why that nigga been looking so hard. I thought after Peaches told him how to reach me he would holla at me. But now I see why he tried to pull that secret agent shit to meet up with you." I laughed at him.

"So did you know about Essence?" I looked at him and giggled.

"How else would I know about Storm?" He smiled.

"So you were jealous and knocked her out for some old shit?" I got up and walked away. He crazy as hell if he thinks I'm jealous of her. He grabbed my arm.

"So is it?"

"No Deangelo, I'm not jealous and she wanted to fight so we did. I knocked her ass out for looking at you if you want to know the truth." He pulled me closer.

"So if you knew about her why did you want to deal with her?" I sat back down.

"Look, when I was with Stacy he told me about her. He said she was really smart and was dealt a bad hand so he wanted to help her. Then when I saw that her business was in jeopardy I really did want to help her. I would want someone to help me. So I did." He sat back watching me like he was waiting on me to say more.

"That's it Deangelo, I promise."

55 STACY

Once my dude told me the email address was linked to a cosmetic company out in New York I was out. They were having some kind of merger party. When I saw Bateador I knew I was in the right place. The next day I sat around waiting to see what the deal was; when I saw my chance I took it. The lady downstairs said the owners were in a meeting and told me where to go. I walked past the office and saw her through the window so I called her and told her to meet up with me. She did and I was good after that.

I was about to head out a couple hours later. When I made it to the airport TSA held me up and gave me a note with DAJ on the front. I don't know how the hell I was that dumb to think Pandillero wouldn't find out. I went over, jumped on the jet and waited 'til it landed. I get off and some nigga name Max told me to get in. I stayed at the hotel that night and the next day chilled out around the hotel. Max came back later that night, he took me to a restaurant and I started to think he changed his mind.

I was about to bounce then I see Bateador come in, not long after Pandillero and Treasure came in. I already know he's gone pull that same old hide the treasure shit on me. It really don't faze me but he know damn well he better hold on.

Even after she went off on me she smiled afterwards then looked away. By the end of the conversation I needed to figure out my next move and quick. Treasure sure doesn't seem too happy the way she was just sitting there. I bounced out and went back to my room for the night. I flew out on the early bird back home.

Shit was running smooth after that. I was shocked that Pandillero didn't let me know what he wanted in return. I figured it was Treasure. That gave me better chances, I know that nigga don't want her fucking with me. So if she doing it on her own I have more of a shot than I thought. I still wanted to get at them again but all lines had been dropped. I was doing my thing but not on the level that I needed. I'm getting money in and I need help working that shit just right. I know between the two of them they can solve the nation's debt problems when it come to managing money.

They the only real hood niggas I know that have hella fucking degrees. Last I heard Pandillero had three Masters and a Doctorate, Bateador had more shit then Pandillero. They always have been smart though. I think I was the only one in the hood that knew they graduated at fifteen.

Everybody else thought they dropped out of school. Those niggas were in college, slanging dope, making money, and dropping bodies all at once. Hell, I guess that shit was passed in their genes, I still don't know if they know they're brothers. I didn't bother to tell 'em, I know how the hood can flip a story so fuck it.

56 TREASURE

He not mad at all, he grabbed my chin and pecked me on the lips. "Don't get it twisted though, if you step out both ya'll asses grass and that's my word." Here we go with more fucking promises.

"I already see you thinking another promise in yo' head. T I'm not playing with you for real. I should kick yo' ass for not telling me he was at the reunion." I looked up and smiled.

"I forgot about that, he was at the reunion." Deangelo dropped his smile.

"Maybe you forgot what happened the night of the reunion. Stacy was the last thing on my mind."

"Yeah, tell me anything T. Like I said it's cool, he'll be here in a minute so hurry up and change so we can squash this." What the fuck he just say?

"Hold up Deangelo, he'll be where? Here here?" He looked up at me then he stood up and carried me in the shower with him. He had me facing the showerhead and he turned on the water. All I could do was hold on to his ass tighter to make sure he feels his share of the cold ass water he sent down my back.

We changed and drove hellas to a restaurant, the second I walked in I saw Stacy ass talking to Corey. "What's up Pandillero, Treasure. I was just telling Bateador ya'll some hard niggas to track down." Deangelo laughed and pulled out my chair, they all sat down.

"Damn Stacy, we hard to find but yo' sneaky ass sho' tracked down my wife." I damn near choked on my lemonade when I heard what Deangelo said. They all started laughing, Deangelo rubbed his hand up and down my back like he trying to get me to burp like a damn baby.

"My bad man, it cost me twelve grand from Peaches ass. Ya'll wasn't responding, I was out that way anyway and had to make this shit happen." I can't believe that bitch; I can't wait to see her sheisty ass.

"Don't use me Stacy to get what you want from my husband, ya'll can sit here and laugh all ya'll want. I don't think the shit funny." They all looked at each other like they don't know what the hell I'm talking about.

"Don't look around and get quite now, it's not funny. Like I told you already, if you want to talk to him then leave me out of it. Here, you can have these back, trust me, I don't need them." I put the box on the table; Deangelo pulled it up and opened it then sat it back down. Corey reached over and grabbed it then looked at Stacy like he wanted to kill him.

"Stacy what the fuck? Don't give her this shit!" Corey said as he put the box in his breast pocket.

"It was a gift that's all. I know she liked the contacts back in the day so I figured I would give her a pair," Stacy said as I looked at him and smiled then looked away.

"T don't wear contacts, besides, if she wanted some I'm sure she can afford them," Deangelo said as he looked over at me, I didn't look up at him. My attention was drawn to Corey because he nudge me under the table. I looked over at him and knew exactly what he wanted. I rolled my eyes big and wide at him and shifted my head, he looked away.

Deangelo pulled me into his shoulder. "Look Treasure, like I said, Peaches said I needed to holla at you to get at Pandillero." I let them talk while I sat there day dreaming about kicking Peaches ass. I know one thing; I was gone hook up her kid's room and just have the shit delivered to her. She got the money to do it now don't she. Yeah right, that bitch probably spent that shit on weed, clubs, and drinks. I can't stand they asses; crabs in a fucking bucket. It's all good though, I'm gone do it anyway and make sure I tell them to circle the amount on the receipt for her dry feet having ass.

I would put my name on the shit but I'll never do that. Deangelo saw me about to do that shit one day and gave me the hardest time about it. He made it like I was throwing it in their face so I never put my name on shit. He always says, when you do things right people won't know for sure if you did anything at all. Once I thought about it I felt better about doing shit for people without them knowing.

Stacy left and we all headed to the club, I was wondering why Corey needed to go home first. But when he came back he was trying to hide somebody behind his back. I don't even have to see who it is, I can tell by the walk as they came over to the table.

"Sammy what the hell you doing here?" Deangelo looked up like I'm wrong about who it is. Then Corey lifted his arm and she slid her ass from behind him. "Don't do me Treasure, what you think?" She put her arms around Corey and he leaned down to kiss her, me and Deangelo both shook our heads and looked away.

I had no clue and Sammy's about to tell me, as soon as we finished dancing with our men they went back to the table and I pulled Sammy around the corner.

"What the fuck Sammy, why you didn't tell me?" She started laughing and licked her tongue out dancing around.

"I thought you knew girl." Yeah right, how the hell would I if she didn't tell me? Deangelo knew but he won't tell me shit about Corey, he always tells me to ask him.

"Stop playing, you know I didn't know. Yo' ass always acting like you so fucking scared of his ass."

"I'm still scared, of that dick!" We were on the wall laughing at what she said.

"After we started working together he wasn't so scary at all. Then when his fiancé died I reached out to him. At first he wasn't having it, we started working closer together. When I came to visit you I saw him and Layla coming into the airport. He was taking her to see his people in the Lou and I was going to see my parents. We flew out together and it was pretty much a wrap after that.

We talked hellas and every day he was growing on me. He asked me to come out after we closed that big deal and I stayed at his house for about a week. I was dying when I had to get back, Layla's so beautiful and he's a big teddy bear. I didn't want to go so they came with me, we pretty much been with each other ever since." I see Corey come behind her and hug her.

"Now you told her nosey ass everything you ready to get out of here?" Sammy was too excited, they started walking away. He turned around and looked back at me.

"What the hell you waiting on Treasure, come on Pandillero not back there." I shook my head and walked ahead of them.

"Stop all that pouting with yo' punk ass." Sammy was laughing as we made it back to the table.

"You find out everything you needed T?"

"I'm good; I just wanted him to stop moping and her to stop sittin' around waitin' for a nigga to fall into her dehydrated lap." Sammy stopped laughing.

"Don't worry about her lap Treasure," Corey said as we laughed at him and Sammy.

"My laps far from dry boo. Everyone's not a freak like you though Bambi!" They both laughed and we headed out the club.

57 DEANGELO

"Alright man she don't know I'm here so give me a minute to get on before ya'll head this way. Don't forget to get that invite in his hand, make sure he know it's a onetime offer. Stay low man, I'll see you when you get back." I knew this nigga was on some slick shit when I found out he was going out to New York. He think he too high profile to go away quite but hell, it ain't shit for real.

We used to be like the three musketeers back in the day. Then that nigga let the power go to his head and we had to walk away. This nigga was shooting mufuckas in broad daylight over a twenty dollar crap game. Smacking ho's that didn't want to trick for his ass, all kinds of shit. Seemed like he was competing with me so hard that he had to go overboard to try and out do me. I wasn't falling for it so he went harder.

After he was signed I was happy for him and even more happy for me. I didn't have to deal with cleaning up his bullshit and looking out for his ass anymore. Even though I can't stand this nigga, I've known him for hellas. He like the step brother that you just hate to be around but don't want to see get his ass kicked. I made sure he stayed the fuck away from T though, every chance that nigga had he was trying to smile up in her face. He had a mad crush on her but I kept her so far gone that I don't even know if she ever picked up on it or not.

I wasn't about to let him get his claws in her and try to get her to trick for his ass. She strong and all but I seen this nigga pull some lawyers under his wing. The nigga was slick, not as slick as me though. Stacy a reckless bastard that didn't even need it, he just did the shit, and Stacy was just doing shit to be doing it.

He thought he was pulling a fast one with that ACL story in the press. I know the nigga was getting hit with hella fines for partying and keeping up bullshit wherever he went. They got tired of that shit after the club fight and that white bitch was killed. He lucky he didn't do time for that shit.

Now he reaching out to us knowing damn well he looking for T. It has to be more to his shit. T still ain't told me she saw him at the reunion, that's been a minute now, almost two years. Even with all the shit that has happened she still ain't said shit. I know she been in contact with people down there about his ass.

I hear the doors close and wait in the galley until we take off. "So you ready to tell me now or should I have Bateador?" Look at my T, she gone straight make me wait. I guess since that shit went down she ain't scared no more. By the way she went off on Bateador; I know she can't be scared.

I let her chill and was trying to see where her mind was at because it's something up with Stacy. I got up early hit the gym with the boys and Bateador. Afterwards they went with Bateador and I went to talk to T. I gave her enough time to get her shit together and the way she bouncing around here she know she wants to tell me.

I stood right in front of the door when I heard the water stop. Look at T; know damn well she didn't have to drop that towel. She not even gone bother picking it up and I damn sure don't care. We danced around and my stick getting heavy squeezing her wet ass.

T looked surprised when I told her he was coming; I don't know why the hell she would think that he coming to the house. That shit will never happen. I know Stacy, and the Stacy I know can only be trusted from a distance so that's how I'm keeping his ass. We walked in and he tried to play it off like he been looking for us, I let him get that shit out. Let me see what this nigga say when I run his bullshit back on his ass.

"Damn Stacy, we hard to find but yo' sneaky ass sho' tracked down my wife." Yeah nigga take it in, you ain't got shit coming this way here! T silly, she thought I was gone let this nigga slid with that shit he pulled. T sexy as hell when she mad, I know she not going anywhere, this nigga just gone have to get over it.

He know damn well he shouldn't be listening that hard to Peaches any fucking way. He damn sho' didn't have to pay her ass. He could've got her a tall boy and a tripe sandwich for that shit. Without the fixing on that bitch; with her simple ass.

I knew T had a box in her purse so when she pulled it out to give it to him I wanted to know what the fuck it was. I saw the contacts and wanted to laugh at his ass. I know damn well T don't wear contacts so for him to give her a pair was weird. Whatever though, I didn't understand why the hell Bateador was so fucking upset about the shit. It's not like the nigga gave her an engagement ring or something.

Hell, I was hoping that's what it was so I could go Mortal Kombat on his ass and finish him like the game. He can smile one more time in her direction if he want to. I plan on Sub Zeroing his ass, grab him up by the neck and pull off his head with his spine still attached. I have to chuckle at the thought of getting at Stacy, this nigga is really trying his luck with me tonight. I sat back and chilled out on the shit.

"Well now you can holla at me and we don't have to worry about it," Bateador said then he looked over at me.

"We know what you looking for Stacy and you know where we stand. On another note, let's clear the air here so I can get it on the table and out the way. This is my wife so if you want to holla at her you need to get at me. I know you want her and that just ain't gone happen, not alive anyway."

"Hold up there Pandillero, let's not go there, I didn't come all this way for no beefin' shit."

"Man we don't have time for beef. What you think we out on the block some fucking where," Bateador said. He getting annoyed and I'm right there with him.

"Like I said Stacy, I know you have feelings for my wife, hell, you probably still in love with her. But you can't have her, that's the final answer. If you don't like that, you can try, and I will kill you! If you can let that shit go we can be cordial. Maybe I can help you and when I need you to, you can help me."

"Come on Pandillero, I'm not into no bullshit, I'm looking for legal shit, I don't need the stress in my life."

"Look at this nigga, they talk about us, this nigga all the way Hollywood on our ass," Bateador said as we all laughed, T didn't find shit funny.

"We not in bullshit, whatever you need, if I can help, I'll let you know. Before I help you I'll tell you what the hell I need. You can take the help or not, it's up to you. Like I said, my wife is not up for discussion and you need to let that shit go. That is if you value breathing."

"It's all good Pandillero, I'll holla at ya'll, I got a flight I need to catch. I'll be in touch." He dabbed us off and hugged T then he was out the door."

58 TREASURE

"Deangelo I want to talk to you for a second." He look like I just smacked his ass.

"What's up baby?"

"I don't want to argue or get you upset but I have to get something out that I've been thinking about." He came from around his desk and leaned against the front of it across from me.

"Go 'head T." Damn he fine, I should say fuck it and swallow his ass back real quick.

"Get yo' mind out the gutter T, let's hear it." I couldn't help but laugh at what he said.

"My mind not in the gutter, shut up." He smells so fucking good though and

I'm digging the hell out the beard he feeling out. I can't help but laugh when I feel that shit come across my thighs.

"Yeah, tell me anything. Me T, not my dick, lookup." I looked up at him and snapped out of it, I'm trying my best not to laugh.

"For real the other night with Stacy, that was messed up Deangelo. I told you I could handle it." He dropped his head and sat on the arm of the couch.

"I didn't say you couldn't handle it. I just needed to make sure he understood what I was telling him."

"This is all I'm going to say and I'm dropping it. I can be around men no matter who they are or how fin——Let me start over. I'm not looking to be with anyone but you Deangelo. You don't have to treat me like I'll fall for any pretty nigga with a big dick. All I'm saying is, I can work with Stacy or whoever without you treating me like I can't." He didn't say anything; he just sat there and smirked. He got up, walked to the door, told Mrs. Bridgewater, his secretary, to hold all his calls and close up. He came back over and sat on the arm of the couch again.

I leaned over and put my head on his knee. "I-know-T-I-just-don't-like-that-nigga!" I fell out laughing at the way he said it, he had to laugh with me. I got on my knees in the couch and moved in between his legs and put my arms around his neck.

"I told you that was cute."

"What T?" I kissed all over his face, he started shaking his head.

"You cute when you're jealous baby." He bit down on my lip then pulled it in his mouth. We kissed and I was on my back G fiving in no time. After he finished dessert he stood up but he didn't want me to move. He held his self up on the wall and was long stroking my ass. His whole body moving and I can feel every inch of him in me. I tried to control it and pull it together, I'm too spread open for that. He know it too, he's taking advantage of every second of it.

He started to go faster and I'm screaming at the top of my lungs, then I couldn't get a peep out. He took all my air away; he sped up and kept at it. "That nigga ain't ever getting my pussy! I know he didn't hit it like this. What was that shit you was talking about a pretty nigga and a big dick? This the only pretty nigga with a big dick you can have. You hear me T?"

"Yes Daddy! Yes!"

"I know yo' ass can, you finna keep feeling me too." I'm juicy as hell, my coochie making more noise than I can.

"I can't hear you T, what you say."

"I hear you Deangelo!" I see he just gone fuck me 'til I can't think straight. He slowed down and wrapped my legs around his waist. He know he's in trouble now, he thought I was done but hell, I hadn't even started.

I had his man good, the look in his eyes were already screaming like a bitch. "Help me up, I wanna ride." He picked me up and sat on the couch. "T, T." I was getting tighter every time he tried to say something, he stopped talking.

He tried to close his eyes but I kissed him and made sure he watched what I was doing. With him still in me I turned facing the arm of the couch so I could hold on. "You like that Daddy?" He smacked my ass so I latched down real firm and started to pulsate then bounced up and down really slow. His head's bobbing up and down; his tongue can't stay in his mouth.

He popped my ass again and I came all over his stick. I gave it more of a bite and started to vibrate. That did it because he hollan, he grabbed my hair but I didn't let that stop me. I dug my nails in his thighs and he let go. I stopped vibrating and gave it all I had with only pressure, he's beat.

He nutted and started screaming my name. He put his arm around my waist holding me so tight I can't move. His shipment's shooting in me hard, fast, and hot. He started to kiss my arm and he won't let me go. Whenever I do move he'll jump and pull me closer, he still nuttin.

We sat there a good five minutes trying to catch our breath; he was still in me the whole time. I looked up at him and his heads back. "I'm not sleep T but I sho' need to be." I laughed and tried to get up; after he did his final jerks he let me go. We cleaned up and were heading out the door. Corey walked up before we made it to the car and said what's up.

"Really, no hug, nothing?" He stepped back, Deangelo started to laugh.

"Hell naw, the way this nigga screaming yo' name I don't want to come near ya'll 'til some water hit ya'll asses. I had to clear out the whole floor fucking with ya'll loud asses." We laughed and Deangelo opened the door for me and we went home.

59 DEANGELO

We headed to the club; I was waiting on Bateador to show up because I know T about to be too shocked to see who he walks in with. I see T happy now that she don't have to worry about Bateador ass anymore. Ever since Jazell died T been asking me how he's doing and if he found somebody. I kept telling her ass to ask him, I know he would've told her he was chillin with Sammy.

I'm surprised Sammy hadn't told her but I guess she was too busy getting it put on her ass. They walked off and we chilled out at the table.

"You know this shit with Stacy not gone turn out right? You should've let me host his retirement a long time ago." I looked over at Bateador.

"He must've forgot that he said he had a flight out because I got a call said he back at the hotel not far from where we met his ass."

"Man I'm not worried about Stacy and I already gave him a fair warning. So if he not gone by checkout then I'll go see his ass myself."

The next morning Bateador called said the nigga was gone so I headed to the office to get some work done. Half the time I come in here and don't know why the hell I have the damn building, I mean an office in the building. We run most of our operation out of here. I barely come in and when I do, seem like I can't focus without hearing the kids running around. I really hate not being able to clear my head and have sex with T when I need to.

Speaking of T, I see her ass coming in the building now. I watch her on all the cameras as she comes up; I'm one lucky man. Every mufucka she walks past turn and look again, even the women look twice at her ass. "What's up wifey, what bring you down here?" She came over and gave me a kiss then sat on the couch. I finished up with what I was doing right as she said she wanted to talk.

After T stopped talking to my man I sat back and listened to what she had to say. I know she can handle his ass but he needed to know that his life's on the line. "...me like I'll fall for any pretty nigga with a big dick."

Really, so she trying to say he's on her mind. I see I have to show her ass a pretty nigga with a big dick. From what I been told that nigga ain't pulling shit close to mine. "Mrs. Bridgewater, I need you to close up now and head out, you know what to do with the calls." I don't know why she don't think I trust her, hell, it's them nigga's I don't trust. If it was me I know what I would do and I know Stacy, he up to some shit that's gone get him fucked up.

T think I'm playing with her ass; she can slip up if she want too. It's gone be hell to tell the captain around this bitch, she gone wish she was dead. I'm about to show her ass what's cute. I'm waxing that ass, made me think back when I was coaching her on breathing. That shit made me want to put it on her some more for all the shit she was talking. I had T calling my name, she knows who cat this is.

She betta let them niggas know and stop playing with me. Oh shit! I thought she was done but I see she been fucking with me. I thought T was gone make me shoot her ass through the ceiling I nutted so hard. I had to hold on so her ass wouldn't fly off. I could tell by the look on Bateador face that he heard us. But fuck that nigga, he betta step his game up with Sammy.

A couple months had past and I kept an eye on Stacy, from what I hear he has some shit going on back home. I was cool with letting T make some calls for him. She knows I don't want her dealing directly with his ass. I'm good and the nigga hasn't crossed that line just yet so he still breathing.

Seem like T been acting kind of strange lately. I took her out to the beach to talk with her. We walked around and I held onto her while she looked out at the water.

"T when you going to check with the doctor?" She laughed but didn't say anything.

"T you know the earlier we find out the better." She sat down in the sand, pulled her knees up and put her arms around them. This the crazy shit I'm talking about right here. One minute she cool the next she balled up like she need to be in a mental ward.

I moved in front of her and pulled her legs around my waist. Seems like whenever T's in deep pain or something she would do this. I hate that I wasn't around to comfort her all the times that she probably has. Once I had her in my arms she looked up at me and said she was scared.

"Okay T, we still need to know so let's go." I stood up with her and carried her up the path to the house. The kids came running pass and we headed to the room. "Here T, let's go!" I gave her a pregnancy test, she looked at it.

"Really Deangelo, you know these things are not certain." I shook my head and walked her into the bathroom and sat on the sink.

"I got you T!"

"Damn Deangelo what you get one of each kind ever made?"

"Nope, I picked up two of each." We laughed, she tried to send me out the bathroom so she can take it but I'm not leaving. Hell, I would've held the damn thing for her, I wanna know more than she do.

After four she said she was done and that was enough so we took a bath and waited. As soon as the timer went off I jumped my ass out the tub and started reading 'em. I looked over at T she was gone, then I hear bubbles, I walked back over to the tub. She had her eyes closed under the water.

I tapped her on her knee and she came up. "So you gone tell me what they say or just sit there?" I helped her out the tub and we put our clothes on and got in the car.

"Deangelo would you tell me?"

"I thought you were scared?" She started to pout.

"I don't know T that's why we going to the doctor."

"How you don't know Deangelo, didn't you read the dumb things?" I stopped the car in the middle of the road and pulled all of them out and sat them on the middle consol. She looked at them then started to laugh. "That's a damn shame how they rip people off." We both laughed.

After we told her doctor that two of them said yes and the other two no, she was more than willing to do the test. I was too happy when we left out of there, T wasn't so happy. The doctor put her on bed rest until further notice.

"T it's not that bad baby."

"Deangelo the boys are three I can't do shit with them but lay there. Shay about to be eight, she already have so much shit going on she barely around. I know you about to be hiding from me every chance you get." We pulled up at the house and I called over Bateador and Sammy they brought over Layla and we all had dinner together.

Once we were finished eating I called everyone into the living room all the staff, kids, everyone. "Alright, listen up!" I stood next to T. "We found out today that we're pregnant and I want everyone to know that T is back on bed rest. So no one for whatever reason will say or do anything to stress her out. You kids hear that? Since T is on bed rest, so am I so leave me the hell alone so I can take care of my wife." Everyone started laughing, I kissed T and put her in my lap while they congratulated us and went back to what they were doing."

60 TREASURE

"Girl I'm too happy you getting married."

"Yeah right, yo' ass happy you out the damn house that's all. I'm surprised Pandillero let yo' ass come all the way to New York with me for the weekend." I looked at Sammy.

"Don't do that big girl, you know he have yo' ass on lock. You better be happy the doctor said you could travel because you know yo' ass wouldn't be here."

"Yeah whatever, he don't have me on lock."

"Treasure please, don't act like you don't see the two dudes walking behind us." I didn't even look back I just started laughing.

"Stop worrying about me Sammy and put yo' game face on so we can close this deal and I can get my fat ass out of these heels. My feet hurt like hell; I don't know why I didn't wear some flats. That's what I get for trying to be cute; if Deangelo saw me he would flip the fuck out on me right about now."

Sammy walked into the conference room and I came in behind her, I was already rettago, my damn feet are killing me. I'm five in a half months along and man what I would do for a deep fried Twinkie with mustard and seasoning salt. I looked up at the investors and my ass all most broke my damn ankle. I recovered while everyone in the room reached over to help me. I'm too embarrassed, we all shook hands, took our seats and Sammy started the meeting.

Two hours later the deal was done, Sammy headed out with them to make arrangements for the close. I'm beat trying to reach down and pull off my shoes. "Let me get that for you Treasure." He took my heels off and sat in the chair, once he started rubbing my feet my eyes were shut. "It's been a minute but I see Pandillero don't waste no time." I can barely get out a laugh.

I put my hand on my stomach to stop the moving, he reached up and touched my stomach and my eyes shot open. Something in my mind said if Deangelo saw Stacy ass rubbing my stomach he'd kill us both and not even hesitate doing the shit. Stacy arrogant ass winked nodded his head and bit down on his lip. I can read his mind, he thinking pregnant pussy.

"Damn Treasure, that baby gone be big." He started back rubbing my feet and there went my eyes.

"Babies." He started laughing.

"Damn, twins again?" I held up three fingers and he really thought that was hilarious.

"You sure Pandillero not trying to kill you Treasure?" I pulled my foot from out of his hand at the thought of Deangelo killing his ass. But just like Stacy, he held on and made me close my eyes again.

"What you doing here Stacy?" He started to laugh.

"Why wouldn't I be here to see my vision take off?" I sat up and looked at him.

"Because you didn't have to be here. So stop playing games Stacy, what do you want from me?" He finished rubbing my foot, kissed it then he put my shoe back on. I shook my head.

"Anyway, why don't you rock the contacts anymore? Don't get me wrong, you fire either way but I thought those were a nice touch. You know what that shit did to me back in the day. So much so, I brought you a shit load, they over there in the basket." I didn't even have the energy to look at what the hell he's talking about.

"Stacy why do you like to play with fire so much? Don't you see I'm about to have six kids Stacy, why even waste your time?"

"Treasure I don't want anything from you but to say thank you. I see you happy so I'm backing off. It doesn't matter if you have sixteen kids Treasure, if you give me a chance I'll show you. I know you don't want to hear it but I love you. There's nothing that has ever stopped me from loving you.

Even now being here with you I realize that I shouldn't have let you go back in Ft. Lee. All this time that's passed and all the shit I've faced I still love yo' crazy ass. Seeing you at the reunion and every time since then my love for you has only gotten stronger. So stop acting like you don't know because I told yo' ass this a long time ago, don't act like you forgot. Come on so I can walk yo' fat ass downstairs."

He helped me up from the chair then stopped and I was lost in his eyes. I saw him come in but I'm not going there again. I pushed him away but I forgot to step back and the chair rolled from under me. His solid chest having ass didn't seem to budge. My big ass tried to grab Stacy ass back and he lunged for me but I'm on the ground. I'm surprised I didn't get knocked out, I'm instantly hollering. My eye hit the metal arm of the chair on the way down, I feel like my hip and ankle snapped. Davis and Jessie came running in the room.

Jessie was about to attack Stacy but I told him to stop and help me up. I can't stand up so Davis carried me out; we were in the car in no time. "Don't say a fucking word; just take me to the airport!" They raised the divider up and I closed my eyes. I can feel my left eye has already started closing from the swelling. I knew in that moment that Stacy was something still to be reckoned with. I'm not going to be able to work with him.

I love my husband but Stacy's his spitting image and something about that feeling is too much. I need to stay as far away from Stacy as I can so home is where I need to be. I want to call Deangelo and tell him to get back but I don't want him to kill Stacy ass.

Even with him warning Stacy I still have love for him and I don't want anything to happen to his crazy ass. After we made it to the airport they opened the door and I tried to stand up but I'm in pain. I see a nurse come from around the corner with Max. He carried me up the steps; I looked back at Davis and Jessie. "GET OFF!" I screamed at their asses. "Talk too fucking much!" The plane was in the air. The nurse looked over me and I had the greenest fucking bruise on my hip, this bitch throbbing. She touched it and I damn near pissed on myself. My left eye is completely closed shut; Deangelo is going to be hot.

The nurse gave me some good shit for the pain and I'm out. It seems like the closer I make it home the more the lightning bolts in my stomach want to spread out. I'm starting to get worried about Stacy and the whole situation. I don't want anything to happen to him because of me. He wasn't trying to hurt me, it was an accident. I know Deangelo won't want to hear any of that.

I started thinking about Deangelo and the pain coming harder, I told Max to take me to the hospital. I was in overnight; I had to sit around until I went to my doctor. Two days had past and Max told me Deangelo and Corey would be in soon, I'm trying my best to play sleep. I know he's going to come in upset at what happened. He told me to stay away but I didn't listen and now my big ass feel it. A sprained ankle and bruising to Deangelo is equivalent to open heart surgery. This shiny black eye is going to be like attempted murder, I just hope he hears me out.

61 DEANGELO

"Baby I miss you and the boys so kiss them for me."

"T you wouldn't be missing me if you hadn't rushed our asses out on this trip so you could hang out with Sammy." She laughed because she knows she only arranged this trip so she can get out the house. I was fool enough to do it, but once she told me I needed to bond with the boys I was game.

"Alright T, you make sure you take care of my babies and don't work too hard." T was too happy about hanging out with Sammy; I know she's tired of being in the house.

"You just make sure you and Corey take care of my babies on ya'll mother land trip." We said our goodbyes and we continued on our journey to the pyramids. The boys loved it; they were running around pointing at everything.

Bateador was like a personal tour guide. He kept trying to school me so we started going back and forth seeing who knew the oddest facts about whatever we talked about.

We had already been gone over a week and we'll make it back the day after T returns home. We sat around at the hotel while the boys fed the animals on the resort.

"You know tomorrow they have that meeting to finalize the contract for Stacy right?" I nodded my head at Bateador.

"Well I just got word that he flew out there?" I nodded again at him.

"So what you want to do?" I looked over at him.

"Nothing!" He sat up in his chair.

"Really?" He laugh like he can't believe what I said.

"Look man, I already told Stacy the rules, if he wants to be fool enough to doubt my word then that's on him. I'm not worried about T she can handle it. Get Max out and keep me informed."

I'm not worried about Stacy I was always ahead of him and I know his games. I know T's helping him make moves back in St. Louis. And I know Stacy's trying to make moves of his own. Bateador wants to end his ass; they weren't as close as he and I were. I want to see just how far Stacy will go to be with T though.

I want her to be happy either way, if it's with me and our family or with Stacy. Of course I'd kill them both if that's her choice. But if he's what she want then I'll make sure they be together.

Early the next morning I took the boys over to my mother so she can watch them. We headed out for our two day trip deep into the Congo, the shit's crazy, all the wild animals, the people. This not our first time being in Africa but it's our first time in the Congo and the site alone is enough. We learned so much and it seems like the time's flying past. "Pandillero, Jesse just called and said..."

I'm pissed it'll take a day to get back to the resort and get the boys before I can go check on T. It's already dark so we can't head out until daybreak. It gave me even more time to boil at the thought of Stacy fucking with my family.

"Did you call Max and see if T was okay?"

"Yeah Pandillero but this com phone is going in and out. He said she wanted to go to the hospital and it went out. I'll keep trying to reach him to see how she doing but we probably have to wait until we get back." I'm on fire, I can't sleep, and all I keep thinking about is the sun. I can't wait for it to show the fuck up so we can get back.

62 TREASURE

I heard him come in and I sat up, I'm too excited to fake like I'm sleep anymore. I waited to hear what he had to say. Look at my baby, just sexy, he has a full beard and his hair is thick and curly. He smiled at me and cruised over by the bed, I tried to get up. I don't want to look like an old lady using the cane they gave me. He picked up his step hugged and kissed all over me, I can't stop laughing.

"Deangelo will you say something? I missed you!"

"I love you T, I was just waiting on you to tell me I could say a word." I started bugging up, those bastards told on me like he my damn daddy. That's why we left they asses back in the states. He stood up and pulled off his shirt, he flexed for me and I'm trying not to laugh. Then he unbuckled his belt and pulled it off real slow. Once he had it off he put it across his shoulders.

"Why you holding on to that for?"

"So I can spank yo' ass with it T. Why you think?" He took forever undoing his pants then he unzipped them and closed it all up again. I'm cracking up.

"I forgot something hold up." He went out into the hall, he came back in and I'm crying. My babies are in his arms and they're too happy to see me. Their hair is all long and curly, they have little fros and all three of them look just alike. That man has some strong ass genes; I already see I'm gone have to put my foot in these lil girls' asses.

We all were in the bed watching TV when Shay came home, she climbed in with us. Deangelo too happy to see her and she just as excited to see them. She climbed up under Deangelo and he held on like she going somewhere. We woke up the next morning, as soon as I open my eyes Deangelo's staring at me. "See T, we need a bigger bed." I looked around and the kids are all over us, August foot is on the side of his head. Shay lying across both our legs and Deangelo's in between us. "Yes we do. Quick!"

We did everything together in the room for three days. It was time for everyone to go back to their regular schedules, the boys hit the gym and Shay went to chess practice. Deangelo came back in the room and helped me to the tub; he sat on the side of the tub in a chair just watching me.

"What's on your mind Deangelo?"

He put his foot up on the tub and tilted the chair back a little.

"The usual! How about you?" I want to laugh because I know what he's getting around to.

"It was an accident. Nothing more than that." He moved closer in the chair and reached down in the water rubbing on my stomach.

"Don't worry about that, you relax." I stopped his hand and moved it over so he can feel what I'm feeling. He put both his hands in so he could feel it.

"For me Deangelo please let it go. For us." He didn't say anything, he washed me up and when I turned he closed his eyes. He shaking his head at the site of the bruise on my hip. "It's nothing Deangelo." He moved in closer and kissed it; he put his arms around my waist and put his head on my stomach. I can feel the babies move and I know by the smile that spread across his face he do too. When he oiled me up I just knew he was about to put it on me but he didn't, he carried me out to the beach.

"Deangelo I know you getting tired of carrying me around."

"Come on T, I would carry all of us and it would be no problem." We laughed and sat on the chaise.

"I look like a whale in this dress." He laughed like I'm telling the truth.

"You look sexy T. Sexier than ever!"

"Yeah, tell me anything." I looked up at him he started to shake his head no.

"My mind is not in the gutter."

"Yeah, tell me anything T."

"Deangelo, look at me." He shook his head no again.

"Why not Deangelo?"

"I know what you about to say so no and stop." I tried to sit up.

"Okay T stay still. What's up?"

"Deangelo for real, I know what you've been doing. It's not working because you have me more worried now not talking than if we talked. I know you're mad so spit it out and stop acting like I can't handle talking to you without getting upset."

63 DEANGELO

Once we landed we headed to the house. "Alright Pandillero three days and he'll be at the office, you sure though? You know my vote but I know you like his punk ass." I grabbed the boys as Ms. Jackson came out they ran to her. "Yeah man, I want to see where this is going." He rode out I headed in the house to see T. Once I make it up all I can see was her eyes and smile, I'm happy she's okay.

"What's up with all the makeup?" She turned her head, I walked away.

"Where are you going Deangelo? Come back I wanna talk to you for a second before you take off." I walked back over to her, when she saw what was in my hand she put her arms over her face.

"No Deangelo, I don't want the kids to see my face like this." I moved her arms.

"Has Shay seen you?" She shook her head no.

"I don't want the kids thinking that it's okay to hide something like you're trying to hide." I moved her arms, kissed her nose and wiped the makeup from her face gently. Her eye was hidden well. I felt my skin heat up the more I cleaned her face and saw the purplish black ring around her eye. My baby look like she was in a MMA fight and got her ass whipped.

"There, all done. Now this is the beautiful wife I wanted to see."

I must've looked different since I let my hair grow out because she eyeing my man like I'm a stranger. I teased her then went to get the boys so she could see them. Their hair is longer than mine; their afros are thick and fluffy. They're too excited to see T, she in tears while they kissed all over her face, the site of them made me happy.

My princess came in and hugged us; I missed her I'm mad that she didn't want to go with us. She has a ton of stuff going on, she reminds me of T with all the work she does so it's alright with me. I watched as everyone slept just happy that I'm lucky enough to have my family together. The peaceful look on their faces made me feel good. It didn't matter that August kicked me in the ear waking me up or constantly moving Deangelo arm away from my shit. I'm happy to have my family; once I saw T waking up I had to tease her about needing a bigger bed.

We laughed at the site of us all bunched up, we sat around together and everyone was good. I still need to deal with Stacy and I haven't forgotten one second of what I want to do to his ass. I avoided getting T worked up about Stacy bitch ass, whenever she tried to talk about it I moved on to something else.

64 TREASURE

"Let's go T!" He tried to pick me up but I told him I wanted to walk. It hurt like hell but he held me down the whole way back. Seem like each step I take I can feel the pain transfer over into him. It was then that I realize just how connected we are. After we changed Max drove us to his office. The building was empty, we walked into his office and he closed the door.

"What are we doing here on a Sunday?" He looked at me for what seemed like way too long. I tried to sit up on his desk so he helped me up.

"What is it about Stacy T that you not telling me?" Do I really want to answer this question?

"Don't get quiet on me now T, what is it about him that has you taking care of him like you've been? I know it's you T, there's no way in hell Stacy hard head ass could've pulled that government contract by his self."

I looked away but he came closer and put his arms around me. "I'm not mad and I would've helped him myself but you were already on it so tell me. What is it T? Do you have feelings for Stacy?" I can't believe he just asked me that shit.

"No! When we were together in Ft. Lee he reminded me of you so much. He helped me feel at ease with what I was going through just by being there for real. In that short period of time it seemed like he was looking for something more important and he needed someone to help him. I'm not in love with Stacy. I just want to see him do well and for him to have a chance to find what's more important to him." I felt my stomach roll, he must've too. He put his hands on it and watched with a big smile on his face and kissed it.

"Now you sure that's it T, you don't want to take your chances, run off and be with him?"

"Deangelo!"

"Calm down T, I thought you could handle it." I calmed down.

"I can. I can handle anything you throw at me. I love you, there's nothing Stacy or any other man can say or do that will make me change my mind about you and how I feel." I kissed him and put my head in his chest.

"You can handle anything T and you sure about what you just said? You can handle anything and it won't change how you feel about me." I looked up at him and smiled and poked my lips up, he gave me a peck.

"I'm sure baby; nothing will ever change how I feel about you." I hear the elevator; he put his hands on my stomach again and asked if I was sure. I pushed him back and told him I was certain. He walked over and sat on the window sill and looked out. The door opened and in ran Stacy. "Treasure!" He

312

has tears in his eyes; he came over to the desk and hugged me. Then he stepped back and rubbed my stomach like he checking to see if I'm okay. He asking about my eye and what the doctor said like he my damn husband or something.

"I'm alright Stacy." He started kissing all over my face and stomach. Corey pissed, he look like he going to kill me. I'm shocked that he would do all this; I'm dodging around him so much I had to clamp my hand on his damn lips to get him to stop.

"Treasure I'm so sorry, I didn't mean for you to get hurt." I feel awkward, here Stacy is holding onto me while Deangelo looks out the window. Corey sitting on the couch across from me, Jesse and Davis are standing by the door.

"Treasure, I would never do anything to hurt you, I love you and I've always loved you. Please Treasure give me a chance to show you how much I love you. I'll take care of you and your kids. I promise Treasure come with me and let me show you. I'll show you I've changed and I can provide for our family. You, our kids and me Treasure, I guarantee I can make you happy again with me." I shook my head no.

"Stacy I love my husband. I don't want to be with you." Just like that, I see Stacy head go to the side and I jumped. I watched the smoke from the end of the barrel of Deangelo's Desert Eagle disappear. I'm beyond shocked at what Deangelo just did; my mouth wide open and all eyes are on me. "Why would you do that Deangelo?" I whispered and started to cry at the site of Stacy body on the floor and the blood pooling around him. He looked at me and handed the gun to Corey.

"Can you still handle this? Have you changed your mind about the man you love?"

I slid forward on the desk and tried to get down; he stepped forward to help me. "GET AWAY FROM ME! DAVIS COME HELP ME!" I screamed at their asses Davis looked at Deangelo. "WHAT THE HELL YOU LOOKING AT HIM FOR? COME HELP ME!" He still won't budge no matter how loud I scream. I reached in my purse and pulled out my Forty and pointed it at him. Deangelo and Corey think the shit funny.

I told them to shut the fuck up and stared at Davis. "You either help me or yo' ass will be next! Jesse you can stop laughing too because after I kill his ass you next!" Then I remembered, I hit my bracelet and looked at Davis. Deangelo nodded at Davis and he came over to help me. "Get the fuck away from me you bastard!" They all looked at me like I'm crazy, not a second later Max burst thru the door. "Take me home."

Max carried me to my bed, I cried so hard I fell asleep. I can't believe what Deangelo did to Stacy. They grew up together; Stacy was like a brother to him. I can't understand it. How could he do something so fucking heartless to someone he considered family? Is that the man that he always kept hidden from me? Is that the man they call Pandillero? The kids ran in the room pulling me out of my thoughts and climbed in the bed with me.

"Momma what's wrong with you? Does your eye hurt?"

"Nothing Shay, just a little sore that's all." She rubbed my stomach as August and Deangelo crawled into my arms. I felt the babies move so they all put their heads on my stomach and laughed.

We laughed every time the babies moved; the kids thought it was too funny. Hearing them laugh made me forget about everything that happened just that quick. Deangelo walked in and saw us all in the bed laughing. He stood there like he waiting for an invitation. They all called him over to join in but he stood there looking at me. He dropped his head while they told him to hurry, I looked over at him. "Come on big baby you know you want to." He popped his head up and smiled then he came over and found a spot to put his head.

He would choose the spot closest to my cat; I can feel each time he sends a cool long blow down on me. He thought it was funny when I moved my leg open a bit. I rubbed his beard thinking about what the hell just happened. A couple hours later the kids ran out to the sound of Ms. Jackson calling them.

Deangelo kissed me and walked them to the door, after he closed it I heard him lock it. He walked over and sat on the side of the bed, I turned on my song by Joe. He turned around. "Can you make me feel better husband?" He made love to me. He took his time and it was better than the first time. He was gentle, caring, passionate and loving. I can feel how much he love me more than I ever could.

The time flew past and we welcomed Corey, Alex, and Rose to the family. After I returned home from the hospital I was on the floor laughing hysterically at the bed that Deangelo surprised me with.

"What happened to my room?"

"This the family room now." The bed is huge it covers almost the entire wall; it has to be close to twenty feet wide. I could not stop laughing. "So where is our room Mr. Man?" He grabbed my hand and we walked towards Shay room, he opened the door and we had all new furniture.

I was on the floor again when I realized he took out all the kids' rooms. "So where my babies at, all the way upstairs now? You know I don't like them being that far away. Why didn't you put us up there and leave them down here?" He looked at me, laughed, closed the door and picked me up putting me on the bed. "I'm a man that's why! You better stop playing like you forgot."

65 DEANGELO

Sitting out on the beach with T she seemed to be really concerned about Stacy. It made me wonder if she had feelings for him, I had to know if she did or not. My curiosity winning and my frustration growing. I told her to come with me. Bateador will be in soon so we headed there. It's time to see where her head's at. "What is it about Stacy T that you not telling me?"

She hesitated and it kind of pissed me off but I'm not going to let her get distracted with what I asked. Of course I lied and said I would've helped his punk ass. I have to find out what she'd say about Stacy. Once she told me that she wanted to help him find what was more important to him, I understood. It really don't make a difference to me, I already know what he's after.

"I'm sure baby nothing will ever change how I feel about you." That's all I need to know from T, I sat looking out the window waiting on them to come in. I listened to Stacy as he poured his lifeless, arctic heart out to my wife. It took everything out of me not to look over at him. I know he has to be holding her or touching on my fucking kids like they're his. "...I've changed and I can provide for our family! You, our kids..."

'OUR KIDS?' After hearing his words I can feel my blood turn to acid, Stacy really wants to be me. Stacy's Judas live in the flesh and don't give a fuck about anyone besides his self. As hard as it is I let him get out what he needs to say. I grounded my anger and let it be for the moment. Stacy has chosen his side. No matter how dangerous that side is, Stacy's going to do whatever he has to to have what I have. I understand what's more important to Stacy; I don't think he understands what's more important to me.

"Stacy I love my husband. I don't want to be with you."

Once she made her choice there was nothing else to be said. I got up and put a bullet in Stacy head and watched his ass fall to the ground. "Can you still handle this? Have you changed your mind about the man you love?" T didn't say anything, she looked pissed and had tears rolling down her eyes, I know it hurt her. To be frank, this should've been done a long time ago. Like I said, I had to know how she felt and just how fucking far Stacy disloyal ass was willing to go to be with her.

She wouldn't let me help her up so I stood back. T never ceases to amaze me. She screamed at Davis to help her and when I looked at him she pulled out her gun. "...can stop laughing too because after I kill his ass you next!" I thought I would fallout laughing. It's a fucked up situation but the thought of her pulling a gun on someone to help her is too much.

"You two jesters need to shut the fuck up with all that laughing. This shit's not funny you fucking assholes! What the fuck is wrong with you two?" I told him to help her get off the desk so she can calm down.

As he walked over I saw her hit her panic bracelet. "Get the fuck away from me you bastard! Deangelo you better keep your flunkies away from me from here on! I'm getting my own security, this some bullshit!" Max ran in faster than I thought he would, I gotta give his ass a raise. He carried her away.

"You think she gone forgive you?"

"I don't know Bateador but I guess I'm gon' find out right?" We laughed as they came in to get Stacy the fuck out my office. Bateador stayed back to make sure his ass will never be found and nothing would connect us to that bullshit. I took my time going home, I wanted to give T enough time to figure out what she needed or wanted to do.

"Daddy come feel the babies, it's creepy!" Shay said once I came in the door, her and the boys kept calling me over. I'm waiting to see if T wants me around her. The last thing I need is for her to reject me in front of them. "Come on big baby, you know you want to." The way she said it made me feel like we'll be okay, I'm happy I still have a chance to work this out.

I haven't had my dessert in almost three weeks and boy am I ready to get a taste. I know she needs the kids so I have to wait. Once Ms. Jackson called for them to head out for practice I walked they asses out too quick. She turned on our song and I knew what time it was. "Can you make me feel better husband?" Hell, I can make you feel more than better. I put it on T; I didn't want to hurt her so I made sure she was more than satisfied. I ran us some water and we sat in the tub.

"Why did you do it Deangelo?" I don't know why she would ask the question, why wouldn't I do it?

"I was only helping him that's all. Ain't that what you wanted?" She sat up and tried to stand up.

"Where you going T?" She said she wanted to turn around so I moved in front of her so she didn't have to.

"Now, what do you mean you were helping him?"

"T you think you know Stacy but you don't."

"What does that mean Deangelo?" I pulled her in closer.

"T do you remember the name of the guy you shot first at the lake house?" She shook her head no.

"Do you remember the police saying the name Demarcus Carr?"

"No Deangelo, what the hell does this have to do with anything? Just tell me where this is going."

"Alright, you may not remember his real name but I know you remember Johnny Boy."

"The guy who took last place? The one Corey knocked out?" I kissed her.

"Good, you remember. When I was fighting him I knew it was something familiar about his style. I couldn't see his face with the mask and I was trying to get that bitch off. When the Officer said his real name, I knew who it was."

"Get around to Stacy Deangelo!"

"If you give me a minute I will. Okay at the Center the police said the nigga in the street was Justin Calvert. Now you don't know Justin because he was never around, he was a corner boy in Murphy Blair. Justin is Stacy stepbrother and Demarcus is Stacy cousin. They were both with Stacy when he tracked you down at the reunion. So I know he knew what was going to happen. You remember when we ran out the house and I hesitated?" She scrunched her face up.

"I thought they went back on the side?"

"No baby, I had more than enough time to shoot but it was Stacy and I stopped. That's why I told you not to come out for anyone." She moved back.

"You lying Deangelo, Stacy wasn't there! He wouldn't do that." I can see she's upset so I stopped talking; we washed up and got out.

I grabbed my phone and plugged it into the television. "Come here T, watch this with me."

She came over and I played it, once she saw Stacy she shook her head in disbelief. "T I told you, you didn't know Stacy like I did. He'd do whatever he needed to do to have something he just wasn't going to have. You were right T; he needed someone to help him find what was important to him.

Once I heard him tell you that you, my wife, was more important to him I knew then I was the one to help Stacy. I waited to see what you would say, to see if you wanted to be with him or not. I had my answer so I gave him what he wanted."

We didn't talk about Stacy anymore after that day, it was like he never existed and I was fine with it. T was in the hospital giving birth and our parents all came over to help with the babies.

"Instead of hiring someone new ya'll need to take me up on my offer and let me help with my grand babies." T looked over at my mother and shook her head no.

"Why not Treasure?"

"Because Ma, I don't want you hanging around here thinking this yo' house." She came over and hit me.

"Shut up, 1 know this not my house boy, and 1 know ya'll have sex, hell ya'll got twenty kids running around here." We laughed T walked away.

"Come on Treasure let me stay."

"Ma' 1 love you and 1 would never stop you from seeing the kids. 1 don't want to feel uncomfortable in my own house with my husband that you already keep hitting on." 1 laughed as my mother walked towards T.

"So what you think you too grown to get hit?" She ran over 1 put her in my arms with my mother standing at my back.

"He not gone save you lil girl," she said as 1 kept T out of her reach.

"That's why you can't stay!" T said as we laughed and sat down.

"Why don't you just move into the villa, it's empty and 1 know you want to be close." My mother jumped up, hugged T then she hit me and walked off to tell the kids.

"Where ya'll two going, 1 thought we were watching a movie?" my mother said as we walked out of the kitchen.

"See, that's what I'm talking about!" T said as she moved on the other side of me away from my mother.

"We about to work on six more so you have a reason to be at the villa!" 1 said as T stopped walking and pulled her hand away.

"Yeah, now yo' crazy ass running to me!" my mother said as T stood behind her. We all laughed and 1 walked over and picked her up putting her across my shoulder. 1 smacked her ass.

"Stop playing; first you were saying 1 didn't want kids now you act like you scared. Now come on so we can get pregnant!" My mother laughed as 1 carried her up the steps.

"Deangelo you crazy as hell if you think I am having sextuplets!" I put her on the bed and got on the top of her.

"You crazy as hell if you think you not! We're not waiting as long as we did after Frick and Frat. I'm talking every year on that ass. I'm starting to think you on that wack ass shot; you know that shit was created as a form of eugenics. I know you not taking it right?" We laughed as she rolled over on me.

"I know that Deangelo and I haven't been taking anything. Baby I know you said you want a ton of kids but I don't have room for that many kids at once. Trust, I want as many kids as I can have with yo' sexy ass." I sat up and pulled her dress off holding her breast in my hands.

"I need more than one T. We have a lot of time to makeup so let's just see how many we can have at a time." She laughed and pulled my shirt off.

"Deangelo really, six more?" I turned her ass over she tried to go on her hands and knees.

"Gone lay back down and put that ass up on those pillows why you're at it."

"You can hit it from the back and I know we'd have at least one."

"I said six, you think I'm playing? You might as well get used to being pregnant, we not taking a break 'til we can't have any more kids." She started to laugh, I went in and she shut the hell up.

66 TREASURE

"Surprised to see me?"

"Girl no, you better brought yo' ass here, what you thought this was?" Sammy hugged me and Deangelo as we walked into their loft, we didn't stay long we were tired from the trip. Or should I say tired from fuckin' all the way over here like two maniacs.

"You okay being back here T?"

"Yeah, why you ask me that?" He guided me out to the porch and we looked out at the Arch.

"Just checking to make sure you know where we at. That's all." How can I forget, St. Louis is home but in the back of my mind I feel those insecurities banging on my heart trying to get out. The first couple nights we all spent time hanging out and enjoying each other's company.

The weekend hit, Sammy and I were out clubbing with the girls while the guys did there thing. When the clubs closed in St. Louis we decided to hit that bridge and keep the night going. The club was packed; we had to get the hell out of there. There were way too many young boys that still wore their pants hanging low. We hit the next best thing, the strip club; we were having a blast in our own world. The girls were wasted we still had bottles coming.

I needed some fresh air so I stepped outside. I didn't see the driver where I thought he would be, I walked around towards the back lot to see if he was parked back there. I turn the corner and was scared to death because I hear some dumb ass move. I look over and see some bitch unzipping some tricks pants, I didn't pay any attention, and I kept going.

"Come on now you doing too much." I dropped my purse, turned around heading toward the voice, I'm hot! I grabbed that bitch by her hair and his eyes are big. "THIS? THIS IS WHAT YOU WANT?" In the process of me asking him the girl got up and hit me right in the face. He reached forward to grab her. "DON'T!" I screamed at his ass while I gave myself some room. I'm so pissed I didn't even take off my heels.

This bitch don't know what she's about to get into. She talking mad shit because she got her hit off on me. She fucked up and ran up again and it was lights out for her ass. I hit that bitch with one good hit to her nose, her legs buckled; she fell back and went to sleep. "Come on T, nothing happened!" He moved forward and reached down to pull her legs from under her. I pulled his gun from out of his waist. "You put one finger on that bitch and I'll kill you!"

He looked up at me while Corey and the rest of the guys were coming our way. I didn't look at them, I'm dead serious and Deangelo knows it. "What the fuck Treasure? What the hell is going on?" They all ran over surrounding me.

"SHUT UP COREY AND MIND YOUR FUCKING BUSINESS!"

"Man give me this fucking gun and stop acting crazy!" Deangelo snatched the gun out of my hands; I stepped back and started to walk away. He grabbed me and I felt that full moon come thrashing out of my body. I kicked my heels off, put my hands up, and I'm ready to get in that ass. He pissed and I don't give a fuck. "Stacy loved me!" I backed away from him and studied his ass waiting on my chance to fuck him up.

I know I said I'd never put my hands on his ass again but this the last straw, after this I'm done. Deep down in my stomach I feel like I'm going to throw the fuck up I'm so irate with his simple ass. I fought like hell to ease my stomach and not let the shit out or get worse. I'm fighting like hell inside to stop myself but I really don't want to. I'm so fucking hurt and humiliated once again all courtesy of Deangelo ass. I've been here before with him and I let the shit go. This nigga even left me afterwards like I was in the wrong, not this time, I'm leaving his ass.

We can call this shit a wrap so I might as well go out with a bang. I wasted damn near all my fucking life fucking with Deangelo half loyal ass. All that training is about to payoff, he may get me in the end but I'm gon' get mine to.

"You want to fight me T? Is that what you wanna do?" I didn't say shit, I'm begging for him to come a little closer. One false move and I'm sure this time I'll get his ass good. Corey came over and stood in between us and before he can get a word out I hit his ass right across the face. Deangelo came from around him quick, grabbed me by the throat and put me against the wall; he has death in his eyes.

"This has nothing to do with him! Calm the fuck down T before you really piss me the fuck off!" Corey pulled him off, I walked over and picked up my purse and was headed to the driver. Then I see Deangelo's white on white Bentley Continental Supersport and decided to take it. He never let me drive the bitch anyway but he really don't have a choice. Hell, I'm debating on running this bitch into the Mississippi if he gives me the keys. Deangelo came walking behind me; if he touch me it's going down.

I stopped at the car and held my handout. "T let's talk! I'm sorry about grabbing you but can we talk, then I'll give you my keys if you still want to go." I still didn't say shit to his stupid ass. He moved fast and pressed his body against me holding my arms, my legs are outside of his. Damn he feels good but to hell with all that.

"Get the fuck off of me Pandillero!" I'm not about to let him see me cry, he looked into my eyes when I said it. This the first time in my life that I've ever called him that. He looked like I had just called him a bitch, he moved away and gave me the keys. I jumped in and pulled away with him standing in the parking lot; I didn't go home I went to where I know he won't find me.

"What's wrong Treasure, what you doing here so late?" I broke down and let all my tears wash over Ethan's chest; he walked me inside and held me in his arms. "So what did he do now?" I can't tell Ethan, I'm too embarrassed to let him know what the hell I'm going through. I closed my eyes and went to sleep.

I woke up because I can hear Ethan downstairs talking to someone so I got in the shower and put on one of his shirts. I walk down to the kitchen and I'm surprised to see that Ethan has company, she said hello and I spoke. "Treasure this is Sharon, Sharon Treasure." Ethan walked over and asked if I was okay, I told him yeah and that I'm leaving out. He tried to get me to stay but I don't want to intrude.

Someone rang the doorbell and Ethan walked over to answer as I turned to go back up the stairs. I hear a scuffle so I turn around and Deangelo has a gun pointed right at Ethan and he looked me right in the eyes. "It's not what you think Pandillero, put the gun down!" Ethan said, I shook my head at the site. Sharon came running around the corner screaming and ran right into Ethan's arms, Deangelo lowered the gun.

"My bad man I thought..." I turned to go up the steps. "No problem, just fix whatever you need to with her." I don't want to hear it, I changed and Deangelo stood there watching me like he's waiting on me to say something to him. I walked right past him and with him still following got in the car and drove off.

I sat around the loft with Sammy while she kept asking me if I'm okay or wanted to talk. Deangelo never came in and neither did Corey. Later that night we hit the clubs like nothing was wrong, I'm on the floor dancing my pain away with no cares in the world.

"Now aren't you a site for sore eyes?" I turned around. "Really? Why you say that?" This guy's too much, I'm sure this guy has to be Brian White. He's tall, light brown complexion, low hair cut, bright smile and I know his full lips have to be soft.

"Come on sweetheart, I know you feel all these brothers in here eyeing you. I'm Sydney and you're drop dead beautiful! I'm willing to let you be the BK to my Mickey D." I can't take my eyes off his mouth, the way the words come out so smooth and direct is turning my wheels.

"Well Sydney, I'm Treasure and it depends on what you're talking about." He stepped closer to me.

"Nice to meet you Treasure. What I'm talking about is letting you have it your way while I'll be loving it." I moved closer to him making sure to put my body right up against his, I can feel Sammy ass looking right at me.

I can't help but blush. "Sydney that has to be the corniest pickup line I've heard in a long time." We both laughed, I sat my Absolute and cranberry down and tried to avoid Sammy and her constant stare. He asked me to dance, I grabbed his hand. "It'll be my pleasure to dance with a man as handsome as you." We danced and had a great time doing it, this man wasn't short stopping. I can feel his stick stretch more and more.

After a few songs we were still on the floor, I'm not a drinker but I put back at least three so far. I feel uneasy like I'm being watched but I don't give a fuck if I am. "So Sydney, you wanna get out of here?" He smiled big and hard, he held my hand and we walked out the front of the club. Before we can make it out I catch of glimpse of Deangelo dumb ass off in the distance. I turned, looked at Sydney and kept it moving on his ass.

67 DEANGELO

"Alright, ya'll ready to hit the streets?" Cap said as we headed out the door, we hit the clubs and watched as the ho's came running. Before we called it a night we hit the strip club and headed to our own room while the dancers came bouncing and twerking. Two hours in I headed out back so I could call and check on the kids and see if T has made it in the house yet. I tried her phone but she didn't pick up so I hung up and was stopped.

"Damn Daddy, let me help you." She squatted down and tried to unzip my pants. I stepped back damn near tripping over a crate.

"Come on now you doing too much." She was about to get up then I see T coming straight towards us fast. She grabbed the girl head and pulled her away. "THIS? THIS IS WHAT YOU WANT?" T beyond talking but I have to try, "T, it's not what you think baby."

This trick stumbled back and hit T, I'm about to beat the shit out of her when T screamed at me. The fight was over once the girl ran back up on her, she hit her and she fell hard. Her body folded back so I started to reach down when I feel T grab my gun.

"You put one finger on that bitch and I'll kill you!"

"Terentia, calm down, it's not like that, nothing happened! I wasn't doing anything with this girl. Can we talk about this before it goes too far? T, put the gun down!" The look in her eyes told me she's had enough.

"After all the shit we been through, all the bullshit I've been through and you about to fuck some stank ass bitch outside a strip club? I should've taken my fucking chances with Stacy! At least I know he loved me and it didn't matter that he was risking his fucking life to be with me."

The guys came out and T didn't move, I took the gun from her and she tried to leave but I grabbed her. Once she took off her shoes I knew she was ready to fight. Usually I'd be on swole when T acted like this but her words mangled my heart. It's been almost a year since Stacy and she throwing his treacherous ass up in my face.

Bateador jumped in to try and reason with her so we could work this shit out. Once she hit Bateador I had enough, I was done. She has Stacy name in my head and the image of her and my kids with that bitch made nigga. I grabbed her ass up and put her on the wall.

"This has nothing to do with him! Calm the fuck down T before you really piss me off!" I could've choked the fuck out of T for that bullshit she spitting about Stacy. I don't care how mad she is with me, Bateador has always had her back and she crossed a line. She got in my car and drove off. "What the fuck Pandillero?" I looked at him.

"I'm not about to fight with you Bateador so give me your keys so I can find my wife!"

"For what so you can hurt her some more?" I'm trying to be tolerant so I didn't say anything, he gave me the keys and I went home.

I waited around for her to show up but she didn't. The sun was coming up and I was getting worried, she wasn't answering her phone. I jumped in the car and traced her, once I saw the address I knew exactly where she at. This whole time I felt something was still brewing between her and this nigga and I know if she gave him a chance he'd take it.

Deep down I know that if any nigga had a chance with my wife it's him. The thought alone is fueling my anger. I'm blistering when I pull up to City house; I wasted no time going to the door. I'm begging to get at this nigga. He answered the door with no shirt on and I see T in a t-shirt going up the steps.

I'm ready to kill them both. "It's not what you think Pandillero, put the gun down!" Before I can get anything out some girl came running to City.

"My bad man, I thought you slept with T. I'm sorry Miss that's my wife I was wrong." I apologized and went to be with T. She didn't say anything she put on her clothes. "T, please baby talk to me. I know this looks fucked up and I really need you to talk to me about this." She didn't respond, when I moved towards her she backed away. Not a word so I followed her outside, when she pulled off I knew she needed a minute to breathe. I followed her to the loft and waited on her to go inside; I went down to Bateador house to think.

"What's up Bateador, Sammy, sorry about last night ya'll." He came over to the couch holding the side of his face.

"Damn man, Treasure knocked the shit out of my ass. I thought Drag ass was bullshitting when he said she tagged his ass, but now I see what ya'll niggas was talking about." We all laughed and Sammy went to be with T.

"Man, I don't know how to fix this shit here. I could beat the shit out that bitch at the club for getting my ass in this bullshit." He started laughing like the shit all too fucking funny.

"Man I don't know how yo' crazy ass always end up with some chick fucking with you. I guess you lost yo' touch." I looked at his ass like he crazy.

"What the hell you talking about? I might be married but these ho's don't give a fuck. You say that shit like I'm one of these busted ass niggas out here?" He laughed harder.

"Man it was a time when the ho's came but the thought alone scared the shit out they asses. Stop playing! Shit, ho's come at me all day but it's the look that makes that ass think twice. You lost yo' look man." I can't argue with that, maybe I have lost my 'beware of danger' sense. Hell, I didn't need it with my family, I love them and they love me. I guess I dropped that shit when I married T. I never wanted her to feel like she had to be afraid of me anymore.

I'm hoping T will stay in so I can go down and talk with her. Sammy came down and said they were all sticking to their plans so I didn't want to disappoint Bateador and not go. Later that night we headed to the club, I told Bateador that I needed to check on T. She still not answering her phone.

We went to the club that they were at and sat in the back. Once I saw T I was ready to pull her ass off the floor. The sight of that nigga touching all over her killing me not to react. I watch as she dance around flirting with the nigga, I'm trying my best to calm down, she walked out with him and I got up.

"Pandillero, I'm coming with you."

"Naw Bateador have fun, this between me and my wife." He sat back down; I jumped in the whip and followed. I could've run the car off the fucking road. Something inside of me is saying she has to make her choice. I followed behind the nigga to see just how far she's willing to go.

68 TREASURE

Once we made it to Sydney car I stopped and watched as he leaned up against the door. "I had a great night Sydney, you ready to go back and have a night cap?" He smiled and pulled me into his arms.

"You sure Treasure? I know that nigga standing in the door over there will be pissed if you came home with me and let me do the job that he can't do." We laughed and I kissed him, I can feel Deangelo coming from behind. I got in and Sydney pulled off before he made his way over.

We made it to Sydney house and I didn't see Deangelo following us anymore but I know he's not far away. We walked in and before I let him close the door I'm on his ass. I'm going to cross that line that Deangelo keeps promising he'd never let me see the other side of.

Sydney put it on me and I loved the thrill behind it all. He working with more than I thought. Even when I throw it back he's up for the challenge and goes right back in. He bent me over and went mouth first into me, his tongues impressive to say the least.

I'm soaked with just the thought of Deangelo coming in the door and killing us both. That didn't stop me though; it only turned me on more. I'm cumming back to back with the image of Deangelo face seeing someone else with his dessert.

Sydney pulled me up by my knees and was holding me in his arms as he thrust his man all up in me. I can't get enough of every second. I dropped my legs and held on to the couch as I crossed them and the friction of him banging my back out had me screaming for more.

He's a beast and he's on a mission to get in no matter how much I tightened up on him. He worked my ass good. I couldn't help but put my leg on his shoulder and watch as he slowed down and kissed all over me while he jabbed my insides.

He kept cumming and changing condoms but he didn't leave me waiting. He ate me out so damn good I'm ready for him to cum again and put his man back in. We went at it nonstop, by the time we finished I'm exhausted, he fell over on me and kissed all over me again. We were breathing hard and laughing like we're little kids.

"Damn Treasure, I don't know what the fuck that nigga did but he fucked up!" I laughed and started to put on my clothes, he didn't want to let me go but I know Deangelo will find me soon. He has a tracker on my phone so I know he can't be far. Last I checked he was less than four miles away from me.

"Sydney this was fun but I have to go before my husband gets here." He stood up and pulled me into his arms.

"Fuck him, stay here, he don't know where you are. Lets hit the shower and go some more Treasure, you know you want to."

I'm tempted but I can't, I looked back at my phone to see where Deangelo was. I asked Sydney the name of his street and when he told me I knew Deangelo was out front.

"I have to go Sydney; can you do me a favor and stay in the house? No matter what Sydney, please stay in the house." He shook his head no and pulled me onto his lap.

"I said fuck that nigga Treasure. If he wants beef I can give it to his ass." I stood backup and pulled away from Sydney and walked to the door.

"Sydney this is between me and him so please just stay here." He put his head back against the couch and I quickly walked down the driveway. Deangelo came out fast heading towards me. I tried to walk past him hoping he'd follow but he continued towards Sydney's door. I pulled his arm around stopping him.

"This is between me and you Pandillero, let him go!" He has fire in his eyes, he tried to reach for my neck but I stepped back. "Not here!" I walked to the car and got in, he got into the driver seat and he banging his hands against the steering wheel.

We pulled up into the garage at the loft and he stopped the car. "T I should fucking kill you for that bullshit back there!"

I looked over at him and opened the door. "Bitch I wish you would," he whispered through gritted teeth. I know he's pissed, the lower his voice is the more irate he really is. I got out and booked it into the building; once I was in the lobby he was hot on my ass. The security guard looking at us crazy, he knows there's trouble. I asked him if he can walk me up, Deangelo's even more pissed. The whole time on the elevator I see him fucking with his gun.

He's debating on killing the two of us and I really don't want anything to happen to the security guard. I got on the phone and called Shay. I know she's sleep but I turned on the speaker phone so he can hear her voice. Deangelo dropped his head and swiped his hands down his face. I continued to talk with Shay as the guard walked me to the door, Deangelo went to Corey house. I thanked the security guard and closed the door, I told Shay goodnight. Before I can make it to the bedroom I hear the door open.

69 DEANGELO

As soon as I saw T walkout the door with that nigga I wanted to beat the shit out that nigga and thrash her ass for going with him. I told her nothing happened. I guess she just don't want to listen and is willing to risk it all on this nigga. I'm trying to keep my cool as I walk behind them, I can't believe she hugged up with him and she knows I'm here.

As soon as I see her kiss him I'm on my way to the car to handle this nigga and fuck her ass up. He pulled off; I jumped in the whip to follow behind. I wanted to run that fucking car off the road; I was on ney ass until they jumped off the highway. I had to get off at the next exit but I'm sure I'll find the car.

If it takes me all night I'll find this nigga and slaughter his ass. I double back and go up the streets in the direction they were heading. After about an hour later, I'm so hot I forgot all about my phone. I pulled it out and checked if they had stopped. Once the address came up I'm hitting seventy to get to this bitch.

Before I can put the car in park she came out. I can tell by the way her clothes are thrown together she fucked this nigga. I'm on my way to destroy him then I'm goin' to deal with her, she pulled my arm. "This is between me and you Pandillero let him go!"

It's cool, I'm gone show her ass just why they call me Gangsta; she wants to go first, a'ight. I can't wait to get her ass back. I got in the car and all I can do is release some of my anger on the steering wheel. I should've beat the shit out of her.

We get to the house she run out the car into the lobby, I wanna annihilate her ass. The only thing that saved her and that bitch ass security guard is Shay. I don't want my princess to hear what the hell I'm about to do. I'm glad that T called her because that'll be that bitch final goodbye to Shay. She better had sense to tell Ms. Jackson to put all the kids on the phone so she can tell them all goodbye. If not, she just assed the fuck out now!

I called Bateador told him to wipe out that bitch ass nigga now and waited 'til I saw the security guard get back on the elevator.

70 TREASURE

"Come here T, you know you den fucked up right?" I stood there not knowing what I would do. I'm not scared and I'm at peace with my decision. He came over and I'm not going out without a fight, as soon as he was in my reach I hit his ass. He didn't hold back this time, he came at me with a backhand. I couldn't get out the way fast enough, I landed on the bed. I still didn't cry as he climbed on the top of me.

"Didn't I tell yo' dumb ass don't fuck up? I see you'll never learn T, I told you don't put yo' hands on someone unless you were ready for them to put their hands on you! You think you ready T? Get the fuck up!" He got up and I kicked off my heels.

"Fuck you, let's go!" He came forward and I'm swinging with all my might, he wasn't even blinking.

He slapped the shit out of me, I kicked his ass right in the nose, he furious. He balled his fist and punched me in the shoulder. I thought I'd die! I have to fight so I took the lamp and hit his ass across the side of the head and came back with two more kicks and kneed his ass in his shit. He went forward and I sent another knee to his face. He went back I got on top of him, he's balled up holding his dick, and I started whaling on his ass.

Anything that's not nailed down I'm grabbing and sending to his ass. I tried to bash his damn head in with the Blu-ray player, he came back and punched me in the face, and I felt my eye swell up instantly. I want to ball up next to his ass and cry. Fuck that shit, this nigga got me fucked up, I shook that shit off and pulled the TV down on his ass. I started stomping the back of it, I wanna kill Deangelo bitch made ass.

He pushed that shit off and was coming for me; I reached for my purse and pulled out my gun. It didn't stop him, he still slowly moving forward.

"So this is how it ends Deangelo?" I have tears running down my eyes at the sight of us.

"I told you T! You don't listen, all this shit and this how you do me?" I wiped my face.

"You get caught up about to fuck that bitch and you come at me over a fuck? Look at my fucking face Pandillero! Look what you did to me!" I'm enraged and I don't really give a fuck about his answer. I stepped back and he pulled up his gun and pointed it at me. Corey came into the room and looked at the two of us.

"What that fuck is wrong with you two?" Corey said as he took in the sight

342

of the room and the standoff we found ourselves in.

"Get the fuck out Bateador, this bitch is dead!" Two shots went off; I dropped the gun and fell to my knees. I looked at Corey and he's on his knees trying to inhale all that he's seen.

71 DEANGELO

I ran down to the house and opened the door. "Come here T, you know you den fucked up right?" I go in the room and she standing there like she don't give a fuck. But hell I don't either, she hit me and it was on. I tried to break her neck when I sent my hand across her dumb ass face.

I let her know that she not getting away this time without meeting her match. I let her up; she kicked off her heels and said fuck me, she right. Fuck me and fuck her too! She swinging and that shit's nothing.

"Didn't I tell yo' trifling ass nothing happened? You fucked this nigga after I warned you what would happen?" I slapped her ass again she kicked me and I'm determined to break her ass before I kill her. I punched her sending her ass back. She came at me with the lamp and it felt like my balls would explode when she caught me.

"Fuck you, all this time and all these bitches you fucked you get mad over one nigga? I earned that fuck and guess what, he was ten times better than you." She pulled the TV down on me; the shit still didn't hurt as much as my heart and my dick. I got up out of pure anger and she pulled her burner out.

"So this is how it ends Deangelo?" T crying but I still don't give a fuck. Her words are still in my head about that nigga.

"Yeah bitch, this exactly how it ends, you better pull the trigger and fast because I'm killing yo' ass if you don't." She went on about nothing.

"...come at me over a fuck? Look at my fucking face Pandillero! Look at what you did to me!" I told her silly ass nothing happened with that chick but she don't wanna fucking listen so I'm about to teach her ass. I look over because I know my gun on the dresser, 1 inch forward.

"All this time Deangelo, I've been waiting on this moment!" I stopped and can't believe what she said; she wiped her face again and smiled.

"Yeah Pandillero, I been waiting on this moment since that nigga raped me because of you. I was never in love with Dominic, he was just a test to see how I would kill yo' ass slow and painful! I was feeding his ass all types of shit. Yo' simple ass thought he was on drugs. That nigga was on more than drugs, I was putting so many chemicals in his ass they thought it had something to do with the fire. I just couldn't get yo' ass though, yo' healthy ass never gave me the chance.

You think it was a coincidence with Sebastian nigga? I knew about his bitch ass when I first met him. I was always protected, I just needed to put that shit together so you would come looking." I can't believe what she saying. I can tell by the look in her eyes this bitch is more than crazy, her ass is deranged. All this time she been playing me.

"Yeah, I'm sorry to say, yo' kids that you love so much, they not yours nigga. You couldn't get me pregnant after all that fucking and years wasted!"

"I'm gone kill you bitch, with my bare hands, you know that right?" She laughed.

"Not today nigga, I'm going to get my kids and take them all to their father, you may know him, and his name is Harlem. See I met Harlem back in Florida when I first left. We fell in love and I kept in touch with him.

I don't know why that fool Dominic thought Shay was his child; he was away when me and Harlem conceived her. It wasn't luck that he was at the meeting, he's always around. I'm fucking him more than I fuck you. Hell, he was even on our honeymoon. Remember yo' silly ass kept having to go to town; he was giving me all that I needed. It don't matter because after I get home, I'm gone kill yo' stupid ass mama for having you." I'm focused on when to make my move and kill this bitch.

"I hooked up with Bunk and Small, they so damn dumb, even with the codes they still fucked up. That's why it was so easy for me to take they asses out. I thought Bunk punk ass told you I set you up but even if he had yo' ass wouldn't have believed him would you? I was so tempted to spray yo' ass that night but I knew I had to wait and make you pay for all the shit you put me through.

You took care of Stacy dumb ass for me though. I knew when you said his stupid ass didn't shoot you he was weak. I begged him to come to New York! Why else would I send yo' blind ass away to the fucking Congo? I was hoping a gorilla would kill yo' ass for me but what fun would that have been?" She laughed more then she stepped back and I grabbed my gun and pointed it at her. I'm still in shock with all that she said and taking it in trying to put the pieces together and figure this shit out.

Bateador came in, I told him to get the fuck out, then I hear two shots, all I can do is smile. I thought back about every fucking second that I spent with this bitch and wondered just when and how this all turned around. She's my wife, the woman I love more than myself. I'd give anything to be with her and protect her. I have to hand it to her; I always wondered why she spent so much time in the gym and at the range.

This bitch an expert handling any heater. I watch as Bateador came to my side, I grabbed his hand as he began to cry. "I, I love you man!" I whispered as he leaned down to hear what I said. Then I see this bitch come forward with the gun still in her hand and I watch as Bateador head flies back.

She laughed like a mad woman as she empties the clip on him. I can feel the blood pour down my mouth. She came closer, leaned in and looked me in my eyes. "Fuck you nigga! I'll see you in hell," was all she said as she stood back up. I saw total darkness.

ABOUT THE AUTHOR

Born and raised in St. Louis, MO. She spent her younger years living in the infamous Cochran Garden Housing Projects. She decided to put her stories on paper after many years of thinking about just how much life has changed since those exciting days in the Cochran.

She wrote her first novel, Lifelong Love: When you know better, you do better and took a long memorable stroll down memory lane. With the help of an over the top imagination she's been busy putting together her next piece of work. Please enjoy Just Another Day: Cochran Affair, the second book of this series which is set to release August 27, 2013. Also checkout Cargo's Flower; Universal Laws and Sins, chapters on Kindle in Amazon. Be on the lookout for the complete book set to release September 15, 2013. You can preorder both books now.

ALSO AVAILABLE
PRE-ORDER

Lifelong Love; When you know better, you do better in stores now.

Just Another Day; Cochran Affair available August 27, 2013. Chapters available Kindle Edition on Amazon.

Cargo's Flower; Universal Laws and Sins available September 15, 2013. Chapters available Kindle Edition on Amazon.

Be the first to review books by Taz Will by sending email to keepitfunkypublishing@yahoo.com, subject: Review for details.

www.ingramcontent.com/pod-product-compliance
Lightning Source LLC
Chambersburg PA
CBHW070407260626
47161CB00001B/311